MOTHER'S BOY

MOTHER'S BOY

Stanley Middleton

HUTCHINSON
London

First published by Hutchinson in 2006

1 3 5 7 9 10 8 6 4 2

Hutchinson
The Random House Group Limited
20 Vauxhall Bridge Road, London SW1V 2SA

Random House Australia (Pty) Limited
20 Alfred Street, Milsons Point, Sydney
New South Wales 2061, Australia

Random House New Zealand Limited
18 Poland Road, Glenfield
Auckland 10, New Zealand

Random House (Pty) Limited
Isle of Houghton,
Corner of Boundary Road & Carse O'Gowrie
Houghton 2198, South Africa

Random House Publishers India Private Limited
301 World Trade Tower, Hotel Intercontinental Grand Complex,
Barakhamba Lane, New Delhi 110 001, India

The Random House Group Limited Reg. No. 954009

www.randomhouse.co.uk

A CIP catalogue record for this book is available from the British Library

Papers used by Random House are natural, recyclable products made from
wood grown in sustainable forests. The manufacturing processes conform to
the environmental regulations of the country of origin

Typeset in Times by Palimpsest Book Production Limited, Stirlingshire
Printed and bound in Great Britain by
William Clowes Ltd, Beccles, Suffolk

ISBN 0091797179
ISBN 9780091797171 (from Jan 2007)

To Brendan and Jean Jacobs

I

A night breeze fluttered front-garden shrubs in the mild December weather.

The tall Victorian villas on both sides of the street towered darkly above John Riley as he walked, though not threateningly so. All was cosy, close, roomy, protected. He had just called in to Holmleigh, Number 38, Rayburn Avenue, a nursing home where his father now lived. He had not enjoyed his visit.

About an hour before, he had been shown through the front door into a hall lit even more dimly than the street, and thence into a large room where four old people, three women and a man, sat paying scant attention to a large television set. They glanced, or rather lifted their heads, toward him, and found him as unattractive as the screen. The guide, a girl of perhaps twenty, pointed him towards the far end of the room, asked him to sit, said she'd 'seek out' Mr Riley for him.

John perched stiffly on the edge of a chair and looked at, then fingered, the curtains drawn over the large bay window. They were faded, but perhaps all the better for that, in that the garish colours, red, purple, blue and beige, in vertical stripes, were still ill-matched but reduced to pastel mediocrity. The place smelt of disinfectant as though some recent accident had been cleaned up near where he was sitting.

He could not make out what the actors on television were saying, the sound being turned so low. The old people must have acute hearing to follow the muttered exchanges. He doubted it. The room was clean with unattractive carpet on which spillages would make little impression. A picture of a copse in winter flanked by a pair of stag's antlers barely broke the arid stretch of monochrome brownish wallpaper. Nothing hung on the wall behind the television set; perhaps one did not need distraction here. On the third wall, above a marble fireplace bricked in and covered with an oriental screen, hung an oval mirror, bought in the Thirties he guessed, its chain still strong.

John Riley must have sat for five minutes, it seemed infinitely longer, before the door opened and the girl helped his father into the room. She held him tightly by one arm and urged him forward with small, musical phrases of encouragement. The other occupants of the room momentarily withdrew their attention from the television in their listless way and then ignored the newcomers. The old man shuffled across the carpet, leaning heavily on the girl, who finally turned and settled her charge into an armchair.

'There, Mr Riley,' she asked, 'how's that?'

The old man made no answer but breathed rapidly, shallowly, as if his short journey had exhausted him.

'It's your son,' she continued, 'come to see you.'

No answer.

'I've been telling him all day that you were coming.'

'Hello, Dad,' John said. 'How are you?'

The old man lifted his head, and stared. He seemed not to recognise his son.

'It's John,' the visitor said.

'It's your son, Mr Riley,' the girl urged, 'come to see you.'

'Ah.'

The small sound escaped the old man's lips.

'How are you?' the son asked. He was answered with a grunt.

'He's got it on him today,' the girl said. 'I can hardly get a word out of him.' She spoke as though her patient were deaf.

'Why's that?' John asked.

'They vary. Often they can't or won't tell you why. He perhaps doesn't feel very well. Have you any pains, Mr Riley?'

The question was ignored.

'Oh, well, if that's how it is,' she said.

The son picked up the plastic bag which sagged against his suitcase, and took out a bunch of grapes. He held them out to his father, who touched them gingerly, and then removed his fingers.

'Thank you,' the father said. 'I've been feeling a bit off.'

'Pain, is it? Discomfort?'

'Something. I don't seem myself somehow.'

'No.'

John delved into his bag and drew out a box.

'Fudge,' he said.

'Is it Thorntons? I don't like anybody else's.'

'Yes. There's the name on the side of the packet.'

'I can't see very well.' Suddenly his mood lightened. 'I used to buy a quarter of this when your mother and I went to the pictures, when we were courting. We'd soon get through it.'

'What luxury,' John said.

'Well,' the girl spoke cheerfully, 'I'll have to love you and leave you. You see he can talk if he wants to.'

The father narrowed his eyes and held out a hand theatrically in front of him towards her. His nails were scrubbed clean if rather long. He began to sing, softly, but with more intensity than with his speaking voice.

'"Madam, will you walk? Madam, will you talk? Madam, will you walk and talk with me?"'

'There,' she answered smiling now, 'you see, you're doing him good already.' She straightened up, brushing at her apron. 'I don't know that song.'

'I used to sing it with your aunt Irene. And your mother played the piano for us.'

'Lovely,' the girl said. 'Ring the bell if you want anything. Or you want to go. We have to be very careful with the doors. There are one or two of 'em who look as if they can hardly get up from their chairs, but give 'em half a chance they'll be out of the front door and halfway down the street like nine-year-olds. That's true, isn't it, Mr Riley?'

She wiped the old man's mouth, and left, pausing only to ask the television viewers if they were enjoying the programme. They whispered unenthusiastically that they were.

John Riley emptied the bag. A box of tissues, two pairs of Lovatt socks, a tube of toothpaste. His father had lost interest, sat leaning forward with his eyes half shut.

For the next forty minutes John tried hard to talk with his father. Sometimes he was rewarded with a monosyllable, more rarely with a phrase or a completed sentence. Often the old man closed his eyes and seemed to drift away. It was clear that William Riley felt ill, feeble, incapable, but that he was unable to describe his infirmity. Only twice did he speak at any length, the first time,

3

suddenly, as if he'd found himself, he curtly described a football match in which he'd slipped in mud and twisted his knee and limped about the world for more than twelve months afterwards. He talked in a flat tone, with few hesitations, his control of words near perfect, but never once looked into his son's eyes. The second time when John mentioned the song he had attempted earlier, William, showing signs of animation, gave an account of how he and Irene had been applauded into singing it again.

'Lovely voice, your aunt Irene had,' he concluded.

'She still has.'

'And good-looking. She had a beautiful bosom on her.'

'Yes.'

'Your mother wasn't pleased. She said we were making fools of ourselves. In front of everybody. "You ought to have more sense," she said, "even if she hasn't." She was sharp. She could be. Your mother. If she didn't get her way.'

He drooped again, breathing heavily, as if the telling of the anecdote had proved too much for him. John looked at the face with its closed lids, its fine wrinkles, its well-shaven cheeks. His father had recently celebrated his seventy-second birthday and though his grey hair was thin he did not look his age once he opened his blue eyes or spoke.

Up to two years ago William Riley had been an energetic man, enjoying his retirement, working on his large garden, decorating his house, helping his wife with the shopping, driving her out each Sunday in his Volvo for lunch in the country. It is true that his memory seemed to be failing, and sometimes he was left scrabbling, unable to find the word he required, but his confident behaviour covered these lapses. Then one morning he had been knocked down by a reckless motorist on a zebra crossing. The accident was of such a serious nature that his family had not expected him to live, but slowly, after a series of operations, he recovered, was able with the aid of crutches to hobble about the hospital and then his home. Physically he seemed to be reaching normality again until a serious fall on the stairs. He could not drive, nor work long hours in his garden; he walked uncertainly, but he seemed as near recovery as they could expect, given his age and the gravity of his injuries.

His memory loss still troubled him, and he resented his lack of mobility. Frustrated, he grumbled as he sat about the house. Ella, his wife, felt sorry that he hated his disabilities so strongly, but spoke sternly to him.

'You could easily be dead,' she'd say when his unending complaints upset her equanimity.

'I'd be better off,' he'd answer.

She'd stare at him, hard, and he'd quail as he never did when he was fit, but she looked after him well, taking him out if only for a few yards on the front pavement, as he began to recover, or to sit in the garden under a blanket.

'I don't like idling about.'

'You'd better learn to knit then.'

'That gardener you've hired has some rum ideas and is as ignorant as sin.'

'At least he turns up when he says he will.'

'That's not much of a recommendation in my eyes.'

They seemed, however, between them, to have come to terms with his incapacities. He struggled about the house and garden, read his newspaper carefully through each day, and accepted that his life of activity was over. He was angry sometimes when he could not lay his tongue to the word he wanted and then found he was equally at a loss as he tried a circumlocution. But he could laugh at himself, or give the impression of so doing.

About a year before, just after Christmas, he was struck down with a further bout of illness, a kind of flu which became so violent in the end that the doctor dispatched him to the hospital.

'What's wrong with him?' Ella asked the GP.

'It will be some sort of virus.'

'But he's been inoculated against both flu and pneumonia.'

'I know. But obviously not against this. He's in the best place in hospital.'

'I don't have much faith,' she said. 'There are superbugs there if we're to believe the papers.'

'Yes. But you couldn't go on as you were. It was too much for you. It wouldn't have been long before there were two of you seriously ill.'

'I think I could have managed. I've done so before.'

'You're a brave, independent woman, Mrs Riley, but it doesn't do to push your luck. You have a good rest. Indulge yourself.'

Ella looked at the doctor, a young man, and attractively smiled.

When the hospital finally discharged him, her husband's condition had deteriorated badly. He could barely walk, needed endless care, had lost all interest in the world, even in his own home, never mind that in the newspapers. He had no time for television or radio, and even when he appeared to force himself to an effort for the sake of a visitor, it made little difference. His dementia grew worse and he often seemed more unconscious than awake.

The GP said he could not account for this worsening of William's health, and suggested that he'd be better in a nursing home.

Ella objected.

'He was a man who always loved his home. And I've noticed that people who are put into these homes grow more rapidly helpless.'

'You must consider your own health, Mrs Riley.'

'I'd prefer to give it a try.'

After a further month or two it became clear that Ella was no longer coping. A bad fall down the stairs settled it for them. She admitted as much to the doctor, and wept. He suggested a nursing home to her, and in due course William moved to Holmleigh. He made much less fuss than his wife expected. She had dreaded an outburst of anger or bitter recrimination from him. This was the house they had moved into when they married, where John had been brought up, a place they had altered and cared for, with a garden that their friends envied; photographs of their holiday haunts hung about the walls. But he said little, muttering to himself as if he was not sure what was happening. He seemed to settle at once in the nursing home, even improved. He now could walk about the rooms, assisted by the girls. He ate little enough, but it was more than he managed at home. He groused, was moody, showed no pleasure when his wife visited him, and when she rang to ask if there was anything he particularly wanted (there was a phone in his room), he made no demands at all, merely grunted. The people in the home looked after him, he said, but he did not offer a word of praise or thanks to them or anybody else.

When Ella questioned the matron she was told that he had settled in well and gave no trouble.

'Does he seem happy?'

'No, I wouldn't say that, but that's often the case with elderly people. They feel the world has passed them by, and they resent it. I think perhaps I'd be the same.'

'Yes. He can't do any of the things he used to enjoy.' She sighed. 'Has he made friends with any of the other people here?'

'No. He ignores them. What did he do when he was at work?'

'He worked for the Inland Revenue at Brook House.'

'Perhaps that's the explanation.'

They both sniggered at the matron's little joke.

Now this evening John tried to hold a conversation with his father, and failed. He told his father what he had been doing at work (he was an accountant) and about a visit to the ballet, a modern American dance company. 'I thoroughly enjoyed it,' he said. 'It was nothing like classical ballet, livelier, more athletic, full of surprising movement.' The old man stared down at his boots. 'And there was a certain amount of full-frontal nudity.' The old man showed no more interest than if he'd been told that attendants collected tickets at the door or sold programmes. John mentioned the local football teams, but his father was not responsive. In the middle of a long drawn-out account of a visit John intended to make, the old man suddenly looked up.

'How's Helen keeping these days?'

'All right, as far as I know. I don't see her much.'

Helen was the wife from whom he was separated.

'Don't see her? Uh?'

His father had lost interest.

In the end, having tempted William to another piece of fudge, and failed to get much more information out of him, John rang the bell. The girl duly appeared, though not immediately.

'I'll have to be away now.'

'Right, yes.' She turned to William. 'Would you like to stay down here, or go back to your room?' She interpreted his inarticulate grunts to mean upstairs. 'We'll see your son to the door shall we?' She cleared his lap of the gifts, packed them into a bag. A grape detached itself. 'Here's a grape for you.' She held it to his lips, but he kept his mouth sourly closed. 'Right, back in the carrier with it. Now, up.' She pulled him, surprisingly quickly, to his feet, hooked her arm in his and set off for the door. Outside in the hall, the party halted.

'Say goodbye to your son,' she ordered.

'Goodbye.' John took his father's hand. 'I'm going to see my mother.'

'The lift's only just here. It's a godsend.'

William was making signs with his free hand towards his son. His mouth stood open ready for speech.

'Give my regards to Helen.' He spoke with clarity.

'He wants you to give his regards to Helen,' she translated, unnecessarily. 'Just stand there. Hold on to the wall while I let Mr Riley out.'

'She's a pretty girl, Helen is.' He straightened himself.

The young woman, never taking eyes off the father, showed the son out of the front door.

II

John Riley rang the bell of the house where he had been brought up. In daylight or darkness the street had changed very little since the time he was born here. He had deliberately left his car behind in London, so that he could mooch about Beechnall on foot or on buses.

The light inside illuminated the stained glass of the front door before his mother appeared.

'Oh,' she said. 'I thought you were never coming.'

'I've been to see Dad.'

'Yes,' she said, arms round him. 'You said you'd do that.'

She took his coat and hung it on the hall stand, instructing him to leave his case.

'I've another visitor,' she said, rather excitedly for her.

'Who's that?'

'Your aunt Irene.' She pronounced it with two syllables. 'She'd occupy you profitably while you were waiting for me.'

His mother ushered him into the living room, where his aunt rose to greet him.

The two sisters were alike in being tall but his mother at fifty-seven looked and dressed her age. She wore a trouser suit of a sombre navy over a white jumper. He recalled that twenty years ago, when he was a boy, she had been teaching in a junior school and had clashed with her headmistress who had refused to let any of her female staff wear trousers. It had become quite an obsession with his mother, discussed frequently, even passionately, with her husband over family meals. He had shown little sympathy with her crusade, saying that though he made no claim to expertise in these matters he preferred women to wear skirts. This riled his wife so that both husband and son suffered the length of her tongue for the rest of the evening.

In the end Mrs Riley won her way, and Miss Cripwell, the

9

head, after a vain appeal to the Director of Education, had to
yield. John guessed that his mother took her victory modestly,
never boasting. She became a close friend of Miss Cripwell, and
they visited each other's homes, went on educational outings
together, exchanged Christmas presents. The headmistress was
even seen on very cold days to wear trousers, to the delight of
the more junior of her staff. When, a year ago, she died, Ella
Riley wore a black dress at her funeral. In the will Ella was left
two Victorian oil paintings, one of the sea and the other of a
rowing boat on a tree-fringed lake with mountains in the distance.
These were judged by an auctioneer friend of William Riley to
be 'quite valuable, sought after these days' and though room was
found for them on the walls of the Rileys' parlour, Ella clearly
thought little of them, once called them 'insipid' in John's hearing
and advised him to sell them once she had died. 'I keep them in
memory of Sally Cripwell, whom I respected and from whom I
learnt a great deal. But as pictures . . .' She had smacked her lips
sourly.

'I'll get you your supper,' she said.

'Not too much, mother. I'm not hungry.'

'If I know you, you won't have eaten anything since breakfast. Can I get you anything, Irene?'

John and his aunt sat smiling at each other, convinced that
nothing would change Ella's views that her guests were underfed.

'How's Uncle Eric then?' he asked.

'Well. Thriving. He's in Afghanistan.'

'Do you hear from him?'

'He'll phone now and again. And I've seen him once on television laying the law down.'

'Is he enjoying it?'

'I can't really say. I tell him it's time he retired and settled
down at home, but that's the last thing he wants.' Her husband
was a foreign correspondent for *The Times*. 'He makes the excuse
that he can't afford to give up until the children are out of
university and well embarked on their careers.'

'Any truth in it?'

'Not really. We're not short. I think he dreads being at home
all day. He wouldn't know what to do except to take a taxi down
to one of his clubs, talk to other old codgers and drink.'

'Do you tell him so?'

'Often. He pays no attention. It's odd. He reads a great deal; I'm amazed how many books he gets through, and remembers, in spite of all his travels. It shames me.'

Irene spoke with an effortless upper-class accent, and sat at her ease. She was a beautiful woman who at fifty still turned men's heads in the street. Whatever her topic of conversation she seemed mistress of it, often surprising her listeners. She had been a journalist and had worked for the BBC. She now wrote a weekly column for the *Independent* and two years ago had published a book on Paris where she had lived for eighteen months with her husband who had been 'dumped' there, his word, by his newspaper. They both spoke fluent French and she had spent her time profitably preparing and writing her book which had been praised as highly in its French translation as in English.

'How's William,' she suddenly asked.

'Hard to say. He has some of his mobility back, but it's difficult to get him to talk.'

'Why is that?'

'He doesn't seem happy. Wrapped up inside himself. Otherwise he leans forward, hands between his knees, staring at the floor. He looks as if he's praying.'

'You never know.'

'I doubt it. I'd no idea what was going on in his head, if anything. He had one little burst of lucidity, or at least a coherent sentence or two. It concerned you, as a matter of interest.'

He waited vainly for her to question him. He did not judge her as indifferent since her face shone with interest; it was as if her good manners did not allow her to interrupt such a narrative.

'You used to sing together, apparently.'

'We did.'

He described his father's attempt to sing in the nursing home. His voice, John said, was remarkably good for a seventy-odd-year-old cripple.

Ella had now returned and stood listening.

'I remember that "Madam, Will You Walk?" It was a favourite of his. I've no idea who wrote it. He wore a bow tie, and used to act the part, bowing and stroking an imaginary moustache.'

'Was he a good actor, then?' John asked.

'To some extent. I never saw him in a play or anything of that sort. Only on-stage singing.'

'I never heard him.'

'No,' Ella said. 'By the time you came on the scene he was too far advanced in his daily work, or so he thought, to be fooling about singing in concerts. He might do the occasional oratorio, *Messiah*, or *The Crucifixion* or *Olivet to Calvary*. And he was doubtful about that.'

William Riley had progressed in the offices of the Inland Revenue, where he had started his working life at sixteen after he'd left the grammar school. He was proud of his promotions, his status.

'He sometimes sang at home when he was working.'

'I would say that he never did any singing at Brook House.'

'I was only a schoolgirl when we performed,' Irene ironically stressed the last word.

'He had a soft spot for you,' Ella said. 'I was courting him at the time, but he'd have given me up for you, young as you were.'

John watched his aunt's face. He, surprised at his mother's bluntness of speech, waited for Irene to show embarrassment, but an amused hauteur was her sole reaction; she might have been watching the antics of some infant urchin in the street.

'Come and sit yourself down, John. Pork pie and salad. I don't suppose they know how to make a decent pork pie in London.'

'Mine was delicious,' Irene said, sweetly.

'I shall enjoy it,' John joined in, trying to erase the anger from his mother's voice.

'Do you want a wash first?' she asked.

'Perhaps I'd better.'

He moved out, swilled his hands and returned to the table. The sisters were standing in silence, but as soon as he sat down, his mother made for the stairs.

'I'll just check that girl has made your bed up properly.'

'What girl's that?' he asked his aunt.

'Erica Partridge. She comes in twice a week to help your mother with the housework.'

He, discovering hunger, ate with gusto. Irene said little, and there were no sounds from upstairs.

'My mother's very quiet, isn't she?'

'She retires to a desk and computer up there.'

'Oh. Why's that?'

'She signed up for some IT lessons when first your father went into the nursing home. Doesn't she send you e-mails?'

'No. Postcards.'

'Interesting?'

'Not picture postcards. Plain, but in an envelope. She doesn't want the postman reading her business.'

Irene smiled blankly. John pushed his empty plate away from him.

'She doesn't sound very happy,' he said. 'Is that just today? Or is it usually so?'

Irene glanced towards the door.

'She feels guilty. Since your father went to his nursing home, she's blamed herself. She says she could have continued to look after him here. I suppose she could, but only after a fashion. It's bad enough to be as crippled as he is, never mind his dementia.'

'I'm not sure how bad that is.'

'No, I'm not. I wonder how much of it is frustration or depression, weighing so heavily on him that he can't bring himself to think straight. Certainly his present memory is poor. He'll ask the same question over and over again. That, I'm sorry to say, doesn't go down too well with Ella. He has been the victim to be interrogated all their married life. How do you remember your father?'

'In what sense?'

'How did he treat you differently from the way your mother did? Or was there no difference?'

'My mother had more to do with me when I was a child. She was more volatile then. You never knew what would happen next.'

'And William?'

'He knew it all. He was something of a reader. He was fond of geography and history and archaeology. He often gave us something of a lecture. He read me a child's story of Robin Hood one weekend, and then said the book was all guesswork, that nobody knew very much about Robin, whether there ever had been such a person.'

13

'Did that spoil it for you?'

'Not one bit. I was pleased to hear both versions. My mother got on to him when they thought I was out of earshot.'

'Did he mind?'

'I suppose he did. He just said, "The boy's got to learn," and that loosed another torrent of words from her.'

'They seemed to quarrel quite often to me,' Irene said, 'and they didn't seem to mind who was there or who heard them. Perhaps they even enjoyed it.'

'I don't think Dad did. He laid the law down at Brook House, and anywhere else given half a chance, but with my mother he was very subdued.'

'She always seemed to get her own way.'

'Unless it was something he thought highly about. His history, or money.'

They heard Ella's footsteps on the stairs. When she entered the room she looked with pleasure at her son's empty plate. He refused her offer of another slice of pork pie, and a dish of trifle, made specially for him.

'You'll be the only one to eat it,' she told him.

'Won't my dad?'

'No. He went off home-made sweet things as soon as you left home. Shop rubbish only.'

'You mean you wouldn't make any more trifle?' John said.

'I would, if he asked for it. But he never does.'

III

Over breakfast next morning John's mother subjected him to her usual cross-examination about his life and work in London. He did not mind this in the least, but answered as briefly and accurately as he could. His mother was sufficiently well versed in the background of his daily existence to be able to expand his succinct sentences into something she understood and which satisfied her curiosity. Sooner or later he knew she would start on a line of questioning he disliked, about his estranged wife and her doings.

'Have you seen anything of Helen recently?'

The question coincided with the arrival of his aunt at the breakfast table.

'I'm not too late?' she asked.

Ella set her sister up with cereals and milk.

'It'll be coffee, won't it? If I know you?'

'If you please.'

Ella poured steadily, filling her sister's cup, then replenished John's, and finally her own. She replaced the coffee pot, and sat ready again.

'Have you seen anything of Helen lately?' she repeated.

'No. Not at all.'

'She makes no attempt to get in touch with you?'

'No.'

'And you don't meet her by chance, at a theatre or a concert?'

'No.'

There his mother dropped this line of questioning, and Irene talked knowledgeably and at length about her concert-going. John had not known she had this interest in music, and asked about it. It appeared that her husband Eric was a keen musician, and came from a musical family. 'When he's at home he spends hours at the piano playing Bach's *Well-Tempered Clavier*.' He had told her that he had no time, or instrument for that matter, at work to

15

spend on music. 'I try to catch up,' he had said. His brother, John knew this already, was James Davenport, the concert pianist. Eric had said, 'Whenever I hear Jim sit at the keyboard and play a Bach fugue, and that's how he starts his practice every morning, I'm full of envy. He thinks nothing of it, but I regret the time I waste travelling round the world, chasing ephemeralities.'

'I think he means it,' Irene said.

'Aren't you sure?' Ella asked. 'His brother must travel a fair amount.'

'My husband changes his mind every ten minutes. He's sincere, powerfully so, about the new idea, whatever it is, but it doesn't last.'

When they had cleared the dishes, Irene said she must write two letters before she set out to visit friends in Lincoln, but she'd help with the washing-up.

'No,' Ella said. 'You go upstairs and write. John will help me with the pots.'

They had hardly started the chore when Ella asked her son, 'Do you know why I mentioned Helen?'

'No. I don't.'

'Guess.'

'Curiosity? And you like her?'

'She came to see me. One day last week. I was surprised when she rang from one of the stops on the motorway and asked if she could call in. I gave her directions and about an hour later she arrived.'

'What was she doing in these parts?'

'I never found out. I guess she deliberately came up to see me. Why she didn't ring before she set off to find out whether I'd be at home and it would be convenient to call I never found out. It was left vague. She brought me a Christmas present, a beautiful antique silver jug. I gave her lunch; she'd had nothing to eat except a bowl of cornflakes.'

'And what did she want?'

'To talk about you.'

He waited for his mother to continue. Typically, having caught his interest, she made him wait, embarking on useless little dashes from sink to shelves and thus to account for her silence. Finally she resumed the subject with a triumphant shrug of the shoulders.

16

'First of all she asked how you were keeping. I told her about those lectures you had delivered in America. She knew nothing of it. She was really interested.' Again she paused, and he waited. 'She said something about accountancy having a bad name recently in the United States. She wanted to know exactly what it was you lectured on, and I couldn't tell her. Then she wanted to hear if you were keeping fit and fully occupied at work. And then she got into a bit of a tangle, was embarrassed, didn't quite know what to say. And that's not like her.'

'No.'

'She asked me if you ever inquired about her, or mentioned her. I said you weren't up here often these days because you were so busy at work. She began to tell me how things were between you before you separated, how neither of you could say anything before the other party misunderstood it. If either of you had the chance to come out with something sarcastic or rude, it was said. You couldn't agree on petty things like, oh, the colour of new curtains she wanted. You were either quarrelling or saying nothing at all. The atmosphere was poisonous, she claimed.'

They had almost completed the washing-up. His mother dried her hands and waited for him to complete his part of the chore.

'She'd kept, it appeared, her apartment, not sold it when you married but had let it out, providentially.' Her son laughed at his mother's word. 'Her tenant was moving out at the time and going to Australia so it was easy to take all her things from your house and live there. I expect you knew all this.'

'I knew where she went to. She owns the whole house. It was her mother's. She had the bottom-floor flat when I first knew her. The other two floors were let out.'

'Nice little income,' Ella said.

'I suppose so.'

'You know very well it is. Now, would you like another cup of coffee?'

'No, thanks. You have one.'

His mother carefully chose a cup, put in instant coffee this time, had the jug-kettle boiling in no time. She motioned John to sit down.

'She said she was glad to get out of your company, to be able to please herself. She dreaded going home to you, and used to

17

leave work in the office for the evening and come home late to avoid your insults. You each got your own supper, she said. And your breakfast. It seemed to me a silly way for educated people, university graduates, to go on. If she's to be believed, neither of you made any attempt to sort yourselves out.'

'No,' John said, 'I suppose we didn't.'

'Do you, did you think you were the first married couple to go through a bad patch?'

'I never put it to myself like that.'

'You young folks, you don't persevere. One hint of a disagreement and you're running for the divorce courts.'

'You told Helen this, did you?'

'I did not. Do you think your father and I never had hard words? We were two quite different personalities. We didn't see eye to eye on every little thing, that I can tell you, but we kept quiet for a bit after a disagreement, until it all blew over and we felt calmer, especially if you were about. And as for my mother's and grandmother's generations, they never even considered divorce.'

'More fools they.'

'You've made your minds up about it, have you?'

'I haven't done anything about divorce, if that's what you mean. I've been far too busy to worry about that. And she hasn't, as far as I know.'

'And you're prepared to leave it there?'

'For the present?'

'It's not because,' Ella now spoke more slowly, 'you hoped for a reconciliation at some time in the future?'

'It never crossed my mind.'

Ella stamped across the kitchen to make some further useless rearrangement inside a cupboard. She stood with her back to him until, finally satisfied with her adjustments, she moved more equably to her original position. Her expression was both assumed and odd; he interpreted it as an attempt at sympathetic concern.

'Have you teamed up with some other girl?'

'Nothing serious. I've taken one or two out. Not this last month or two when I've been run off my feet with work.'

'But you never wished to have Helen back?'

'No.'

'Well, it's not so with her.'

Ella took up a stance that would not have been amiss in the pulpit of her father's Nonconformist chapel. Her face depicted certainty.

'When you split up she said how relieved she was at first. There were no arguments as soon as she opened the front door. She could please herself. She realised that she had done the right thing by walking out on you. She could bring work home to occupy her whenever she liked, and it made all the difference knowing no one would interrupt her, that she would not be worrying when you'd come storming round the house blaming her for something that had gone wrong, or leave her to sit wondering what you'd quarrel about next. Do you know what she said? "He has a cruel tongue when it suits him." I thought, "Six of one and half a dozen of the other."'

'Probably.'

'But now after you've been apart six or seven months she's beginning to feel differently. She feels, she said, lonely and vulnerable.'

'There are other people in her house, and she has plenty of friends.'

'That's not what it sounded like. She felt deserted. Alone. Adrift.'

'She left me.'

'Whoever,' Ella said, like the good class teacher she had been, 'was responsible for what had happened in the first place, it makes no difference now to the way she feels. She's all alone, and doesn't like it. She blames herself, no doubt, but she sees herself as neglected. Does this come as a surprise to you?'

'Yes. But why did she come and tell you?'

'She daren't approach you, because she thinks, with some justification, that she's responsible for her own trouble.'

The two sat in silence. John drummed his fingers lightly on the table in front of him. His mother watched him closely, waiting for her moment.

'That's what she feels at this minute. Are you going to do anything about it?'

'Such as?'

'See her, talk to her. Or at least write her a note. Then she'll know I've mentioned it to you.'

'I'm perfectly satisfied as I am.'

'And so you'll do nothing?'

'I think so.'

Again silence fell after these last brief exchanges.

'Do you think that's wrong?' he asked.

'It's not for me to say. You must make your own mind up. But as you thought enough at one time of her to marry the girl, you might just make an inquiry now to see why she's changed her mind.'

'Won't it make it worse if I listen to her and then tell her I'd prefer things to stay as they are?'

His mother drew in breath.

'It might. But at least she will know for certain what you think. At present she's frightened and alone and I guess that with this comes the hope that perhaps you may have changed your mind to some slight extent and are prepared to give it another try.'

'I don't think I am.'

'Well, that's it, then.'

At that moment Irene came into the kitchen to announce she'd 'scribbled her two notes' and would post them and then set off to visit her friend. No, she did not know when she'd be back, but she'd phone through in good time.

'You won't be home for lunch then?'

'Oh, no. But you knew that.'

She wished them both a courteous good morning and left.

Immediately her sister had gone, Ella pulled a sour face.

'Not in favour today?' John asked.

'She never has been.' His mother, in and out, now embarked on her preparations for lunch.

'Why does she come up and stay here?' he asked.

'To flaunt herself. That word just suits her. She's had it far too easy in her life. She's always had money. My parents gave her too much when she was at Oxford. Far more than ever they gave me when I was at teacher training college. And she and her husband earn fabulous amounts for their journalism and appearances on the television. Ridiculous sums they get.'

'Do you ever read what they write?'

'I've something better to do. Eric is interesting sometimes. He seems to travel everywhere. And I think he's in danger quite often. But he's that sort of man.'

20

On her next return from the pantry where the freezer stood, she stopped awkwardly in front of him.

'I'd be glad if you'd go to see Helen or at least write her a note.'

'I'll think about it,' he replied peaceably.

'You know I've always liked her. If you see her again, you might feel differently about your marriage. While she sat here, I was really sorry for her. And I thought she'd make the ideal wife for you.'

'She didn't leave after one flaming row, you know. Or one fit of the sulks. We'd been getting on each other's nerves for months on end. I tried to be reasonable about it, but I tell you when she upped sticks and left I was relieved. And, if I'm any judge, she was worse affected than I was. When this man in her flat gave notice that he was going to Australia, the news must have been a godsend. Remember it was she who left.'

'I'd still like you to get in touch with her. It would please me. I'd feel, then, that everything that could have been done had been done.'

'I'll see.'

'Thank you.' His mother was her most placatory. 'Now, how are you spending today?'

'I shall go into town. I've a bit of Christmas shopping to finish. And then I shall visit Dad again after I've consulted you. I don't want to ruin your plans. You'll have plenty to do with both Irene and me here. You're not going to visit him, are you? Today?'

'No, I go twice a week, Wednesday afternoon and Sunday evening. Of course I shall go on Christmas Day.'

'Do they have a party?'

'No. I expect they'll lay on a special meal. And perhaps organise a sing-song for them. Carols and old-time songs.'

'Do the old people sing?'

'A few might join in. They seem to enjoy it. Mrs Jones, the matron, is something of a singer and she invites some of the members of a choir she's in to come round and lead the choruses.'

'Does Dad enjoy it?'

'Well, as you know, he wasn't in there last Christmas, but he grumbled about a sing-song they had soon after he got there.

"Pack Up Your Troubles" and "It's A Long Way To Tipperary". He said he didn't want to be singing rubbish like that, as if he was in a pub. Not that he ever went into pubs. He was a cut above public houses.' She sighed. 'He's very much worse since then. I doubt if he'd know what they were singing now.'

'Would you have liked to have gone into the pubs with him when you were younger?'

'Not really. We'd call in when we were on holiday, for a snack and a drink, that sort of thing. Neither of us had anything against alcohol. In moderation.' She spoke slowly, separating word from word.

'I'll think about this Helen business,' he said.

'Oh, thank you.'

IV

John left his mother to her cooking and immediately wrote to Helen. He carried with him two or three Christmas cards and in one of these, a Madonna and child, issued by Oxfam, he informed her in his best script that his mother had spoken to him about her visit to Beechnall. If she would like to see him he'd be back in London two days after Christmas, and perhaps she would phone. He hoped she was well. He signed it 'Yours, John' and felt a proper neutrality had been preserved. He posted it in the town centre so there would be little doubt about its prompt arrival. He felt slightly virtuous after this, but did not expect any great change either in Helen or in his way of life.

He completed his shopping and went into the Bell Inn where he ate a substantial meal, including Christmas pudding, washed down with a pint of lager. He had been in this room with his wife for lunch two Christmases ago, but the room seemed quite changed, appearing both larger and lighter. It had obviously been redecorated. There were pictures on the wall of mediaeval scenes: a knight setting out for a Crusade, a knight and his lady being amused by a jester, a knight kneeling in vigil in a Gothic church by the body of a comrade, or perhaps a king. These were large and in black and white, and spread across the wall opposite to where he was now seated, exactly the place he and Helen had occupied two years before. At the end of the wall, right by his table, hung a smaller oil painting of a man's head and shoulders, rather amateurishly done and faded. The sitter wore a not very elaborate wig. When the waiter brought his main course John asked about the portrait and who the subject was. The waiter stared at it as if he had never noticed it before.

'No idea,' he answered pleasantly. 'I'll ask about it.'

When he returned with the Christmas pudding he immediately volunteered, 'Nobody back there knows. They reckon the gaffer must have picked it up at an auction. But both he and the missus are out just at the moment.'

'I thought it might be some eighteenth-century landlord,' John said.

'Possible. One of life's little mysteries.'

Warmed and in good heart he made his way on foot to Rayburn Avenue to visit his father, and to present him with a newly bought gift, a smart knitted pullover. His mother had given him the measurements before he set out. The old man, who seemed in better temper than last time, took it and felt it gingerly with his finger ends as it lay unopened across his knee.

'Isn't that lovely now?' one of the carers said as she passed. 'Is it a Christmas present? My, you aren't half lucky.'

William Riley responded with a nod to her cackle. She was not, John noticed, the same girl who was on duty the night before. He could barely force a word out of his father who yet seemed not entirely displeased. Now and then William smiled, a mere slight shift of the lips unaccompanied by any sparkle of the eyes. Again he hummed to himself, conducting faintly with his right hand, but the son could not make out the tune he murmured.

John plied his father with questions, receiving monosyllabic answers. No, they were not having a Christmas party. No, the carol singers had not called. No, they did not drink wine on high days and holidays. Yes, there was a Christmas tree in the dining room. When asked what his favourite carol was, he clamped his lips tight and raised his nose in scorn. He must have heard the question, for after a minute he touched his son on the arm and said confidentially, 'That man on the end chair,' he nodded in the direction, 'is a musician. He knows about fugues and things.' There was no conversation of any consequence between the two. John tried question after question, without result. William initiated nothing, though his expression remained pleasant.

'My mother will be up here to see you on Christmas Day, and she'll bring Irene with her.'

'Irene,' the old man repeated the name as if he had not heard it before.

'Her sister. Ella's sister.'

'Oh, Ella's sister.' Baffled still.

24

'You used to sing with her. Years ago. So you told me.'

No reply. John's chin sank to his chest.

'Do you know who I am?'

The old man jerked upright, staring almost wildly.

'John. You're my son John.'

'Where do I live?'

At this moment the carer brought them each a cup of tea which she put on a table she drew up near to William's chair.

'Sugar in the bowl,' she said. 'Do you want any, William?' She juggled with the spoon, and as he nodded let a large spoonful trickle in from four or five inches above the liquid. 'That'll sweeten you up,' she said. 'Though he seems quite cheerful today.'

'Is there any reason?' John asked.

'Why are you so pleased with yourself?' she shouted. She spoke much more loudly to patients than to the visitors.

William ignored her, stony-faced.

'All right then,' she said. 'Be like that.'

She raised a cheerful hand to John, and went off with a flourish of her tray.

They spent the next half hour in silences and questions briefly answered. William had to be encouraged to drink his tea, and this drew from him his single original comment.

'They have no idea how to make palatable tea.' He offered his remark without malice, still with the smile on his mouth.

'Too strong for you?' John asked.

'Cheap tea. Sweepings from the floor.'

'What did you have at home?'

William turned his face away from his son as though the topic had lost his interest.

John tried listening to the other patients, but they rarely spoke. They'd respond with a dry smile to the pleasantries of their nurses. No one but his father had a visitor at this time in the afternoon. The television set was switched on, but John could not see the screen, which had been turned from the position of the evening before. Perhaps this was deliberate and meant to stimu-late in its small way the interest of inmates who, excluding meals, would occupy the same chairs in the same room day after day.

'Do you ever watch television?' he asked his father.

'No.'

25

'You used to like *Panorama* and the gardening programmes and *Horizon* and the news bulletins.'

For all the change in expression on his father's face he might have been speaking Chinese. Seconds later William's eyes were closed and he was asleep. John looked at him with pity. When his father woke, he was no more communicative.

On Christmas Day in the afternoon Irene drove her sister and her nephew down to see the old man. The television sets were in full use; the programme seemed to be an American thriller. The number of people in the downstairs sitting room was larger than usual though visitors looked nearly as comatose as inmates, and spoke in whispers. William Riley occupied his usual chair; he showed a marked livening on the appearance of Irene, but that soon evaporated. After helping him unwrap his Christmas presents, which were received with a marked lack of interest, Ella went upstairs to collect his washing and put away the clean clothes she had brought in for him. He refused a chocolate and a biscuit with a dull shake of the head. They stayed half an hour and he spoke coherently only twice, both times to Irene. He kept his eyes closed and his pale, wooden face showed no vivacity at his visitors, their presents and spurious excitement.

As they left the home Irene said William had deteriorated markedly.

'Last time I was here he could talk sensibly. Now he's half asleep all the time,' Irene said.

'There's nothing much to stimulate them.'

'When William was in his prime he'd plenty to talk about. Is he in pain now?'

'I don't think so, or no more than usual. His mind's going.'

'Do you ever take him out?' Irene asked.

'I've got rid of the car. I hardly ever used it, and I could see no sense paying out good money to keep it rusting in the garage.'

'Shall I run him out tomorrow? The four of us? Is there anywhere he particularly liked?'

'Brook House, the Inland Revenue headquarters.'

Irene gave up. They reached home in sullen silence.

V

By the last post before Christmas, John Riley had received a card
from his wife. She thanked him for his communication and asked
him to telephone her when he returned home and then perhaps
they could meet, at her home or his, or at some place acceptable
to both. The writing was neat, the expression totally understated.
He showed it to his mother, who perked up immediately, and
said, 'There. It was worth writing. She's replied, at least. Nothing
may come of it, but at least you've both tried.'

'Not what you'd call enthusiastic,' he said, pointing to the card.

'Don't you go and spoil it. The opportunity is there. You've
both responded. It's up to the pair of you to make of it what you
can. I liked the girl. And she seemed clearly upset when she came
to see me.' She walked away, turned suddenly. 'Let me know
how you get on.'

'I will.'

'And don't you forget. I know you of old.'

He left it a day before he rang Helen. She, like him, had taken
the whole of the Christmas week off work and suggested she
came round in the evening.

'I feel more myself then,' she said.

'Shall we go out for a meal first?'

'No.' Her answer was immediate. 'Send out to that nice Indian
takeaway near you. It's only ten minutes walk there and back.'

'Right. I'll order for seven o'clock. If you could be here, let's
say, by six-thirty you can warm the plates while I fetch it. What
would you like?'

'I'll let you choose for me.'

'I'm no expert. Would you like wine, or are you coming by
car?'

'I'd like wine,' she said. 'It improves everything.'

'Six-thirty, then,' he said.

'Thank you.'

The conversation ended there. They might be schoolchildren hesitantly angling for a first date.

Helen arrived five minutes behind time. He had laid the table in the dining room, and had lit a small fire in the lounge, with some difficulty since this was a rare event and the chimney must have been damp. The room had smelt of smoke for an hour or more afterwards, but now the coke fire glowed red. He had surprised himself by his uneasiness during the whole day as if a certainty of failure obstructed his every move. He had eaten little, polished his furniture, hoovered every carpet and even cleaned the windows, though he knew by the time his wife arrived all his curtains would be drawn against the winter evening. He had chosen the meal at one p.m. after consultation with a polite Indian, who explained the explanation on his bill of fare. 'Tandoori dishes,' this read, 'are first marinated in freshly ground spices and yoghurt sauce for a few hours, then cooked in a clay oven. Served with a side salad and mint sauce.' John chose the most expensive, tandoori king prawn, inquiring sarcastically if there would be time for preparation of this dish. The proprietor, wagging a delicate hand, said there would be no doubt. The customer indicated he would call in exactly at seven to collect the meal. He would leave the choice of the vegetable side dish to the experts. 'Have you a favourite, yourself?' he asked. 'Aloo gobi,' the man replied. 'What's that?' 'Potatoes and cauliflower. Delicious.' 'I'll take your word for it.' He then said he had an important guest, so that the meal must be ready for seven, when it would be eaten not fifteen minutes later. 'I understand, sir,' the man answered. 'All will be prepared.'

At the ringing of the doorbell, he walked leisurely to answer it. He held out a hand to greet his wife. He had decided on that. Kisses meant nothing these days, but he did not want either to deceive his wife or commit himself too soon.

Helen wore a brilliant red coat over a black dress. Her hat was unusual, a comic Robin Hood misshape with a feather, perched at a jaunty angle. He hung up her coat and hat with care. She clasped her handbag to her as if she expected him to snatch it away. She seemed smaller than he remembered as he stood in the hallway and her hair, always fair, now bleached, shone. He asked about the weather outside. She said it was cold, but not unduly so.

'Not raining?'

'No. I couldn't see the stars.' She looked about her. 'You haven't hung the Christmas decorations?' she asked.

'I've no idea where they are.'

'At the far end of the back bedroom wardrobe in a hatbox. Or they were.'

He signalled her forward into the lounge.

'This looks cosy,' she said. She took an armchair in which he had never seen her seated before. She sat neat and self-possessed, her handbag on her lap. She declined a drink, telling him that while he was out she'd stretch her legs and enjoy the fire.

'Central heating is very good,' she said, 'but one can't sit staring at a radiator.'

They chatted, not easily, for the next ten minutes when he said he'd put his topcoat and scarf on and run down to the takeaway. He told her to make herself comfortable, and she replied that she'd every intention of so doing.

On his return – they had kept him waiting nearly a quarter of an hour at the Taj Mahal Tandoori – Helen slipped on her shoes again and helped him put the meal on his largest plates. They carried it, each separately, into the dining room while he took the wine from the refrigerator.

'I chose prawns rather than their chicken or meat for you,' he said as they began the meal. 'You used to prefer that.'

'Yes, thank you. It's delicious. There's rather a lot, though.'

'I always get my money's worth.'

'You won't mind if I don't finish it, will you?'

'No, not at all.'

She ate delicately, smiling, elbows busy.

'And the wine?' she asked.

'Verdicchio dei Castelli di Jesi Classico.'

'Good gracious,' she said, like a Sunday-school teacher. 'Is that special?'

'Don't worry. Straight out of Sainsbury's. It looks like water.' He sipped. 'It's dry. It said it was on the label. I hardly drink wine these days.'

She expressed her satisfaction with his choice.

He could not get used to the brightness of her bleached hair. It suited her, emphasising the swift intelligence of her features. He congratulated her and she appeared pleased.

'My dumb blonde period,' she said.

'I was just thinking how brainy it made you look.'

'I'll try to live up to my appearance.'

They did not talk a great deal, but the tandoori king prawn kept them well occupied. He finished first, and soon afterwards she laid down her knife and fork confessing herself beaten.

'You don't mind?' she asked.

'No. They specialise in large helpings.' He gathered the two plates. 'Now I have a trifle in the fridge. Would you like that?'

'No, thanks. I'm full.'

'So am I, now I come to think of it. A cup of coffee?'

He reinstalled her by the lounge fire. When he returned with the coffee, her eyes were closed.

'It's too comfortable in here,' she said, stirring. 'I feel sleepy.'

'Late nights?' he asked cheerfully.

'No. Not at all. It's the fire, I think.' She stretched her legs. 'It really is a luxury.'

All the time he sipped his coffee he wondered when he should begin the serious talk. Was it up to him? She had made overtures first. As he sat opposite her, warmed to the bone, he knew that he'd be quite satisfied if she left in an hour's time with not a word of their problems touched on. She looked pretty, decorative, with her bright hair (he could not come quite to terms with that), petite, contented, thoroughly womanly, her eyes wide now, delicate fingernails shining.

When he had poured second cups for them both he leaned back. He owed it to his mother to question Helen. He did not expect any permanent good to come of it, but he felt curious, wanting to know what it was that troubled her.

He narrowed his eyes.

'My mother said you wanted to talk to me,' he began. That was neutral enough.

'Yes,' she answered, in a childish, withdrawn tone.

She wasn't going to help him out, he decided. They were at loggerheads after a single sentence from him. She had clasped her hands and looked unblinkingly at him.

30

'She told me that you were lonely, felt vulnerable. I think that was her word.'

'I did say that.'

'Did you want to come back here?' No answer. 'Or, at least, talk about it?'

'Yes, in a way. I wasn't certain.'

'Why didn't you tell me? You don't live too far away. Or you could have written to me.'

'I wasn't sure of my reception.'

'What does that mean?' he asked.

She took in an audible breath.

'I wasn't sure of how you felt, and as I had to make a call in Beechnall, I arranged to meet your mother. She was very kind to me.'

'And what was the advantage of seeing her?'

'I thought perhaps she'd pass my message on, and I'd be able to judge the possible outcome from your attitude. I didn't want,' she hesitated, 'to create trouble.'

'No,' he said. 'I understand that.' He wriggled in his seat, settled himself more comfortably. 'Has this evening, so far, made any difference?'

'I was apprehensive about coming back to this house. We lived here together for more than two years.'

'I don't suppose the place has changed much. I've not consciously made any great alterations.'

'You've moved one or two of the pictures round in this room.'

'That's right. But I expect we'd have done that if you had stayed.'

He decided such snippets of conversation were the best he could expect.

'You felt you'd like to come back here?'

'Yes. Or at least I wasn't comfortable with myself. We'd been apart for some months, and I still couldn't help thinking about you. After all we were in love.' She paused; he said nothing. 'Weren't we?'

'Very much so.' That struck the right, encouraging note. 'But I remember what we were like when you left.'

'So do I. And yet within a month or two I was uncertain. I feared somehow that I'd let you down.'

'We had just got on each other's nerves.'

'But we didn't try to sort it out. We just let matters get worse and worse.'

'Do you think we were capable of that? I was so angry I could barely exchange a word with you without starting a row. I don't think, you know, we should forget that.'

'You don't want us to make up, then?' she asked.

'I didn't say that. We were fighting and nagging all the time in that last month or two. I found it hell. I could no more have made it up with you than flown over the houses. Now we've been living apart for some months, it doesn't mark us in the same way. We tell ourselves that we didn't try hard enough and that now we're older, more experienced, we could perhaps make a better job of it the second time round.'

'Did you miss me?' she asked, stressing her verb.

'Yes. But I was glad the constant argument was over.'

'Did you think about it often?'

'Yes, I did. In the first weeks after you left. And I sometimes wondered how we managed to get into such a tangle with each other.'

'And did you come to any conclusion?'

'I blamed you,' he said. 'You were unreasonable.'

'In what way?'

'If I made a suggestion about pretty well anything you'd veto it or pour scorn on it. Things that you said you enjoyed when first we married you now mocked or dismissed just because I suggested we do them again.'

'It didn't seem like that to me.'

'How *did* it seem?' he asked.

'You had no time for me. I was a nuisance, an incubus.'

'I thought an incubus was a male spirit forcing himself sexually on hapless women.'

'That's what I mean. There you go again. Correcting me.'

'I beg your pardon.' He lowered his head. She spoke like an adolescent in trouble, not a sharp solicitor.

They sat speechless for a few minutes in the warmth of the fire which comforted them, dried bitterness from their exchanges. John, with legs stretched full out, was in no hurry. She had asked for the meeting and must now take the initiative. He looked her over as she sat opposite him, perhaps three yards away. She made an attractive picture in her armchair; that he admitted. She still wore their wedding ring, he noticed. Her hands were small and beautiful and a faint, unobtrusive perfume sweetened the air. What would happen if he made a physical move towards her? She'd yield, he guessed, but he was not tempted.

Now and then one or the other of them raised the purpose of their meeting, but the topic petered out as if they did not dare to take the matter further. Soon after ten she said she must go. She said she was beautifully warm and would go straight to bed.

'I'll run you back in the car,' he said.

'Oh, don't do that. There's no need.'

'I'm not sure the streets are safe for women walking alone.'

She did not argue, and seemed grateful. Before she left the car after the short journey, she unbuckled her seat belt, leaned over and kissed him.

'Thank you for a lovely evening,' she said in a little girl's voice.

He watched her speedy retreat up the steps to her apartment. She did not turn either to speak or wave, but unlocked her door and slipped inside.

He wondered what story he'd tell his mother when she questioned him. When he had reached home and garaged his car, he too was glad to turn his back on the night.

VI

Just after New Year's Day, a week later, Helen rang John to ask if he'd like to accompany her to a concert.

'I felt in your debt,' she said, 'after that delicious evening you provided for me. I came across,' the words puzzled him, 'two tickets for this violin recital. I know you like fiddle players.'

'Who is it?'

'John Taylor.'

'Who's he?'

'He's a young man. A professor at the Royal College. They say he's outstanding.'

'Who are "they"?'

'Ronald Hoare who works in my office. His wife's a violinist.'

She gave him details of the concert and they arranged their time of meeting, had two minutes of pleasant reciprocal inquiries after health, and then rang off. No sooner had he walked into the next room than the phone fetched him back. This time it was his mother, inquiring if he'd seen or heard anything of Helen.

'If you'd have rung fifteen minutes back the answer would have been no, but she's just phoned to invite me to go with her to a concert.'

'Where's that?'

'St John's, Smith Square.'

'Well, go on; what sort of concert?'

'A violin recital by a man called John Taylor.'

'What's he playing?'

'A Beethoven sonata and the César Franck. He opens with the Vivaldi variations on a theme of Corelli.'

'What Beethoven?'

'The Kreutzer.'

He answered briefly, puzzled by his mother's curiosity about the details of the programme. She herself rarely patronised a

34

concert these days and never used her CD player. Her piano lid remained shut for weeks on end. This close questioning must in some way be connected with her interest in his and Helen's welfare.

'How is Helen?'

'She said she was well.'

'And her attitude towards you?'

'Well, she did invite me to the concert.'

'And how do you feel about it?'

'I shall enjoy it.'

'I'm not talking about the concert. Do you detect any change in the way you view Helen?'

'Detect? No. We've had no contact since we met in the Christmas holidays.'

'But she must be friendly towards you, or she would not have invited you out with her.'

'Yes. Very likely.'

'Are you taking this seriously? You hardly give me any sort of real answer, and then you make out you misunderstand me. You don't seem in the slightest bit concerned about the state of your marriage It's a serious matter, John.'

'I answer you as best I can.'

'I don't think you do.'

'It's a week since we met and talked. We were friendly enough, or at least we weren't scratching each other's eyes out, but we came to no sort of conclusion. I remember how we were before she upped sticks and walked out on me. I don't blame her. But when she left I was relieved, as I believe she was.'

'Don't you detect any slight change, symptoms of improvement? I'm very fond of you both, and I'd like to see you happily married again, as you were at the beginning. You could barely keep your eyes or hands off her.'

'We were better than a few months ago, but we could hardly be worse.'

'You should be positive about this, John.'

'What do you mean?'

'You are married to Helen. You made vows to her in a church. You should be on the sharp lookout for any and every opportunity to make it up with her.'

He did not answer, and his mother kept silent, at least for a short time, believing perhaps she had gone too far. When she did speak again it was less abrasively.

'I'm very glad you're seeing her again. When's this concert?'

'Tuesday of next week.'

'Let me know how it goes.'

'I will. How's Father making out?'

'Much the same as when you saw him last in the holidays. Neither better nor worse. Have you seen anything of your aunt Irene? She said she might call in to see you.'

'She's never visited me once since I bought this house and that's six years ago.'

'That's what she said: she ought to make a start.'

'We'll see.'

'She'll ring, I expect.'

'She'd better.'

He gave his mother no encouragement here. He'd wager she'd been pressing her sister to go round to inspect his house, and then report back to her about the squalor or extravagant decor of the place. He was fairly certain that the sisters did not get on well with each other, but they were sufficiently alike to gang up on him.

When his aunt telephoned he answered pleasantly enough. Yes, she could visit him a week on Saturday, one of the dates of her choosing, and he'd be delighted to provide her with a meal and he'd show her round his house.

'It's you I want to see, not your house and garden.'

'Whence the sudden interest?' he asked.

'I saw you at Christmas, and was favourably impressed. Your mother and I discussed your character and idiosyncrasies at length.'

'I feel flattered.'

'I'll come to lunch, if I may. These days that's my main meal.'

'Have you any objections to anything? You're not a vegetarian, are you?'

'No. I ought to be, but I'm not. Plain food. I'm not a big eater.'

'I see.'

He wasn't certain whether Irene would report this conversation to his mother.

The violin recital exceeded expectation. John met Helen exactly on time so that they had no need to hurry. The soloist was admirable, with a rich tone of almost orchestral dimension. His accompanist, with what John considered the plebeian name Henry Jones, was equally accomplished. It all reminded John of his schooldays when he was allowed into the local celebrity concerts in Beechnall for a small fee by the kindness of some earlier patron of the school who had left money 'for the artistic education of members of the sixth form'. He even remembered some young lady prizewinner playing this evening's opening item, the Corelli-Vivaldi variations, as an encore. Helen seemed equally charmed. She was brilliantly turned out, in tartan and black, with a scarlet silk scarf and a Russian hat. He accompanied her home, not wishing to leave her out alone in the streets late at night. She invited him in for a nightcap, and he accepted, grudgingly knowing he had to be up at the crack of dawn for tomorrow's work in Reading.

'Are you coming in for a drink?' she asked, outside her house.

'I'd better not. I've a big day tomorrow.'

'Please.'

He yielded.

They drank cocoa together, a beverage he'd not tasted since he was a child. They talked about the concert, John excitedly.

'I don't know what I've been missing,' he confessed. 'I ought to go to more recitals and theatres.'

'And football matches,' she mocked him.

They laughed together, like conspiring friends.

'Why don't you go?' she asked.

'Work. I've been too busy. I feel pretty well exhausted by the time I get home.'

'What time's that?'

'Often eight or nine o'clock. And then it's too late, or too much bother to go out.'

'You managed it tonight.'

'You invited me. I cleared my decks for tonight's outing. But until we actually went, I'd no idea how much I was missing.'

They talked thus for half an hour, friendly, smiling, and then suddenly he said he must leave. Helen's face showed her disappointment.

'I've a big job on tomorrow. I shall have to be out of the house by seven-thirty.'

She watched him.

'You could stay here for the night,' she said. 'After all, we are man and wife.'

'All the papers I need are at home, and I promised to pick up one of my team. It's a large affair. The police will be involved, I guess, when we've finished.'

'It's not dangerous?' she asked.

'Not at all.'

'I'm so frightened these days. People act like gangsters. A man was shot dead in a pub not half a mile from here only last week.'

'I read about it in the *Standard*,' he said. 'Wasn't it a case of drugs?'

'I think so.'

He was on his feet, and making his way out to the hall. She followed at speed. Before he had time to take his coat from the stand, she had flung her arms round him.

'We must go out together again,' she said.

He felt her weight on him. Her breasts pressed into his coat. He squeezed her, but without passion, like a brother.

'Next week,' he said. 'I'll ring you Friday night, if I'm back.'

They kissed, meaning it. He hurried away into the dark street, warm, pleased, puzzled at his own reactions.

VII

Irene Davenport turned up exactly on time for her visit. She looked strikingly impressive in a green coat and dark trouser suit. Her large BMW added distinction to the street. She looked her nephew over with an air of satisfaction.

'This is a really pleasant house,' she said. 'These big bow windows make it so light.' First blood to me, John thought.

She drank a glass of dry sherry, but told him that was all the alcohol she'd take; she wanted no wine with her lunch as she was driving. He had prepared a beef casserole which she praised and followed this with fruit salad and thick custard. She ate small portions but clearly enjoyed the meal. She drank iced water.

'Is this from the tap?' she asked.

'Yes. A hospital nurse told me that it was the purest water you could drink.'

'And you believed her?'

'Yes. Is it not right?'

'As far as I know. When Eric's home we have bottled water. He lives in such strange places that he's suspicious of anything that's not bottled and sealed.'

'Is he still in Afghanistan?'

'Yes. He's been warned that he may be moved to Paris shortly.'

'Is he pleased about that?'

'He doesn't complain. He finds something interesting wherever they send him.'

'I thought he liked the wild places of the earth.'

'The editor thinks he's as fit as he possibly can be, and has had so many injections that they can send him anywhere they like with no ill consequences. He loves to be pushed around from pillar to post. "It's the way I learn," he informs me. It wouldn't suit me, that I can tell you.'

'You sound just like my mother,' he said.

39

'Your mother knows her mind and speaks it. Teachers are quite often like that. Your father know his income-tax law, of course, but otherwise as you know, he let your mother rule the roost in the house. She chose the colour of the paint, the wallpaper, the carpets, the furniture. She decided on the holidays or the meals for the day.'

'That wouldn't suit your husband?'

'Oh, I don't know about that. When he arrives home from some foreign assignment, he's usually exhausted, and for two days he'll lounge about the house like a ghost. If I fed him on, oh, let's say cheese sandwiches for every meal, he'd eat them and be thankful. If anyone asked him he'd answer that he was used to meals of that sort. But after two days he'd have thrown off his tiredness and be himself.'

'Which would mean fancy food?'

'Not really. Eating's not all that important to him. He'll have enough to keep him lively. No, he's always searching after something new, different, difficult.'

'Such as?'

'He'll see something in the paper, some archaeological dig, or murder case, or unusual happening, an earthquake or landslip, and he'd want to go off and investigate it. That's the wrong word. He'd be on the lookout for a new slant on the story. He'd want to find out how ordinary people reacted to out-of-the-way occurrences. He can't sit still.'

'Has he always been like that?'

'Yes, always. I knew him first at Oxford. He was two years ahead of me.'

'Studying?'

'Greats. But he was always off at the weekends on some mad scheme. They'd climb a mountain or two, or take a rowing boat out to sea and sail from one port to another whatever the weather. Silly things, but different from sitting at a desk reading Aristotle in Greek. His tutor used to tell him there were still exciting discoveries to be made in these old writers, but they weren't obvious to him. He said he quite enjoyed sorting out philosophers and their ideas, but they didn't hit him hard enough, surprise him sufficiently for him to spend the whole of his life studying them.'

'And this wildness attracted you to him?'

'When I went up to university I was a little provincial mouse. I was quiet, wouldn't say boo to a goose. I enjoyed having my own room, and different friends, and I worked hard at my French and German. There was plenty to fill my time up. And then he started to show an interest in me. I could hardly believe it. I was a nobody. And he was older than I was, and it was said that some of the dons were afraid of him.'

'What was the attraction, then?'

'Physical, I suppose. Sexual chemistry. He seduced me. I was a virgin. From what I had been brought up to believe by your grandparents and my teachers and friends, that should have been the end of it. He'd had what he wanted from me, and he'd be off on his next conquest. But it wasn't so. When he left university he set out on some sort of trip to the Antarctic. I thought I'd heard the last of him, because he hardly wrote a word to me. Once I'd graduated, I decided I'd work at the BBC, I went on a typing course in London. That's the way we did it then. Got in at the bottom, and worked our way up. In the end he came back to me just as I was about to fall in love with somebody else. He knew people at the Beeb, and got me climbing on the news-journalistic ladder. We weren't married for another two years, and then he went immediately to South America. He wrote a very good book about his time there. About the Amazon, mainly. Have you read it? I'll lend you a copy. It's fascinating. He writes as he talks.'

'You obviously admire him.'

'I don't know if "admire" is the word. I know all the draw-backs. Marriage isn't too easy an institution, as you'll know yourself. We spent a good bit of our lives apart.'

'Didn't he ever offer to take you on his expeditions?'

'Once. When he did a month or two in New York, but I had just changed my job, and didn't want to go anywhere until I'd thoroughly settled and knew what I was doing.'

'It all sounds interesting,' he said.

'Yes, it was. In its way. And how is your lady wife?' She altered her tone of voice to emphasise her old-fashioned, polite sarcasm. 'Your mother is hoping for a reconciliation there, or so she tells me.'

'My mother lives in a world of her own making.'

41

'But how are you and Helen getting on?'

'We've met twice, once at my house, once at a concert, and we both enjoyed ourselves. There were, however, no earth-shattering changes.'

'Your mother seems very fond of Helen. Unusually so.'

'Just a stick to beat me with.' Irene laughed nervously at the sharpness of his tone. 'My mother is not exactly pleasant with me these days.'

'What wickedness have you been indulging in?' Again her voice underlined the artificiality of her words.

'I'm not to blame. She thinks life has dealt her a poor, dirty hand. As you know, William is pretty well disabled, mentally and physically. She has no idea how to spend her time away from her school. She begrudges all the dusting, and hoovering, and cooking and polishing she does. Moreover, she expected Helen and me to be starting a family, grandchildren for her to coo over, and what do we do but split up? She has always seemed to me an intelligent woman, and when she retires at sixty, if she does, she could take up new interests with the WEA, and the University of the Third Age, if that's what they call it, or join classes which do tapestry or painting or calligraphy, or she could join music societies, or theatre clubs or even gymnasia. But no. Not her. She moans and groans about Father and me, and for all I know, about you, and everything else.'

'Something in what you say,' Irene agreed.

'I feel sorry for her,' he said. 'She's worked hard all her life for her husband, for me, for the schools she's taught in, and what's left to show for it? Nothing. Absolutely nothing.'

'She's doing the garden now?' Irene asked.

'Yes. With help.'

'Does she know anything about it?'

'There are plenty of television programmes and dozens of books. And she seems willing to learn.'

'That surprises me.'

'Well, come outside and see my garden.'

They went out through the door of his modern kitchen. A burst of sunshine with a stab of icy wind greeted them.

'It all looks very neat,' she said from the yard. She showed no keenness to move further.

'Come and walk round. We'll be sheltered from the wind.'
Irene took tiny steps.

'There's not much to be done at this time of the year. Even if
I had time.'

'You've looked after it so far?'

'I have a man who comes in if I'm going to be away. He
admires my designs. Or so he says.' She listened, but shivered.

He led her indoors. She congratulated him on the warmth of
the house.

'Will the flowers be out soon?' she inquired.

'Yes. Snowdrops and then crocuses, depending on the weather.'

'It looks so very neat,' she said again. Her interest in gardens
was small. 'I have a man in to deal with mine. Eric says he knows
nothing about it.'

'Ambiguous,' he said. 'The man or your husband?'

She frowned slightly in puzzlement, then suddenly understood
him.

'Oh, the man's ignorant, not Eric.'

He suddenly pictured her husband. Tallish and rangy, not an
ounce of superfluous weight. Eric Davenport's eyes were ice
blue. His brown hair, slightly touched with grey, was cut short
like an old-fashioned public schoolboy's. He could stand perfectly
still, but when he moved he did so with energetic speed.
Sometimes he wore a pair of glasses, though John had never
made out for what purpose. John remembered watching his uncle
do a difficult climb in Scotland on television, easily mastering
nasty overhangs. Eric had moved without hurry, pausing only
now and again to comment on his interest in the climb. He had
barely seemed out of breath and climbed over the tough rock
face so securely that the watcher felt no tremor of fear, merely
admiration for the confident movements of body, limbs and head
forging upwards.

'Is he climbing in Afghanistan?' he asked.

'I don't think so. Or not seriously. If he's thinking of a stiff
ascent he practises for weeks before.'

'Every day?'

'That's not always possible, but he's out every minute he can.
He leaves nothing to chance. No, he's there now reporting on the
political situation after the war. He's learning Pashto.'

43

'Is that the local language?'

'Of some parts. He knows some Hindustani already. He seems able to pick a language up in no time. His paper sends him to a local college for a crash course.'

'For how long?'

'A few weeks. They have all these technical aids in their language labs. I think he thoroughly enjoys acquiring a new language. He says it's not altogether necessary these days, with English so widely used.'

They were sitting now by the garden window of the dining room drinking black coffee.

'What am I to tell your mother?'

'How fastidious I am about dusting and polishing the furniture.'

'No, you idiot. About Helen?'

'What I've already told you. This last expedition has given me a taste for concerts. I shall go more often.'

'With Helen?'

'It's possible. She made an ideal companion. She knows quite a lot about music. But don't encourage my mother to draw any out-of-the-way conclusions from that.'

'Did you have sex with her on the two occasions you met?'

His face showed his surprise at her question which she delivered without emphasis as if she were asking, for instance, had they managed to obtain good seats for the concert. She showed no embarrassment at all as she sat waiting for the answer.

'No,' he said.

'And you weren't tempted? Neither of you?'

'I can't speak for Helen,' he said.

'No.' Long drawn-out, judicious.

'I don't think for a moment,' he said, determined to get his own back, 'that my mother will ask you any questions about that.'

'I don't suppose she will. I ask because I'm interested. But I see that you regard my question as impertinent, even impudent.'

'Well.' He drawled the word at length. 'Let's be generous and say "unusual".'

'I thought you were a modern young man and wouldn't be put out.'

'It's not really your concern, though, is it?'

'None of it's my business, really, but your mother seemed troubled and I'm interested; curious is perhaps a better word.'

'You have your answer.'

'I think perhaps it throws some light on the situation.'

'Oh, good. I'll add this: when we lived together, the sex was good. In fact, it was just about the best thing in our marriage, all things considered. We spoilt it, of course, in the end.'

'Have you a photograph of Helen? I saw her only once, at your wedding. She certainly looked very pretty then, but I don't think I'd recognise her in the street.'

He stood and made for a drawer from which he took a postcard-sized, steel-framed photograph which he passed over to his aunt.

'Try that,' he said.

Irene carefully looked, then searched in her bag for a pair of spectacles. She donned these then scrutinised the picture again.

'The pair of you,' she said. 'Very handsome.'

'I'm only there to show you the scale.'

'A good photograph. Have you any more?'

'Dozens.' He was still standing by the drawer. He took out two framed photographs which he passed over. The first and larger was a head-and-shoulders of Helen, taken about three months before they split up.

'She looks very vivacious here. And happy.'

'Yes. She wasn't. We were constantly quarrelling at the time.'

'I couldn't deduce that from the photograph.' Irene looked at the other, a sarcastic smile about her lips. 'Ah, portrait of wife in bathing costume. Where was that taken?'

'In Bournemouth, about eighteen months ago. We went to visit an old aunt of Helen's, great-aunt really, one weekend. She had a large bungalow, a little way back from the coast, which had a swimming pool.'

'Well-to-do?' Irene queried.

'I'd guess so.'

'So Helen has expectations there?'

'It was never mentioned.'

Irene nodded, almost sympathetically, but said nothing.

'The old girl was very lively. She wrote children's books.'

'And a husband?'

'He died not long after he'd retired and they had moved to Bournemouth.'

They talked for perhaps an hour until Irene stood to announce that she must be on her way.

'I've really enjoyed it here. I'm amazed at your house; it's so beautifully clean. I expected the usual bachelor pad and its detritus.'

'I'm not at home sufficiently long to make the place dirty. And Mrs Thorpe comes in Tuesdays to do the bedrooms, and Fridays the ground floor.'

'Does she do your washing?'

'Yes. And I guess her own at the same time. I cook a bit, as today, and usually the only places I use are my office and the bedroom.'

'Could you manage if your cleaning lady was ill?'

'I could. I have done. I wouldn't want to, because I haven't the time. This last three months I've been inundated with work, and it's likely to get worse.'

She looked him over, then asked mildly, 'Is accountancy boring?'

'Not to me. Perhaps it suits my personality. All jobs have dull periods, but there's enough to keep me interested and my brain at work.'

'And I presume it's well paid?'

'Not compared with football or television journalism, but yes I think I'm reaching a stage where it's reckoned that this labourer is worthy of his hire.'

'And it doesn't depress you that you'll be doing it for the next thirty years?'

'I never think about it. Never crosses my mind.'

They walked out together into the hall, where she put on her elegant coat and after a search in her large handbag jangled her car keys. Smiling broadly she held out her arms for John to kiss her.

Her lips were soft, and she seemed in no hurry to break apart. Then, astonishingly, her tongue forced its way sweetly into his mouth. When they let go of each other, he was amazed to find he felt nothing but delight in the last few minutes' performance. This was his mother's sister, twenty years older than he was, another man's wife, a famous man's, and herself distinguished in her own field. They had acted like schoolchildren.

'We must try that again,' she said, drawing on her gloves.

He did not know how to answer that.

Irene marched to the front door, and had negotiated the two fairly complicated locks in no time. She moved into the garden path. At three-thirty the day was already darkening. The large car drew away.

John stood in his hall, breathless, thoughtful. He had even put a hand on his aunt's buttocks. She had responded. He could not help wondering what kind of report his mother would receive. He learnt three days later when the postman delivered a card, decorated with roses, which read: 'Your aunt was amazed at the exceptional neatness of your house. It puts both of ours to shame. Your cooking, too, was above praise. With love, Mother.'

VIII

For the next fortnight John Riley was kept busy at work. The job at Reading turned out to have no serious consequences for the firm concerned, and the police were not called in. The task had been complicated but he had demonstrated in the end that the owners of the firm were honest. They were delighted, for they had feared the worst, and had paid their accountant rather more smartly than they had settled with some of their other earlier creditors. He warned them that they had been foolish, and suggested a more straightforward way of keeping their accounts. 'It will save you money and time,' he told them. The two brothers who owned the factory looked like crooks to John, had been struggling to keep their business solvent but had now begun to make a profit and had taken on two new hands. They had been careless about their books for the past two years, chiefly, John guessed, to hide their losses.

They smiled at him now, and he recommended to them a young local accountant who had worked in his office soon after qualifying.

'Won't you do it for us, Mr Riley?' they begged. 'You have no idea how you have set our minds at rest.'

'This young man will do the job as well as I do, but it will be cheaper.'

That settled the argument. They presented him with a set of plastic trays, one of their 'lines', but in his view aesthetically satisfying. He congratulated them on their taste and craftsmanship.

'That's our trouble,' the older said. 'We're basically artists, not businessmen.'

The three days he had spent in Reading left him tired. He began his next job, a much larger but more straightforward business, without enthusiasm. He wondered if he was losing his appetite for accountancy, but finding he had time on his hands in the evening rang Helen to see if she had any good ideas about spending an evening together. She seemed reluctant, saying that she had been out twice this week, to a musical and then to a film, both of which passed muster, just, and had promised to go to a dance. A young man she knew, a doctor, attended a ballroom dancing class, and the school had laid on a dance so that the pupils could demonstrate their skills to themselves and to the wide world.

He felt disappointed, and wondered who the young doctor was. He was surprised that he felt jealous.

One evening, having an hour to waste, he went to the local pub, the Cross Keys, an unusual practice for him. He claimed that it was no use visiting such a place, unless he had friends already with him. As he moodily walked along the street he caught sight of Helen arm in arm with a man in a raincoat. Helen, he guessed, would have seen him, and in the old days would have waved or shouted to catch his attention. Tonight she looked away and hurried her partner forward. John stopped to watch the couple reach the street corner where they turned out of his sight.

The pub was almost deserted; the muzak groaned low; the beer tasted sour. Two pallid, middle-aged men argued over the relative merits of teams at the top of the Premiership. They conducted their polemics without enthusiasm, and the favourite expression of both was 'you know'. Neither said anything of interest. When John had finished his pint, he returned his glass to the bar and, buttoning his topcoat to the neck, slipped unnoticed out of the door.

The street struck cold, and it seemed to be growing foggy. Passers-by slapped their feet onto the pavement to keep warm. The windows of the closed shops were only half-lit, having an air of dereliction. A beggar sat on the pavement, head in a knitted balaclava, a mongrel dog on the ground by his knees.

'Have you any small change, sir?'

John stopped, looking down. The local council had been advising the public not to give their money to beggars, who would waste it on drugs. It was specially advisable not to be charitable to those with dogs. There were homes provided where these characters could find a night's lodging if they put themselves to a little trouble to apply.

'So I could get myself a hot drink,' the fervourless voice implored.

John dug into his pocket and dug out a handful of change. He stared at it, noting two pound coins on top of the rest. That was right; he remembered dropping these in the pocket where he kept silver.

He carefully placed the coins in a round shallow tin the beggar had in front of his right foot. They filled the receptacle which before had held two or three coppers.

'Thank you, sir. God bless you, sir.'

The man did not once look up. John did not move away.

'What's your dog's name?' he asked.

'Sam.'

'A good name. Goodnight.'

No answer. The dog, which had stirred at the mention of his name, settled down comfortably.

Back at home it was, at least, warm. He made a cup of instant coffee. He picked up the morning's paper, but threw it down again. He did not feel tired, only disheartened. He compared his lot with that of the beggar in the cold street, but drew no comfort from the comparison.

The telephone rang. John rose slowly. He was not expecting calls on this Saturday evening. If a colleague was too ill to work, he or his wife would announce it on Sunday. His mother was unlikely to ring at this time of night, unless in emergency. Perhaps it was Irene. Perhaps not. Without enthusiasm he picked up the phone.

Helen.

She spoke plainly. Just by chance, she'd been looking through the Royal Shakespeare Company's new programme. They were beginning in Stratford until the end of January when they started touring the country. She had suddenly decided she ought to see another Shakespeare play, especially as the ones they were offering were unusual.

'What are they?' John asked.

'*The Merry Wives* and *Coriolanus*. I've never seen *Coriolanus*.'

'Have you seen *The Merry Wives*?'

'Yes,' Helen answered with pride. 'And Verdi's Falstaff.' She paused. He listened. 'It would mean taking two days off from work and staying the night in Stratford.'

'Have you thought about dates?'

'Yes. I will tell you my choice if you think the idea's viable.'

'It's possible. You may even mention days I can take off. I owe myself a little holiday.'

He took out his diary and they fixed a date.

'That's to see *Coriolanus*,' Helen said. 'You realise that?'

'I think I'd prefer that.'

'What's it about?'

'A very proud man who hates the common people.'

'And?'

'They and their tribunes throw him out of Rome, and so he joins with his old enemies to attack Rome.'

'How do you know so much about it?'

'Remember I did it for A level. Maths, English and Economics.'

'You couldn't have done that mixture at our school,' she said.

'I didn't know what I wanted at that age. So I added Economics to the two I'd done best at in GCSE.'

They talked in this vein for a few minutes and arranged who was to get the tickets and who to book the hotel room.

'We're taking a room together, are we?' he asked.

'If you don't mind.'

'No. I'll see to the hotel. I did some work in Stratford earlier last year, and had a very satisfactory, comfortable place. As soon as you've booked the tickets, I'll see to that.'

'I'm glad you can go,' she said with simplicity. 'I was a bit doubtful about asking you.'

'Why so?'

'I was a bit niggardly about going out with you when last you raised the matter. I was very pushed for time at work, and worried about a client who was acting unwisely, and try as I might I couldn't stop him.'

'I know the feeling well.'

'Good. That's fixed then, if I can get hold of the tickets.'

She waited.

'I saw you earlier this evening,' he said. 'You were walking along Branscombe Road with a young man.'

'We'd been to a rugby match.'

'Did you enjoy it?'

'Not much. I didn't understand the rules. It was the first time I'd seen the game. It seemed very rough, and the players were puffing and panting and swearing. I liked it when they threw the ball in and they lifted the players up to catch it.'

'Who won?'

'George's hospital.'

'Never heard of it.'

'George was the young man who took me. George Walker. He's the doctor I mentioned to you.'

'Does he play?'

'He did. But he doesn't now. He did something to his leg.'

'How long did the match go on? It must have been seven-thirty when I saw you.'

'We'd been out for tea. With some of the players. An enormous meal, sausages and bacon and beans and fried bread.'

'That sounds more like breakfast than tea.'

'It was. It was in a café near the ground. They always go in there after the match. And then on to the pub. We didn't, though.'

'Exciting.'

'I don't know about that. Very friendly and noisy.'

'Were they all doctors?'

'Yes, or students or one or two people connected in some way with the hospital.'

'A good team?'

'I don't know. I'd no means of telling. I shouldn't think so. There weren't very many people there watching. Not like the time you took me to see Arsenal play at Highbury. George brought me home but he had to go back to the hospital. He was standing in for a friend.'

'What does he do?'

'He's a senior registrar in neurology.'

'Impressive,' he said.

'Yes, they say he's clever. But slightly foolish. He oughtn't to be spending so much time on rugger at this stage of his career.'

'How old is he?'

'Thirty-one.'

They talked for a few minutes more. She'd deal, she said, with the tickets first thing on Monday, and let him know the result.

'Thank you,' he said. 'You're a treasure.'

His spirits had lifted; he walked round the room and began to sing. He did not choose his song, merely sang it.

> Wrap me up in my tarpaulin jacket,
> And say a poor buffer lies low,
> And six stalwart lancers shall carry me
> With steps solemn, mournful and slow.

It was a favourite of his father's, who sometimes hummed it about the house, and it had a story attached. When William Riley was in the fourth form of his grammar school he'd taken part in the school play. He did not have a leading role, he was in fact a footman, or serving-man of some kind, and he had been chosen because he was tall for his age. John had no idea what the play was, but his father had appeared three nights of the week before full houses, parents and fellow-pupils, stiff and upright without speaking a word.

After the last performance the cast and technicians had celebrated with a small party on the stage. William was by far the youngest and had sat on the floorboards proud as a peacock amongst the six-formers and the three beautiful girls borrowed from the neighbouring girls' grammar school who had taken the leading parts in the drama. Two young masters had organised both the play and the party. They ate a rock bun or two and drank lemonade; in those strict days nobody thought of beer on educational premises. And they had talked and laughed and told jokes and had sung this song 'Wrap Me Up'. William Riley had never forgotten this event, when prefects had spoken to him as a human being, almost as an equal, and one of the girls had smiled at him and inquired if he often acted in public. The party had lasted not much more than an hour before the caretaker, a grim and disgruntled figure, staggered round rattling his keys to indicate that it was time to lock up, but William had felt this to be a high point of his life, and sometimes sang the song the great ones had taught him, and had told his wife and son once or twice in moments of adult pleasure of that momentous evening.

Now the sad song had come unbidden to the mind of John Riley because he had heard from Helen. He still did not know whether he wanted her back as a wife, but disliked the idea of sharing her with a neurologist or anyone else. He slapped the table top as he walked around the room. That hour of partying on the stage had taken place nearly sixty years ago at the end of a World War and had left its mark through his father on him. He shook his head, glad and nonplussed.

IX

Towards the end of January and just before the projected visit to Stratford, Ella Riley rang her son at ten o'clock one evening. He could tell by the tone of voice and her breathless delivery that she was excited.

'Where have you been all day?' she demanded.

'At work. Where else?'

'Until this time of night?'

'Yes. I left soon after nine.'

'I've been trying to get hold of you all evening.'

'I'm sorry. But you have me now.'

His mother breathed heavily.

'We've had some excitement here.' That was typical of his mother. She delighted in allowing you a period for guesswork or tantalising anticipation before she made her announcement which, she hoped, would be more exotic than your guess.

'Yes?' Polite, but not encouraging.

'It's your father. And I didn't know until this afternoon.'

John wondered what the news would be. Perhaps William had fallen on his head, and cured his dementia. He dismissed that as unlikely, and waited for his mother to continue with her tale.

'They had a fire at Holmleigh on the evening of the day before yesterday.'

'Was it serious?'

'The fire itself, no. It was on the second floor and the fire brigade soon dealt with it. But one poor woman died from smoke inhalation. And another is quite ill. They rang me to tell me that your father was all right, unaffected. They don't quite know how it started. They think perhaps it was a cigarette end.'

'I thought they weren't allowed to smoke.'

'They're not. Except in the small lounge. Never in their bedrooms. But some of them are quite irresponsible. They're not

55

allowed to keep either matches or cigarettes; those who smoke have to deposit their supply with the staff, and to ask if they wish to indulge.'

'And how does Dad come into it?'

'This afternoon, I'd just had my lunch, when the front door-bell rang and already there was a reporter from the local news-paper. Apparently he wanted a photograph of your father. I questioned him, and he said that during the fire at a nursing home, your father had been responsible for the rescue of two old ladies.'

'How was that?'

'It seemed extremely unlikely to me, but I didn't say so to him. I said that I knew there had been a fire, that my husband was unhurt, and that was all. He said the fire was on the second floor, and black smoke was billowing all over the building and the alarms were ringing. Your father, as you know, was on the third floor where there were two other patients. They'd been put there because their legs were adjudged fit to walk up two flights of stairs. Your father wasn't in bed; it was only about nine and he sat watching the television. He went outside, saw all this smoke, saw that it was impossible to get downstairs through it, and went and knocked at the doors of the two women. One of them was up and about but the other was undressing. She's very slow, and uncertain. The matron said it took her an hour to get dressed in the morning, and as long to get ready for bed in the evening. This other woman and your father bundled her into some clothes. He told them it would be very cold outside, and made them put on scarves and hats as well as overcoats. Then they made their way along the corridor to a door which your father had undone in no time. Outside there was a fire escape with a small platform at their level. Your father climbed out first, and they had a terrible job to get the infirm old lady out. She was terrified and screaming and hitting out at them. It was rather dark, but your father had a torch with him. Apparently he said that the only good thing was that they were out of the choking smoke and into the fresh air.'

'What then?'

'The two of them forced the hysterical lady down the steps, but it was a nightmare. They struggled to make her move her feet and by the time they did get her down the other poor lady was in tears The fire escape, which was metal, did not go all the

56

way to the ground. There was a gap of four or five feet. Why
this was so I just can't make out. But your father managed to
jump or fall off. How he did it I don't know, because he can
barely shuffle about on the flat ground. And then he lifted the
other two from the ladder. By the time he was dealing with the
second a maid came round and gave him a hand.'

'He seems to have been able to move easily.'

'I'm amazed. He could get about without difficulty, they said.
Do you think it was the adrenaline at work in all the excitement?'

'Possible. But he's been so slow of late.'

'According to this reporter the sensible lady said he was as
cool as a cucumber. He issued orders, knew exactly what to do,
made them put on warm clothes, closed all the bedroom doors
to keep the smoke and fire out of their bedrooms, took the bar
off the door leading to the fire escape without any trouble. She
said she'd no idea how to do this, and if he hadn't been so sharp
they would have been dead of smoke inhalation. He was a real
hero, and she thanked God such a man was up there with them.'

'Where were the staff?'

'There were only two on duty at night. The matron and her
husband were in bed at the top of the house in a converted attic.
They dashed down the fire escape, but couldn't open your father's
exit from the outside. The woman who died was on the floor
where the fire was. She had taken in so much smoke she was
dead by the time they rescued her. They think she might be the
one who'd started the fire. She must have sneaked a cigarette
and matches upstairs. They're all very upset about it in the home.
I think they expect trouble at the inquest, and the fire authorities
will now insist on all sorts of expensive alterations.'

'And how does my father seem to be taking it?' John asked.

'He's just as he was before it all happened. He's slow, and
hardly says a word, except to grumble.'

'And what do the doctors say about him?'

'Doctors? What do you mean?'

'There he was dumb and immobile, but when the fire comes
he regains his wits, his voice and the use of his legs.'

'It appears so.'

'If he can become normal and rational in the fire then why
can't the hospital restore him to good health?'

'Our doctor is as surprised as I am. "I didn't think it possible, Mrs Riley," he said. "There he was only able to shuffle about, and yet not only could he clamber about on the fire escape, but he helped that practically bedridden woman down the steps as well. He must have been using muscles he hadn't employed for months. It's beyond me," he said, "quite out of my ken."'

'And Dad doesn't say anything?'

'No. Except the first lady he rescued is always round him now, making a fuss, bringing him little gifts. I think he quite likes that.'

'He's somebody to talk to.'

'He doesn't want to talk to me.'

'Ask the psychiatrist you occasionally take him to see and find out if he's come across other cases of sudden, temporary recovery like this. It seems all very odd to me.'

'Odd? What do you mean?'

'I wouldn't expect a man who's broken both his legs immediately to start to walk normally.'

He was as puzzled as his mother.

She sent him a cutting from the local paper: 'Nursing Home Hero Saves Lives of Two'. The picture was of his father in his prime, taken ten years or more ago, when he looked out over the world as if he owned it. There were no quotations from William who clearly had offered no comment to the reporter. The sensible lady had been eloquent in his praise. 'Mr Riley,' she said, 'whom I had always known as a very quiet, reserved man, judged exactly what was to be done and because of that he saved our lives. We could not go down the stairs because of the billowing smoke, and it would not have been long before we'd been overwhelmed by it. He knew exactly what steps to take, and encouraged us. My friend Mrs Smith-Tenby suffers from vertigo but he managed to lead and support her down three storeys like a hero. That is my word for him, because that is what he is.'

John's aunt Irene rang him about his father's exploit.

'Well, then,' she wasted no breath on an introduction, 'what do you think of your father now?'

'Hero of the hour,' he said.

'Has your mother sent you the cutting from the newspaper?'

'She has.'

'You've not been up to see him yet?' she asked.

'No. But mother describes him as exactly as he was before all this happened. Laconic in the extreme, and in just as much trouble as ever he had in getting about.'

'I don't understand it,' Irene said. 'I thought dementia was a one-way affair. If you lost your legs in an accident you wouldn't suddenly be able to walk again.'

'That's what I thought. But we were obviously wrong. Human beings are all very different. My mother's doctor said he didn't understand it at all. But I suggested that if he could suddenly pull out of his lethargy and disability they ought to see if they can't treat him in some way or other to get him back to normality.'

'Exactly. Unless his depression is self-inflicted or even assumed. And the fire jolted him out of it for that few minutes.'

'Which theory do you favour?' he asked, sarcastically.

'I've no opinion. He always seemed a limited human being to me. I wouldn't have liked to have to work for him. He'd be a terror to his underlings. I would have guessed he would have hated being put into what he'd call "an institution". What does your mother think?'

'She's as baffled as we are. He could barely get about at home. That's why he went into the nursing home because of his lack of mobility rather than the dementia. She says that that has become worse since he went into Holmleigh, perhaps because he hasn't had sufficient stimulation. I don't think for a minute that he's putting an act on.'

'I see.'

'Was your mother glad to put him into a home?'

'I think she saw no alternative. She couldn't lift him and push him and carry him about the place. And he seemed unhappy.'

'And what does she say now all this has happened?'

'In her odd way I think she's rather proud of him. He rarely appeared in the newspapers, except perhaps in a small-print list of Inland Revenue people at a dinner, or at a funeral. But now here he is a hero, saving the lives of these two women, ordering them about, putting his arm round them to help them down the fire escape, then lifting them off at the end. When she heard all this from the reporter it crossed her mind that this was a miraculous cure, and that he'd perhaps be something like his old self again.'

'And that would have been good, what she wanted?'

'Hard to say. I'm never quite sure what's going on in her head. She was so stressed when he was at home, that she was glad to get rid of him. She was physically drained doing everything for him. She'd done her best to keep him at home, but it had proved too much for her. She didn't like that at all. She always said you could do anything within reason if you wanted it badly enough, but she learnt that wasn't so.'

'What did your father think about having to leave home?'

'I wasn't there,' John said, 'at the actual time of moving. He'd been pretty miserable before when I'd seen him. I had no doubt that a nursing home was the best solution.'

'And you told your mother so?'

'Yes. In no uncertain terms. She has this nonconformist conscience. It was her duty to care for her husband, in sickness and health, for richer, for poorer. She'd promised to do so at her wedding. And so she was very unsure. She realised the job was getting beyond her strength, but she had to do her duty.'

'I wonder,' Irene asked, 'why she married him in the first place?'

'Love,' John answered. You should know more than I. You were there. I wasn't.'

'I've told you before he wouldn't have suited me. He was dull, and rather pompous even as a young man. I think he saw our family as a cut above his socially and so he always had to be on his best behaviour. He was genuinely fond of your mother and always did his best for her. And for you, for that matter. But he hadn't many social graces. He wasn't very good company. Even when he tried to be, as at Christmas parties and the like. He couldn't wipe the serious look off his face. Our father was a parson, as you know, but he knew how to laugh.'

'Was my mother's marriage not a happy one, then?'

'You should know. You were there; I wasn't. She was probably suited. Ella has some peculiar ways. She looked on me as flighty. I think she was jealous that I went to Oxford and she didn't. I don't suppose I was very much cleverer than she was, if at all. I was nearly eight years younger and though we went to the same school it had improved by leaps and bounds in the eight years between us. A new headmistress, for instance, who picked younger, better qualified staff. But your mother did well enough. She became a successful head of a school, and William made good progress in the Inland Revenue, so they were never short of money. But your mother always seemed glum about it all. As if she bore the world a grudge.'

'She married the wrong man?'

'I wouldn't say that. No. I guess Ella has always been at cross purposes with the world. She never as a grown-up seemed in the best of health. As far as I could make out there was nothing seriously wrong with her, but she acted as if there were.'

'She went into hospital at least twice while I was a boy.'

'Yes. Womanly things. D and C twice, I remember. And once for an operation on her toes. Her ill-health was nervous, if anything, and I guess inborn.'

'You never got on with her, did you?'

'We were fine while I was young. I suppose as she was so much older, I did as she said. It's not until I went to university that she seemed to turn against me. She lived in a house that was just as spacious as mine. Ours was in St John's Wood and yours in Beechnall and that makes a tremendous difference to the price these days. I know she envied me my jobs, though sometimes they were less well paid than hers, especially when I started. Then when I clambered on to the television news and the journalistic ladder, she felt I was overpaid. She often told me so. She felt, probably rightly, that teachers were undervalued in this country.'

'That wasn't your fault.'

'No. But I exemplified the faults. Even if at a distance.'

They both laughed, enjoying their non-conclusions.

'It's about time you came round to visit me,' she said. 'I owe you a meal.'

'Not at all. I enjoyed your visit.'

'Then you won't come?'

'Of course I will. One weekend if we can find dates that fit.'

They rang off, not unpleased with themselves. He walked about his house humming, glad that he had impressed his aunt.

Later the same day he received another call, on this occasion from Helen. He was surprised, since they were to go to Stratford in three days. Was she calling that off? They worked through introductory, trivial inquiries about health and work and weather before she said, 'The reason I'm really ringing you is because my aunt sent me a cutting from the *Evening Post* about your father saving two women from a fire in the nursing home. It *is* your father, isn't it?'

'It certainly is.'

'Tell me all about it.' Her voice had a childish ring about it.

He gave a short, dry, unexaggerated account of the fire at Holmleigh, and his father's part in the rescue of the two women.

'He really did rescue them?'

'I've no reason to think otherwise.'

'He always seemed so quiet, so reserved. As well as crippled.'

'Still waters run deep.'

'So you were not surprised? I thought he had difficulty walking. You must be very proud of him. Does bravery run in your family?'

'My mother once waded into a river to rescue a child. She received a certificate from the Lord Mayor.'

'But not your father? Nor you?'

'Neither.'

'Do you know, John, there's something remarkable about your family. Both your father and mother have saved lives. And yet you've never boasted about it. You've said not a word.'

'My father's escapade has only just happened.'

'There you go again. You call it an "escapade". That means something like a mischievous adventure, not a brave act which saved two lives. You speak of it as a joke, some bit of foolish behaviour.'

'My father could hardly walk, and he seemed little interested in other people, and yet he led these two women to safety. How he did it and why, I am at a loss to understand.'

'You seem to begrudge him his little claim to glory.'

'I don't mean to. I just don't understand how he managed.'

'Have you spoken to him?'

'Not since this happened. I hope to go up the weekend after next. You can come up with me if you like. My mother would be pleased.'

'Oh, John, thank you. I'd love that.' Her voice fluttered, 'I love you.'

X

The trip to Stratford went without mishap.

They argued, of course, about *Coriolanus*. She thought that setting it in Japan with the hero a samurai warrior added reality.

'I can't see any sense in it at all,' he ventured.

'It makes such a man seem possible. Foreign but possible. We tend to think of the Romans as people like us.'

'I don't. They were cruel, even barbarous, at the time of Augustus, never mind in 490 BC or whenever this took place. They'd be as outlandish to us as any samurai warrior.'

They quarrelled over this, but mildly. He praised the company's rendering of late Shakespearian verse, saying that the effect on him was powerful. 'That's what's important about Shakespeare. The verse. Shakespeare's language.'

'Don't you think he overdoes it sometimes?' she asked.

'I'm sure he does. But he is dealing with desperate events and people's reactions to them.'

They slept together after the play in a hotel room that was large, light and comfortable. John feared that their absence from each other might have made this sexual reunion difficult, disappointing. They engaged naked, and he was able to restrain himself sufficiently to arouse her to orgasm before he had finished. She squealed her pleasure. They then, at his bidding, solemnly, almost as in a rite, resumed their pyjamas and slept. They woke early and made love again. This was good, skilful on the part of both, but he found almost as much satisfaction in the cup of coffee he had hopped out of bed to make for them once the sex had finished. He sipped at that, and she smiled over at him. He felt at peace, but only ephemerally so. He could not account for this.

They ate an early but slow breakfast. The rest of the morning they spent looking round Stratford, or as he put it, 'You "beguile

the time and feed your knowledge/With viewing of the town,"'
or, again leaning on the knowledge of the play he studied at
school: "'Let us satisfy our eyes/with the memorials and the
things of fame/That do renown this city."' Helen, easily impressed,
congratulated him on his knowledge, but did not recognise the
play from which he quoted.

'*Twelfth Night*,' he answered on her inquiry. 'Knocked into my
head by the constant tests our English master inflicted on us.'

She seemed modestly delighted, and could barely keep her
hands off him. Her arm slipped constantly through his as they
walked, and she pressed against him at every opportunity. Her
night with him had clearly aroused her. She was, he thought, like
a child with a new, expensive, unexpected toy.

He had never before been in Stratford in winter. The cold wind
raced round every corner, so that they were glad to find a bus
which provided a tour of what he called the reliques of this town.

'I didn't expect to see all these people about at this time of
the year,' he said.

'As long as the theatres are open there'll be people here.'

'I suppose so.'

'There are a good number of foreigners,' she said. 'American
and Japanese. What must it be like in the summer?'

He enjoyed the visitors as much as the rooms in the birthplace
which they trailed round. They asked questions by the dozen:
'Was Shakespeare rich?'; 'Did he love his wife?'; 'Why did he
leave her his second-best bed in his will?'; 'Are there any of the
Shakespeare family living still in England?'. The questioners did
not know much about the plays, but were desperate to absorb
snippets of information about his life, his wife, his father's occupation and religion, his mother's social status, his children.

The visitors pressed the guide hard.

'Would you say that Shakespeare was a friendly man?'

'He was very quick with his tongue, witty.'

'That's not the same thing?'

'No. But he was referred to as "Sweet Mr Shakespeare".'

'He could hold his own in business, couldn't he?'

'Yes. And in the courts. He made sure that any property he
acquired was properly his. There was no foolery about it; he'd
have you before the magistrates quick enough. And he bought

the biggest house in Stratford ready for his retirement. Quite early in his career.'

The guide then regaled them with the story of the clergyman who pulled down New Place in 1759, presumably so that he shouldn't be troubled by bardolators. 'It seems a feeble enough excuse to us now, but . . .'

'Do you know the name of this idiot?' a voice inquired.

'Francis Gastrell, of Frodsham.'

That silenced them all, and the guide beamed with self-satisfaction. Helen grasped the tweed of John's overcoat as if the name could bring bad luck on them. The guide now let fly a list of names connected with Shakespeare. Sir Hugh Clopton, John and Susanna Hall, Thomas and Judith Quiney, Thomas Russell and Francis Collins, Gerard Johnson or, more correctly, Geerart Jannsen, Heminge and Condell, Martin Droeshout, the witnesses of the will, Collins, July, Shaw, Robinson, Hamnet Sadler, Whatcott. He gabbled information about that as if it were too important to be delivered portentously to people who within an hour would have forgotten it. He gave a curious, brief, garbled survey, delivered over the heads of his audience, of the mystery of Anne Hathaway and Anne Whateley, and his explanation. A further question drew from him the story of the nameless ignorant baker of Warwick who married a descendant and thus inherited a box full of Shakespeare's manuscripts which he allowed to go to rack and ruin before a great fire consumed them. Coughing behind his hand, he then withdrew the tale saying no corroborative evidence supported this story. By the time he dismissed them he clearly had had enough of his listeners.

'We had our money's worth there,' John, out in the cold street, whispered to Helen.

'He spoke far too quickly at the end,' she answered. 'I don't think he wanted us to follow him. It was just a gabble.'

'But one which made us aware of his knowledge.'

They ate a solid lunch, cod in breadcrumbs with chips and peas, salad on a side plate, ice cream and coffee before they collected the car from the car park.

'What shall we do now?' he asked.

'Go back home.'

'Do you mean that?' he asked. 'We've another day off tomorrow.'

'It's so cold here, about the streets.'

They returned to London to Helen's house which was warm, and quickly made warmer. Over a large cup of tea she asked, 'Do you think that was a success?'

'Oh, yes. We saw some fine acting, and I learnt a great deal. I would have liked to have questioned that guide privately.'

'Was he an educated man, do you think?' she asked.

'No. Self-educated. He'd certainly read and remembered a book or two. And listened to the experts.'

'He seemed to be losing patience with us.'

'You know the feeling, surely. You're explaining something to a group of people, and pitching it at the lowest common denominator so that they all understand. Then some clever dick pipes up to complain about the simplicity of your answer.'

They talked amiably for a short time, slightly embarrassed in this new situation. When she asked what he'd like for their evening meal, he answered, 'Fish and chips filled me up for the rest of today, thanks.'

'You're going to stay the night here, aren't you?' she asked.

'I'd like to slip back home and look at the post and e-mail and answerphone.'

'But you'll come back, won't you?'

'If you want me to, I might consider it.'

They sat slightly uneasy, neither daring to look straight into the other's eyes.

'Why are you always so awkward?' she said. 'Didn't you enjoy Stratford?' No answer. 'Did you?'

'Every minute of it.'

'Well, then?'

'I don't want us to rush things. I remember what it was like before we split up. That did neither of us any good.'

'Why must you make everything so complicated? We enjoyed each other in Stratford, and we should work onwards from that. But not you. You're frightened of your own shadow.'

'I just don't want to rush into anything that will leave us worse than we were. It's true our temperaments are different. I'm cautious and careful, on the lookout for snags. You're more generous and quick-natured than I am. But we ought to bear those differences in mind.'

'Bear in mind,' she scoffed. 'Bear in mind.'

'Yes.' he answered. 'I don't want us hurting each other, and fighting.'

'Oh, go home then. Go home and play with your computer.'

Suddenly she was crying, with huge tears splashing down on to her blouse. Just moments ago she had been angry, her face set in scorn. Now she seemed broken, out of control, sobbing, her body shaken.

'I'm sorry, Helen,' he said. 'I meant it for the best.'

He received no answer to that, and his excuse seemed inadequate enough to him. Her hands were clenched, and up before her face. He stood and tried awkwardly to put an arm round her shoulder. She leaned back stiffly against her chair to prevent this. He put a hand on the shoulder nearest to him; she tried violently to shrug it away. He left it lightly in place. She now struggled, as if to rise, and scrabbled for a tiny, lace-edged handkerchief with which she dabbed at her eyes.

'Can I get you a drink or something?' he asked.

He spoke hesitantly and she did not answer. He stepped away and stood by his own chair, one hand on the arm. Her snuffling had ceased, though her cheeks were blotchy and her wet eyes red.

'I do apologise,' he said again.

She looked up at him, mouth trembling.

'I didn't come here to quarrel,' he said. 'But now we seem not to be able to disagree without hurting each other, without tears. I didn't want that. That's why I didn't want us to overdo it at all because we both know how we were. I didn't—'

'You had sex with me, and now you don't want it any more,' she burst out.

'That's not true.'

'As soon as we're back here you want to be shooting home to your work and your computers.'

'That is so,' he said, voice placatory. 'There's one bit of tricky business at work that I'd like to check up on.'

'There always is with you. There always will be. You're not like a human being. You're a machine.'

Now she was crying again, wringing her hands.

67

He took a step away from his chair, but not towards her.

'You want me to go?' he asked, softly.

Helen did not answer, but turned away from him. He watched her agony as she wept now without noise. He dropped his head and moved quietly out into the dark hall. Clumsily he looked round for the switches. The only illumination came from a street lamp through the stained glass panels in the front door. He groped on the wall, where his fingers met a bank of four old-fashioned switches. He pulled one down; a light flashed on high upstairs, perhaps two floors above; he tried again and was successful. He put on his plaid scarf and overcoat, and picked up his case.

Standing in the chillier air of the hall he decided he could not go without a last word to his wife. He laid down his case, and quietly stepped into the sitting room.

Helen was seated in the same chair, but now she held herself upright with her eyes closed.

'I'm going now, Helen,' he whispered.

She opened her eyes, but said nothing. Her lids fluttered.

'Thank you for these last two days,' he said, desperately. 'I shan't forget them.'

Silence again. He waited. Her eyes were open.

'Thank you,' he continued, almost breathlessly. 'We must try it again.'

Nothing.

'Goodbye then.' She sat like a rumpled doll. 'Many thanks.'

He tiptoed from the room, left the light on in the hall, and reached his car. Outside the cold cut into his flesh.

Back home he turned up the heating, boiled the jug-kettle and made a cup of coffee. As he sat with this in a Windsor chair he again felt breathless, as if his lungs were failing to function. He sipped the hot drink and felt better for it almost immediately. His spirits withered as if he had skimped some task he had meant to do thoroughly, and was now called to account. They had quarrelled so easily. He had made a perfectly reasonable request that she let him off for an hour, after which he'd return and their holiday would continue. She ought to have understood; she was a solicitor and needed to be conscientious even at the expense of her convenience or pleasure. But no, without warning she had insulted him and then burst into passionate tears, after which she refused to give him any answer at all. That was not the behaviour of a reasonable person. Was she always so irrational, or had he done something that had suddenly upset her? He had tried to be as conciliatory as he could, but she had made her mind up to repel him. She had acted like a spoilt child.

And yet in Stratford their arguments about the play had been pleasant, adding spice to the day. He had felt no fear that she would become angry with him, accuse him of awkwardness. They did not agree, and that was perfectly natural. They enjoyed their difference of opinion.

He finished his coffee, still disgruntled, then made his way upstairs to his office. Neither answerphone, e-mail or post made any reference to the business matter about which he had worried. The two young men, clever but still trainees, had failed to find any fault. He flicked through the rest of his correspondence. There was nothing of importance. He dealt glumly with the two most urgent pieces, and left the rest easily available. He shuffled downstairs and wondered vaguely whether he'd be well employed cooking an evening meal. He decided against this. A cheese and pickle sandwich would have to do. He slumped back into a chair. He'd left his morning paper at Helen's house, curse her.

The telephone rang. His mother, and on the warpath.

'I hear you have quarrelled again with Helen,' she began, grimness in every word.

'Yes.'

'She rang me about a quarter of an hour ago.'

'Go on then,' he said. 'Let's hear what she told you.'

'Never mind what she said.' There was no sympathy in his mother's voice. 'Let me hear your side of the story.'

'We, on her suggestion, mark you, decided to come home a day early. We did so, and went to her house.'

'And?' Relentless.

'She invited me to stay the night, and I agreed.'

'There was no disagreement between you?'

'No. Not then, nor at any time we were in Stratford.'

'What happened then?' The last word was snapped out.

'I just suggested I went back home for an hour. There was a piece of business I was rather worried about. A couple of my young men were dealing with it and . . .'

'Who?'

'Price and Widdowson.' She wouldn't know the names.

'Go on, will you.'

'I was worried about this account they were looking into. I thought there might be some snags. A firm called Perkins. It's a new account, and I knew nothing about the firm. I put these two young men in; they're bright; they both did well in their finals and they've been with the firm for something over a year. Just before I went to Stratford, they rang in and said there might be something tricky going on. They weren't sure. I told them I should be away for three days and told them to leave a message on my e-mail at home if they wanted me to look into something immediately I got home. I even gave them my mobile number in case they needed help or advice before that.'

'Did they ring?'

'No, not on my mobile. I expected a report of their progress on my computer at home, but there was nothing.'

'So you went rushing back home for no reason at all.'

'We shall see. They'll ring in to the office tomorrow. But they weren't unduly worried, or at least thought that they could deal with the matter.'

'So you left Helen for nothing?'

'You could say that. I thought she'd see I was concerned and needed to check up.'

'But you needn't have been worried?' his mother asked.

'Neither of us knew that. And if I had not gone home, I should have been left thinking about it.'

'Supposing you had found that there was something amiss. What would have happened then?'

'I'd have rung one of them up, discussed it with him, and said what I thought should be done next.'

He heard his mother breathing heavily.

'Did you not realise that she'd think you placed your business above your marriage, above your private life?'

'It never crossed my mind. But now you mention it I'll say this. If she is going to place her whims first then that's not a very sound basis for marriage. She's a solicitor; she ought to know that some pieces of business need careful handling.'

'And you ought to realise that you were just beginning to mend a relationship and now you've thrown away your chance.'

'I asked for an hour off. I even thought, insofar as I thought at all, she might like an hour to herself to make preparations for a guest staying overnight.'

'She had probably done all that before you set off for Stratford.'

'It didn't seem an impossible request on my part. An hour to slip home. I might have wanted clean underclothes or pyjamas or handkerchieves.'

'You didn't say that. You told her you wanted to look into something connected with your work.'

'And you think that was unreasonable?'

'On this occasion, yes.' She smacked her lips. 'You should have been more considerate, at this time of all times.'

'And she was upset?'

'She was.'

'What remedy do you suggest, then?'

'Remedy. Remedy. You do choose some odd words, John. This isn't something that can be cured by swallowing a pill.' She paused. He made no answer. In the end she yielded. 'If I were you I'd be on the lookout for some event or treat she would enjoy. Write and phone her. And don't leave it too long.'

'And if there aren't such events immediately available?'

'Make one. She's your wife. You owe it to her.'

His mother lectured him. He wasn't sure where her sympathies lay exactly. He suspected that she judged Helen to have acted unreasonably, but that he should have submitted to her, pandered to her foolishness and thus made the extent of his love clear. At the end of the sermon, he glumly asked how his father was shaping.

'I think he's doing slightly better. He talked sensibly to me. Usually he says next to nothing. But he said he felt that his life had been taken away from him.'

'What did he mean?' John asked.

'He tried to explain. It was as if all anticipation, expectation had disappeared. Not only was he physically feeble, he would never recover, and therefore nothing worth doing or having would ever happen to him again. He did his best to explain all this. It was the longest, most coherent conversation we'd had since he'd been in the home.'

71

'Poor old chap. Did he mention the fire?'

'I did. He didn't seem interested. Mumbled on about this woman who keeps dropping in on him. He's grown tired of her and her ways.' Another pause. He could hear his mother blowing out breath. 'You're going to visit your aunt Irene soon, aren't you?'

'Yes. This Saturday.'

'Eric is coming home, isn't he? I don't know when.'

He did not know either. The conversation petered out. He made his cheese sandwich, and scanned the evening newspaper for some event, to tempt Helen. His evening stretched ahead.

XI

'Come in,' his aunt said at the front door. 'Eric's back home.'

'If it's inconvenient, I'll go.'

'Inconvenient? Not at all. He'll be glad to see you. We're boring each other to death already.'

'Is he back for good? Or did my mother say something about Paris?'

'They won't make their minds up about him at *The Times*. The original idea was to send him over to France when his spell in Afghanistan had finished. But he's made such a good job of it that they may well decide to extend his time there.'

Irene had now hung his coat and scarf out of the way.

'Does he seem tired?'

'No. No more than usual. I can't tell what he wants to do next. I think he's considering a book on Afghanistan, and so he'll go back there without a murmur.'

They turned into a very pretty sitting room, half in darkness in the dull winter light. Eric Davenport had spread himself out in an armchair in front of a handsome gas fire. He leapt up from his chair to shake hands firmly with John. He wore denims, jacket and trousers, and his shoes had been admirably polished. After an inquiry about John's health, he sat down athletically, rubbed his hands together and shouted, 'Welcome to St John's Wood. I'd almost forgotten what a comfortable chair was like. Do you come here often?'

'This is my first visit.'

'You surprise me. I'd have thought Irene would have had such a personable young man up here paying court to her most week-ends to add to the gaiety of nations.'

'No. We meet occasionally at my mother's.'

'Your mother's. Yes. I hear that your father's been indulging in heroics, saving hapless maidens from the fire.'

Why his uncle-in-law used such stilted vocabulary baffled the nephew. Eric's dispatches in *The Times* were unusually well written, with nothing of whimsy or cliché about them. John gave a short account of his father's performance on the evening of the fire. Eric listened, bright-eyed.

'That's splendid,' Eric said. 'He must be in his seventies. The fire department will be after the owners of that home. Did it surprise you that your father acted as he did?'

'Yes. Whenever I've seen him in the last year or two he seemed very unwilling to talk, or incapable of doing so. And I had the impression that he could barely get about at anything above a shuffle. That's why he went into the place. It was not so much his dementia as his immobility that made it impossible to live at home.'

'I see. Was he a courageous man when he was younger and physically fit?'

'I don't think that courage of that sort was ever put to the test. He always seemed reserved, content to do his job in the Inland Revenue competently, and keep his garden in good order or help about the house.'

'He was proud of his home and family,' Irene said. 'I also had the impression that he felt he had done well with his life. After all, as you know, he came from a poor family; his father was a navvy though sensible enough to see that his son went to the grammar school after he'd passed the eleven-plus. I don't think there was ever any chance of his staying on until he was eighteen and then to a university or training college. There wasn't the money.'

'Interesting,' Eric murmured.

'He went into the income tax business and set about doing well there. He passed all their exams without any trouble, put time in at night school and all the rest.' She smiled. 'He always said that the matric examination he passed at school was a marvellously good foundation for any sort of further education.'

'You seem to know all about his qualifications?' Eric queried.

'He used to tell Ella all about it, and she passed it on to me. He told her that all the other people of the same rank as he held were university graduates, but he never felt at a disadvantage amongst them.'

'Are you like your father?' Eric asked, cocking a curious eye at John.

'Well, I went to university.'

'And what did you read? Accountancy, wasn't it?'

'Yes. And then I completed my professional qualifications.'

'Do you enjoy your work?'

'Yes. And recently I have been asked to do little jobs outside the usual run of accountants. I've lectured at university here, and in America, and have examined recently for the Institute.'

'Of which you are a Fellow?'

'Yes.'

Eric Davenport did not seem to like him, John suspected. He could not decide why. Irene, no longer in the room, was presumably in the kitchen preparing lunch.

'You're married, aren't you?' Eric began.

'Yes. But we have parted.'

'Parted? Do you mean divorced?'

'No. Not even legally separated. We just do not live together.'

'I know at least two pairs of properly married people who have kept their own homes. They live amicably enough together when they want to. Presumably they have sexual relations, but they don't share homes or, I guess, bank accounts. But they see enough of each other to make a marriage contract the symbol of their intentions. They would presumably move in and look after their spouses if one became ill. In both cases, I admit, these were second marriages by all four parties.' He yawned as if bored by his own conversation. 'Do you see anything of your wife?'

'We went together to Stratford to see *Coriolanus*.'

'It didn't work out?'

'We enjoyed it, but as soon as we came back we quarrelled. Over next to nothing. My mother thinks it was my fault.'

'She was always judgemental, wasn't she, Irene?' This to his wife who had been standing in the doorway listening. 'If you don't object to the word?'

'She was always free with her advice,' Irene said.

'She told me to take her to some place, or offer to, where she wanted to go.'

'Such as?' Eric asked.

'A play.'

'*Timon of Athens*?' Eric, with sarcasm.

'An opera. *The Magic Flute*, if it were on. It isn't. Or a concert.'

'You should have brought her up here today for lunch,' Irene spoke enthusiastically.

'She might not have liked that,' Eric said.

'No, but you would. She's a very pretty girl.'

Eric narrowed his eyes.

'Somebody's getting at me,' he said. 'These two sisters are devils for criticism. They'll set you right, whether you fancy it or not. I blame their father, The Rev J. Whitworth Stokes, Bachelor of Divinity. He's much to answer for. Did you know your Grandfather Stokes?'

'No. Or my grandmother.'

'She was very like your mother, in looks and temperament.'

'And is Irene like her father?'

'Not in looks, thank God.'

'He was a handsome man,' Irene claimed.

'You didn't like him much?' John intervened mischievously.

'He died just after we left Oxford,' replied Eric. They used to come up once or twice a term for a start. He was the sort of man who kept you on your best behaviour.'

'He didn't succeed too well with you.' Irene laughed, as if disparaging her criticism of her husband. 'Eric, get up please and offer our guest a glass of sherry. And by the time that's done, lunch will be almost ready.'

Her husband did as he was told, and the two men sipped together. Eric's mood lightened.

Over lunch Eric gave the other two an account of his spell in Afghanistan. He liked the wild country and the people, but doubted whether peace would ever be found there.

'Did you see anything of the Taleban?' John asked.

'Not recently. After the Russians had been thrown out, yes. They didn't interfere with me at all. They meant what they said. They were fundamentalists.'

'They gave women a rough deal,' John said.

'Yes. I suppose they could see no sense, no advantage in teaching women to read and write and cipher. Not in their country. There was no call for educated women.'

76

'They're short of teachers and doctors, aren't they?'

'We tend to think of our own country where the nearest school is fifteen minutes away and a hospital not more than an hour. Not there. People are very much more self-sufficient than we are. Not that I'm suggesting that we take that sort of life up. People die younger; life's austere compared with ours; their pleasures are very restricted.'

'Isn't there money to be made growing opium?'

'The Taleban stopped that at first. Then economics overcame religion. There'd be argument about it, I don't doubt. That's one of the matters I want to look carefully into, if I get sent back.'

'Are your superiors undecided?'

'They thought it was time I had a holiday. So they wheel me back here, and then set about questioning me. They're first-rate employers. They've suggested Paris to me. My French is a sight better than my Pashto or my Arabic. I'm no great linguist. It's a drawback, that. You have to depend too much on people whose English is as bad as my local lingo. One can easily get it all wrong. They keep the women out of your way, and you learn, in my experience, a deuce of a sight more of what's basic to life in a foreign country from women than from men.'

'Aren't the women kept in ignorance, from what you say?' John asked.

'Sure, sure. But the food, the drinking water, the care of children or old folks who've managed to survive into age: they're important if you want to know what life's really like.'

Eric described at length two journeys he'd made, one of them to see the statue of Buddha the Taleban had destroyed, in a four-wheel drive, rather old, which he said only just kept going over the rough country.

'And when you got there?'

'I don't think I would have thought much of the carvings when they were still extant. Large, impressive in that way. But it was vandalism. They were intensely religious people who didn't want to leave remnants of an older creed. They thought they might mislead the simple; I don't know. So that bit of the country's history is blown up, blown away. They believe in what they say they believe, and act on it. Fanatics? Yes, they are.'

'You seem in two minds about them.'

'I am. Their beliefs are of no importance to me. They wouldn't do in this country. But I can't help but admire people who live out their cherished faith.'

'You could admire the Spanish Inquisition or the Nazi Party on those same grounds.'

'I could. I don't, but I could. Half the trouble with the people of this country today is that we don't believe in anything much. Football, perhaps, television, celebrities, a comfortable life, money in your pocket for the pleasure of your family, or yourself.'

'Oh, I don't know.'

'I know your sort,' Eric answered. 'Liberal. Tolerant. I hate his views but I'd give my life for his right to hold and propagate them. That's good, sounds fine but it soon deteriorates into a kind of wet hedonism. You do as you like, and so will I, and that'll be wonderful as long as I've the necessary money to spend on myself.'

'And how would you cure it?'

'I'd reintroduce National Service, where you live under discipline and sometimes in danger, where you eat what you're given or do without, where the living conditions are constantly against you. Out there, sand in dry winds. It clogs everything. Gets into your clothes, your food, your weapons, your machines, so that the most elementary procedures of everyday living seem impossible. Nothing works properly.'

They had finished their dessert and were thinking about coffee when the phone rang. Irene jumped to her feet, returning to say that Professor Briggs of the School of African and Oriental Studies was on the phone.

'Good,' Eric said, 'just the man I want. Hold the coffee till I come back.'

Irene explained that her husband was spending his leave in England reading up on the history of Afghanistan. He was down at the London Library most days.

'Are there many books?' John asked.

'I can see you're like me. You think that two or three would be the sum total. But no, according to him there are dozens and not all in English.'

'Can he read them?'

'Yes. He's good at languages.'

78

'He told me he wasn't.'

'Oh, yes, he is. French and German and Italian. And he had a spell in Moscow. He's not afraid to try his tongue out on them. Anyway, he's down there each day grubbing at the books and maps. Or at the Royal Geographical Society.'

'And all this means he'll be going back?'

'I wouldn't be too certain. If they offer him some interesting line in Paris, he'll be off there like a shot. Or Prague. Or Washington. But he says knowledge is never wasted. He thinks that his book on Afghanistan may well take years to write. "It might be finished off when I retire," he says, "if I have the energy." He doesn't like to sit around doing nothing. This Professor Briggs is a scholar he's picked up on the way. Somebody introduced them. He's an expert on Islam and very learned, Eric says. He has some sort of interest or connection with Afghanistan, and has recommended obscure books and pamphlets.'

'But useful?'

'Oh, yes. I think so.'

Eric returned, rubbing his hands.

'What's he found for you this time?'

'Some chap at the British Museum who's spent quite a lot of time out there. And a couple of German scholars who might give me a different slant. A man and wife. They lived there for years.'

'Have they written a book?'

'Yes. I've read it. But they've agreed I can go and talk to them.'

'Where do they live?'

'Bournemouth.'

'Where?'

'You heard. Bournemouth. They're pretty old now and they've settled near their only son, who's more or less an Englishman by now. But Jack Briggs says they're really interested, and will be delighted to talk to somebody like me who's been there so recently.'

Irene made the coffee.

All the time Eric Davenport talked and questioned. He seemed excited, perhaps on account of something Briggs had said. He was quite different from the man who an hour ago had seemed both hostile and indifferent. He'd perhaps decided that John, nephew John, was worth talking to. When they had finished coffee John said that he must go.

'It's hardly worth your coming,' Irene objected, 'Just for a couple of hours.'

'If you live, as I do, on your own, there's always work to be done.'

'I've enjoyed your company,' Eric said.

'But not learnt much about the Afghans.'

'Don't you believe it. You asked about law out there. And about poetry and literature. The old folks in Bournemouth have done some translating I believe. It always does me good to talk to intelligent people. They ask about things they're interested in, and I am not, or not particularly. It gives me a slant on what my prospective readers will want to think about.'

'I see.'

'He was going to a football match,' Irene said, 'until I told him you were coming.'

'Are you interested in football?' John asked Eric.

'Everybody is. Even some Afghans. You can get Premiership results out there as quickly as you can here. If you know your way about.'

Eric shook hands and made his way at speed up the wide stairs.

'He must have some book he particularly wants to read,' Irene said.

'He's very energetic.'

'He's been like that ever since I've known him. And he hasn't seemed to slow down at all. It has its advantages in his job. I'm not so sure that it's altogether compatible with domestic happiness. He's always on the brink of going elsewhere, doing something new and exciting.'

John did not know how to answer this. In the hall he donned and buttoned his topcoat.

'Would you mind if I got in touch with your mother to see if we can't get Helen to visit us here in your company?'

'Why would you want to do that?' he asked.

'I thought you were the ideal couple, and would like you to have another try.'

'I don't know whether you'll get anywhere with this scheme of yours.'

80

'But you've no objection?'

'No, but may I remind you that we didn't split up for no reason. We could hardly bear the sight of one another.'

'Yes. I understand that,' Irene said. 'You have seen that Eric and I are not the ideal married couple either. If he weren't away so much, I doubt if we'd still be together.' She giggled at her slightly grotesque play on meaning. 'You've no objection then?'

'No.' He didn't know what he felt about the idea.

'Get your diary out. What about next Saturday? Is that free?'

Without much argument they decided on three or four free dates.

'You'll have to hurry,' he said. 'Helen's pretty busy.'

'Your mother doesn't waste time. And I'll do my best. I'm used to deadlines.'

She patted his buttocks, without much effect through the thickness of his winter coat, kissed him on the lips and let him out of the door into the dull ferocity of winter's cold.

At nine o'clock that same night Irene rang him.

'It's all fixed up,' she said cheerfully without prelude.

'When?'

'Next Saturday. You are to drive round to her house and bring her here for lunch.'

'What sort of suit am I to wear?' he asked sarcastically.

'None of your impudence. Best bib and tucker. Now is there anything that she particularly likes or dislikes? In the food line, I mean?'

'No. She has a good appetite and was brought up to eat whatever is put in front of her.'

'Good. I expect your mother will ring you up before too long. With good advice.'

'You haven't invited her to inspect how your little plan works out.'

'No. It was not even considered. I guess she would have preferred it at her house, but that would have taken too much organising. So. Noon next Saturday outside Helen's.'

'Thank you.'

'You don't mean that, do you?' she asked.

'We'll see.'

Both grinned, unobserved.

XII

On the day before their visit John rang Helen to fix the time he was to pick her up. Uncertain of his reception he tried to sound businesslike. Helen on the other hand, was almost garrulous; she had been following Eric Davenport's dispatches from Afghanistan, said how well they were written and asked what sort of man he was. John described his energy, his bookish researches, his chasing round to interview people.

'It's not very restful for your aunt while he's at home?'

'No. He follows his own devices, and I guess this break might be rather short, and so he's setting about his book on Afghanistan whilst it's all fresh in his mind.'

'Is he a good talker?'

'When he wants to be. I had the impression, and maybe I'm wrong, that he'll speak like an angel if he sees advantage in it to himself.'

'He writes beautifully,' she demurred.

'On his best behaviour. I had the impression from Irene that *The Times* rates him highly. They fetched him back from Afghanistan to give him a holiday.'

'Had he asked for it?'

'Not as far as I know.'

'Anyhow, I'll look forward to meeting this paragon. I don't know your aunt very well either. I have met her. She seemed quite beautiful, and I can't say that of too many women of her age. Is she like your mother?'

'In temperament. She looks about twenty years younger. Dresses quite differently.'

'What's the difference in age?'

'My mother's about seven years older than she is.'

'I'm rather looking forward to this. Are you?'

'Yes,' he said. 'They're an interesting couple.'

'Good. Twelve o'clock here then.'

He arrived at Helen's house exactly on time, and was invited in. She was not quite ready, and dashed upstairs to complete her preparations. She did not keep him waiting long, and appeared in a well-cut trouser suit in darkish grey. Her hair had been professionally treated that morning. She looked pale, but smart, intelligent, a lawyer alert for you, and, under the rather severe guise, beautiful. He expressed his admiration for her appearance. He spoke briefly, but there was no mistaking his sincerity.

'You look good, too,' she said, taking his arm to lead him in front of the large mirror. She was friendly, exceptionally so, as she grasped his arm tightly.

They drove out to St John's Wood with less difficulty than he expected on a Saturday afternoon. Helen made every effort to talk cheerfully to her husband. She sat neatly upright, commenting on pedestrians, shops, traffic lights, in a sharp, enthusiastic way as if she had determined to impress her husband with her pleasure in his company. No trace of old disputes resurfaced.

As they approached Irene's house Helen commented favourably on the district and said she wouldn't mind living there.

'Pretty stiff prices,' he said.

'Oh, I know that. But I think if I took on a very high mortgage so that I couldn't afford to go out, I could put up with my hardship in an area like this, in houses like these.'

'What would you do?' he asked, amused.

'Read a lot more than I do. I picked up a facsimile edition of Shakespeare's sonnets.'

'"His sugar'd sonnets amongst his private friends",' he quoted.

'Yes. I've been spending some time on them.'

'Is it difficult?'

'Yes. But I cheat. I also have a modern edition with notes.'

'How did you start on this, then?'

'I read a biography. It had an unusual title: *Ungentle Shakespeare*. I'd always thought he was a thoroughly well-liked man, that's what you said. But this outlined some of his quarrels. It's also a play on words. Shakespeare, because he was only a player, had difficulty in becoming a gentleman. He wasn't allowed to put the Ardens', his mother's family, heraldic bearings on his coat of arms, when he finally did become one. And that was apparently done by the Garter King of Arms, a Sir William Dethick, who wasn't appreciated by his fellow heralds, and was finally removed from office for his outrageous behaviour early in James I's reign. Mark you, he was given a very handsome pension.'

'I knew Shakespeare became a gentleman and purchased the honour for his father.'

'Yes. But Katherine Duncan-Jones, who wrote this biography, thinks that Shakespeare's difficulties in getting himself recognised had a powerful effect on him, and this is shown in *Twelfth Night* where Malvolio, a mere steward, aspires to marry his mistress, Countess Olivia, who in the end calls him "gentleman", and is locked away as a madman for his presumption.'

'Interesting. I've never heard that before.'

'It seems possible to me. Shakespeare was looked on as a mere player, a nobody, not even a university man, liable to mistakes, a kind of servant. He was highly regarded, according to this biography, by the young undergraduates of the time, and always saw to it that his plays were popular, caught the fancy of the groundlings as well as the aristocrats and the men about town, the lawyers, the courtiers.'

'What else did she say?'

'I tell you a thing that did surprise me.' They had now stopped by the tall privet hedge in the Davenports' front garden. 'I'd always thought that Shakespeare at the end of his life had retired and spent his time in his garden, a man who'd succeeded in the wide world and now could end his life in comfort, at peace with the world.'

'But he didn't?'

'No. She thinks he was ill, and drank to kill his pain.'

'What was wrong with him?'

'She thinks heart and circulatory problems. He was rather overweight. And also she guesses that he was suffering from syphilis.'

'Is there any proof of this?'

'No. And she's very fair in pointing out that there isn't. His son-in-law, a highly respected doctor, would have treated him, and though he kept meticulous notes of many of his patients' illnesses, there's no mention of Shakespeare. She says, very plausibly, that if he had taken notes he would have destroyed them. He didn't want them to fall into someone else's hands. She thinks that the bad-tempered nature of the will and its alterations give us a clue to his depressed state.'

'He may not have liked the idea of dying,' John objected.

They got out of the car which he carefully locked.

As they were walking up the garden path, she suddenly said, 'He was depressed because he felt his life had been wasted.'

'Why did he think that? He'd made money and a big name in the theatre.'

'His sonnets did not sell or create the interest he expected.'

'I shall have to talk to you again about this. It's fascinating.'

'I've started reading about Shakespeare since we went to Stratford. There's a man in our office who's vice-president of the local Shakespeare society. He's quite an expert.'

'Who's that?'

'Robert Friend. He was the one who suggested reading *Ungentle Shakespeare.*'

They rang the bell. John felt pleased beyond measure. It was as if Helen had forgotten their quarrel and subsequent silence, and remembered their trip to Stratford because it had led her to a new interest: Shakespeare's life. He saw himself as responsible in some part for her departure. She was an intelligent girl, a very successful passer of examinations. She'd read the Duncan-Jones book with care, probably more than once. It had changed her view of the poet, and to such an exciting extent that she wished now to spill out her discoveries to her husband, whom she had banished in anger a week or two ago. This was the Helen he had loved in the first place, not much given to rapid changes of mind or whimsical or irrational choices, but a clever girl who, having discovered something worth investigating, wanted to share her enthusiasm with someone she judged capable of understanding the attraction of the topic and sensibly commenting on it. Helen stood at his side, her face alight, dressed with a taste which enhanced her rare beauty. He could have put his arms round her in the grey coldness of this bleak February day.

The door opened and both Eric and Irene stood there to greet them.

Irene kissed them on both cheeks and ushered them royally indoors. Her husband stood in the background until Helen approached and kissed him. He was dressed in a dark grey lounge suit with a white shirt and tie. Irene led them into the hospitable warmth of the drawing room, lit by a chandelier against the darkness of the early afternoon. They took to chairs and Eric provided glasses of sherry. When all were seated, Helen by Eric, John by his aunt, they searched round for sociable talk.

'What are the two of you up to?' Eric asked Helen.

'Work,' she replied. 'I expect John's just as busy as I am.'

'Ah, well,' he said. 'I've been ordered to make a start next week. They've directed me to Paris.'

'Was that unexpected?' Helen asked.

'No. Not at all. And there's a political conference in a month's time.'

'Will your time in Afghanistan have prepared you for that?'

'Not a bad way to get ready. Journalists have to sound as if they know it all. They can't, but if they're any good they'll mug it up quickly.'

Eric Davenport gave a fascinating account of his research. John admired the clarity of delivery, the understanding he showed, the variety of topics, his almost miraculous memory of what he'd read. He attributed his facts to their sources or reeled off opinions without difficulty, often quoting one expert's view against another. It was a tour de force which the man delivered in a modest, correct-me-if-I'm-wrong manner which made his learning the more impressive. He presented his brilliant mini-lecture without a trace of boasting.

'Will you have finished your research by the time you set off for Paris?' John interrupted.

'I hope so. Or enough for me to mull over before I go out east again.'

'Will the paper send you? Or will you go on your own?'

'No telling. But I shall do my best to get out there. It's absolutely necessary.'

'Do things change much there?' Helen asked.

'In some ways, no. The country dominates. That's what the Russians found when they invaded. They didn't know what they were in for. The Americans were better prepared. They booted the hell out of every obstacle, geographical or human, before they moved the ground troops forward.'

86

Helen continued with her questions as if her interest was really caught. Eric answered her with zest, concentrating solely on her, ignoring his wife and her nephew. John enjoyed her cross-examination and the quick yet complete answers as much as they appeared to. In the middle of one of his eloquent flights, Irene looked across at John and shrugged. A few minutes later she asked him to give her a hand with the serving of the lunch.

'They're getting on well,' he said drily, unsure about his attitude.

'That's Eric at his best. With an audience of one pretty girl he's determined to make an impression.'

'You sound as if you don't altogether approve.'

'I've heard him at it for a good many years now. It tends to pall from minute to minute. But I must confess that he sometimes manages to impress me even now. He's a very good talker, and he knows it.'

Over lunch Eric continued to talk. He castigated the universities as places which had outgrown their usefulness.

'I can't say much about the scientists or the medics. I wouldn't trust most of them further than I could throw them, but that's prejudice on my part. I read Greats, and the people who taught me didn't earn their pay. Some of them were clever, though not all by any means, but they set you the same old topics they'd be doling out for years, and they'd comment, sometimes quite accurately, on where your essay failed to deal adequately with the subject. But one man I had as a tutor had lost any interest in history that he once had.'

'What did he teach you?' Helen asked.

'Virtually nothing. He might now and again correct some fact or conclusion if he could be bothered. He once commented unfavourably on the style of one of my essays, but I put that down to bad temper or a hangover or some mishap.'

'And what about the good ones?'

'They tell you about your mistakes, suggest some further reading, and one or two might say what examiners might think of your efforts.'

'They didn't tell you anything that was remotely connected with your present life?'

'I wouldn't say that. But what happened in the time of the

ancient Greeks hasn't much relevance to my life now.' He laughed at the expression on Helen's face. 'Go on then. Prove me wrong.'

They argued with obvious pleasure. Helen spoke to him like a trusted old schoolmistress, reminding him that these pedants, even the idle ones, had taught him to read carefully, to summarise, to make a case one way or the other out of the reports, the bits of evidence which had come down to us from those old and different classical times. He returned with zest to his case, pleading for more modern exercises. He'd read *Hansard* by choice. And he knew some of the speakers and why they delivered their speeches in the way they did. They laughed out loud when she said it did not seem much of an education to plough through the ill thought out, often extempore, rhetoric of politicians.

The two seemed to have found an affinity which allowed them to disagree and yet on the most pleasant, appreciative terms. Helen had abandoned her rather quiet lawyer's appraisal of his efforts, and exaggerated, over-coloured her answers, even their vocabulary. Eric spoke to her as if he was amazed at her quick retorts, her ability to laugh at him as she made fun of his arguments, gave the impression that he did not hold many opinions seriously, but tested them out on her to see what she could handle and master. They paid little attention to either Irene or John, but conducted this rapid crossfire of polemics as though they were the only people at the table.

John watched, interested, even jealous at Helen's blossoming. She had always spoken to him, even in accusatory or quarrelsome mood, in that low, clear, unhurried voice that he imagined she had practised to use on her clients. Now she was livelier, talking at a higher pitch, ready to break into laughter at some clever piece of repartee from her opponent. Irene spoke only as a hostess inviting them to second helpings of roast beef, Yorkshire puddings or gravy. Helen and Eric were too preoccupied with each other to concern themselves over-much with food, though both, in time, cleared their plates.

Once when the two were arguing whether it was sensible to risk one's life climbing mountains, Irene asked John quietly whether he had planned his main holiday this year. She spoke in a quiet, unemphatic voice to John who was sitting next to her. Before he had time to answer the other two had stopped their rapid-fire talk and were staring across at Irene who had dared to venture her trivialities when the experts were in full voice. Irene dropped her eyes; John vouchsafed her no answer. The principals after a slight hesitation continued where they had left off.

After the meal they retired to the drawing room for coffee and, at Eric's request, brandy. John refused this, saying mildly, 'I've had the one glass of wine I allow myself when I'm driving.'

'You have your strict rules for the conduct of your life?' Eric asked, sarcastically.

'Yes, I'm a man of habit.'

'And do you find that satisfactory? Do you ever break your rules?'

'As little as I can manage.'

He thought, as he spoke, how priggish he sounded.

'You're missing a treat here,' Eric said, lifting his glass to Helen who raised hers in return. Irene, John noticed, did not even bring in a glass for herself. They talked this time about the honesty of politicians. Eric dropped names and anecdotes without appearing to boast. He seemed quieter, though from time to time he touched Helen's arm or hand as he spoke to her, as if to make up for his lack of liveliness. Irene now came to her own. A week or two ago she had begun her column in *The Times* about shopping, and how she carefully compared prices and quality of goods sold in supermarkets, old-fashioned shops and market stalls. She had preferred the supermarket except for meat and fish, and had claimed that she only shopped elsewhere when she felt in need of exercise. The article had aroused some interest and controversy, and not a little correspondence, some of it rude. Irene explained all this in a gentle voice, and John noticed that Eric had dropped off to sleep.

'Wake him up,' Irene ordered Helen, who sat nearest to him.

'Oh, no. I daren't.'

Eric opened his eyes. In that moment before he quite realised what was happening or where he was, his face seemed old, lined. By the time he spoke his jawline had hardened.

'I had a poor night,' Eric excused himself to Helen.

'Napoleon had the habit of nodding off,' she said, 'and was much brighter for the little rest.'

His face twisted sourly.

'I ought to go to bed earlier,' he said.

'What time do you usually go?' Helen.

'The small hours. What with the books.'

'And the bottle,' Irene added, with quiet authority.

'And the noisy friends.' He seemed determined to damn himself.

The conversation went on for another half hour. Helen spoke in a lively way about some eccentric woman who had buried her husband in her back garden, put steps and iron railings round the grave, and decorated it with two enormous headstones. Irene seemed quite taken with the tale, surprised that it was legal. Helen explained the laws and by-laws.

'Won't it lower the value of the property?' John asked.

'We explained that we were certain that it would, but she wasn't interested. "Such relatives as I have pay no attention to me while I'm alive, and those who are expecting me to leave them something when I'm dead will lose out when Ted's corpse has reduced the value of my house."'

'Is she sane?'

'As you and I are. She knows what she wants and what she's allowed. "It's difficult for me to get to any of the local grave-yards, and I'll go the few yards down the garden path to sit by my husband's mausoleum, if that's what we can call it, every day. That's what Ted would like."'

'Where did she get the word mausoleum from?' Irene asked.

'She's obsessed, and spends hours telling people what she wants. It would be a wonder if she hadn't heard it.'

'What's the derivation?' Irene again. 'I did know, but I've forgotten.'

'Some king or satrap called Mausolos. His wife built this great tomb for him. It was, if I'm not mistaken, one of the Seven Wonders.'

'Satrap?' John inquired. 'What's that exactly?'

'I think it was a governor of a province in Persia. I do believe that the bits and pieces of this tomb that survive are in the British Museum somewhere. Not that I've seen them.'

'What's in the British Museum?' Eric asked suddenly, waking.

'The remains of the original mausoleum.'

'Oh.' He lost interest again.

When the visitors were ready to leave Irene showed them to the door. Eric did not even rise from his chair, but raised a hand lethargically to them, and muttered a farewell.

They drove sedately enough towards Helen's home through streets that were already darkening. They barely spoke, except when once they passed a police van dealing with a smashed Ford which stood half on the pavement and, nearby, a Honda equally damaged in the gutter.

'I wonder what's happened there?' he asked.

'The road's wide, and there doesn't seem much traffic. An overtaking accident, I'd guess. Though the cars are in odd positions.'

'Perhaps the police had to move them.'

'A possibility.'

She spoke deep down from the coat which muffled her. Her situation on the front seat was awkward, askew, as if she expected any minute to have to leap from the car.

He drew up outside her house; it had now begun to rain and the windscreen blurred his view of the street.

'There we are then,' he said, cheerfully. 'Safely home.'

'Are you coming in? If you're not too busy.'

'Thank you.' He owed it to his mother. He did not in himself relish the idea of sitting there listening to her showering praise on Eric Davenport. 'If it's no trouble.'

At least her house was warm. She drew the curtains, and scurried off to the kitchen to make tea. He sat upright in his chair listening to noises about the house, presumably from the tenants upstairs. A book lay open on the small table. He looked at the title: *William Shakespeare: A Compact Documentary Life*, S. Schoenbaum. With it another, *Shakespeare: A Life* by Park Honan. Once she started on a subject, Helen did not easily give up. He replaced the books and was about to sit down when his eye caught sight of a small, thin, brown book. He picked that up; the facsimile edition of Shakespeare's sonnets. He opened it carefully; it looked old and about to disintegrate. The typeface and spelling gave him trouble.

'And tender chorle makſt waſt in niggarding.'

Helen entered with a tray, which she placed on a Regency table by her chair.

'Can you read this?' he asked.

'What is it?'

'Shakespeare's sonnets.'

'Oh, the facsimile edition. Yes. I'm getting used to it. At the start I used a modern version with notes. I'm gradually getting the hang of it.'

'What's "chorle"?'

'Show me.' He did so. 'That's churl. A rustic. One lacking in polite manners.'

'Makes some sort of sense,' he said.

She smiled, and began to pour the tea from a silver teapot.

'How do you want it?' she asked.

'Weak, please. With milk and no sugar.'

'No change there, then,' she said, pouring.

'No.' He waved away the biscuit barrel. She took her cup and sat down opposite to him. She sipped. He remembered that she enjoyed her tea scalding hot.

'What did you think of Uncle Eric?' he asked.

'You never called him that,' she said.

'No. It's how my mother always refers to him when she's talking to me.'

'I see.' She prepared to answer his question. 'He seemed exhausted. Do you think he is?'

'I hardly know him. From what they said he'd had a hectic night with some of his friends. Like Shakespeare. It killed him off.'

'My experts don't seem to accept that.'

'Oh, why not? Who spread the story, then?'

'A man called John Ward, who was both a doctor and parson, came to Stratford in the 1660s and said that was the local tradition.'

'Who were the friends?'

'Ben Jonson and Michael Drayton.'

Both now concentrated for a short time on their teacups.

'Eric will be older now than Shakespeare was when he died,' John ventured.

'I suppose so.' Her eyebrows rose high. 'He looks as if he's worn all the nature out of his flesh.'

'He's still very handsome.'

'Oh, yes,' she agreed. 'Very.'

'What did you think of him?' John asked. 'Impressive?'

'Well, yes. He knows a great deal, has been everywhere, and he talks well. I expected that. I read his articles on Afghanistan in *The Times*. He writes really well, both lucidly and expressively.'

'No faults?' he queried.

'He's a bit too fond of the sound of his own voice for my liking,' Helen answered.

She spoke without heat. He felt suddenly glad.

'Perhaps we caught him on a bad day,' John said.

'Very likely, but it doesn't alter him, basically. When he was talking to us over lunch, you could see that he was out to shine.'

'But if that was to our advantage?'

'It didn't suit me. That's all I know. And I didn't like the way he just sat by the fire with his brandy and abandoned us.'

'He was fagged out, poor chap.'

'He didn't make much of an effort.' She was adamant. 'How does he get on with Irene?'

'I don't really know. They don't see a great deal of each other, I suspect. He doesn't take her with him on his foreign expeditions. Not that she wants to go to the Amazon, Chechnya, Tibet or Afghanistan.'

'Do they quarrel much?'

'Not as far as I know.'

'Have they been married long?'

'Ages. The wedding wasn't long, I believe, after they left university.'

Helen sat opposite him, lively and interested. He admired both her clothes and the admirable confidence with which she wore them. On working days she was invariably smart, sober, subfusc, not drawing attention to herself. Then it was her efficiency, her knowledge of the law, her understanding she wanted people to notice, not her beauty, her figure, the liveliness of her features, the variety of expression in her voice. Here was someone, her whole attitude suggested, who would consider your predicament in the light of her considerable knowledge of cases similar to yours and advise you to your advantage. She did not wish her physical beauty or presence to be the main source of attention or attraction.

'Do you like him, John?' She rarely used his name.

'He's made a reputation for himself. He appears on the television, and so is something of a celebrity. My mother is greatly
impressed by him. He answers your questions without hesitation,
and it's your question, the one you asked, which he answers, not
something irrelevant to the topic. She also always says that he's
not afraid to say that he doesn't know something.'

'Is your mother a sound judge?'

'Within her limits. She's intelligent, but she's always been too
keen to accept what life offered her without complaint. I guess
she was under the thumb of her father, a man who'd had to fight
for an education, and never stopped reading and teaching himself.'

'You didn't like him either?'

'I'm working on hearsay. But my mother and Irene used to
talk about him sometimes. I say talk, but often it became argument. Irene in her quiet way used to claim that her father's mind
was too restricted, too conservative to accept new views. I think
she, Irene, thought the same about my father. He was another
autodidact.'

'Aren't such people to be admired?'

'I suppose so. The newspapers always argue that education
should be learning for yourself, and there's some truth in that.
But if you remain in educational institutions, be they schools,
colleges or universities, your contemporaries fling their ideas
about at you and you get used to trying to make sense of what
they tell you, and then to find out, one way or another, what's
wrong with their views. It makes you both careful and rash, liberal,
let's say, open to new ideas.'

They smiled at each other.

'Tell me,' he said, 'what you've been doing recently.'

'Work, mostly.'

'You're not short of clients? Are we getting more litigious, do
you think?'

'Yes. With our encouragement. Divorce rates are high.
Neighbourly quarrels can't be settled by common sense. Doctors
and employers are chased for compensation. It keeps me busy
and well paid, and so I don't complain. What I don't know is
whether society as a whole is better off.'

They talked away; she seemed in no hurry to be rid of him.

94

They argued like trusted friends, one wanting to get the better of the other but bearing no ill will over their differences.

'Let's go out for dinner,' he suggested suddenly.

'Thanks. I'd love to, but I've a lot of work to do. It'll take me all this evening and probably the whole of tomorrow.'

'Interesting?'

'Not really. But it's the sort of thing I'm best at: being careful, making sure I've got the whole story in mind.'

He was aware of her beauty, her attraction as she spoke modestly about herself. He wanted to put his arms round her. He stood and announced he'd better go and let her get on.

'I've really enjoyed this time we've had together,' she said. 'It's made me feel that I shall be able to sort these cases out properly now.'

He pulled her into him, and she allowed it, though he felt some faint resistance, some stiffness about her body. They kissed, deeply, until she put her hands on his shoulders and gently eased him away.

'Not now,' she said, sadly, as if regretting her words. She kissed his cheek with a brief peck of apology.

As she showed him out through the front door she said, 'Thanks so much for this little outing today. You don't know how much good you've done me. This morning I felt so low I couldn't have worked properly. I barely felt able to start. Now I'm more like myself.'

'Do you get lonely?' he asked.

'Yes. Sometimes it's unbearable.'

'You should ring me. I mean that. Promise you'll never allow yourself to become so depressed without giving me a call. I may not be the most sympathetic man on earth, but I'll do my best. Promise, now.'

'Thank you. I will.'

She spoke soberly but as one in command of herself and the situation. They kissed again, and he left. Before he had taken the few steps to the front gate, she had closed the door on him. He was disappointed as he looked back, and the weather under the rain and street lights spread bleakly cold.

XIII

Though he knew she would be impatient to hear from him about the visit to Irene's house, John made no immediate contact with his mother. He could not exactly reconcile this behaviour with his sense of fairness, and though the outing had been a success as far as he and Helen were concerned, he did not wish to talk about it, particularly to his mother who would want it served up to her in perfect detail. She saw her world in black and white; to his mind his relationship with his wife was at present limned in the palest pastel colours.

On Tuesday Ella rang him.

She asked after his health, and received his usual non-committal reply.

'Was it a success? You know what I mean.'

'I think so. Helen and I had no hard words with each other, and we had a pleasant cup of tea at her house after I took her home.'

'Then why didn't you ring me and tell me all this?'

'Carelessness, mainly. Thoughtlessness. I've been pretty busy.'

'Even on Sunday?'

He did not answer.

'I also thought,' he said, 'that you might have contacted Irene or Helen or both, and that they would have satisfied you with their stories rather than my biased account.'

'I have heard from Irene.'

'And what was her verdict?'

'It was not her place to give judgements. She said that Eric had really put himself out to interest her, in spite of the fact that he wasn't too well.'

'What was wrong with him?'

'She didn't say. She said you were very attentive to Helen, but rather quiet. She thought how nicely both you and Helen dressed.

Her husband, she says, is never well turned out. I suppose it's living in places like Afghanistan.'

'It's no use polishing your boots out there. They'd be covered in sand and dust inside ten seconds.'

'That's another thing. Eric apparently never cleans his shoes. She has to do them for him every single morning.'

'Another unsatisfactory husband. How's Dad?'

'Much the same. He's more and more vague, though sometimes he'll appear to speak sensibly. He asked me, for instance, why you and Helen hadn't been in to see him. I said you lived in London and were both very busy. He then kept repeating the word "London" over and over again as if he'd never heard it before.'

'And how are things going on in your school?'

'Quite well. There's a lot of illness about at this time of the year. And amongst the staff. That means I have to take over some of the teaching and neglect my other duties.'

'Such as?'

'You've no idea how much a head has to do these days. The paperwork is tremendous. It's not a case of filling in a few lines in the logbook these days, you know. And the parents and the governors, who have some power, are always coming up with some madcap scheme or other, or quarrelling about some decision.'

'And the Director of Education?'

'He's no trouble. On the rare occasions I've seen him he's been sympathetic and helpful. We've an inspection coming up after Easter. Some of the staff are beginning to worry themselves to death about it.'

'Does that do them good?'

'What do you mean? Anxiety never did anyone any good. Especially to conscientious people.'

'I meant the idle ones.'

'Not of necessity. We did pretty well in the seven-year-old tests last year. I had congratulatory letters from the Director, and, believe it or not, the Lord Mayor.'

'Well done, that woman. Though aren't the pundits against examinations these days?'

'Some are. They say we should be widening the cultural horizons of the children with art, music and literature. But most of the Ofsted people I've spoken to think as I do, that these exams set reachable standards in maths, science and reading. And once you can read you can teach yourself if you're so minded. You'd be surprised how many illiterate adults there are in this country. It runs into millions. And that is a disgrace.'

'The thing I noticed the couple of times I visited your school was the decoration. Pictures, bright colours on the walls, tables with beautiful cloths under the displays, flowers, plants, models, pieces of verse. I thought how marvellous it all looked. And quite unlike the rooms I was taught in with drab paint fading on the walls and chalk dust everywhere. Presumably grammar schools didn't need art or culture of that sort. Latin verbs and differential calculus were enough for us. Music and Art once a week in the junior years. After that Greek or Physics.'

'The secondary schools aren't much better now. Bare walls. Uncleaned windows. That annoys me. I get my teachers to clean our windows on the inside at least. Some of them don't like it; they say the caretaker ought to do it. But don't get me on to that. The chairman of the governors and I are often at loggerheads about such matters. He says they should be covered by insurance. One of these days I shall come straight out with it and tell him that the parents would do the school more good coming down one evening and cleaning the windows than sitting round a table talking rubbish about what they're ignorant of.'

'You ended that sentence with a preposition.'

'You're as bad as they are. Anyhow how are you and Helen shaping? Have you made arrangements for any more meetings?'

'No. We were both very cautious. What I can't seem to get you to understand is that we didn't separate over nothing. We could barely abide being in the same room together. That's gone now, in my case, though I don't know about her. So we treat each other with circumspection. I enjoyed talking to her. We hit on a subject we both were interested in, and that got us off on the right foot.'

'What was that?'

'Shakespeare. She seemed quite the expert. She can't half take in information. And retain it.

'She knows a lot about it, does she?'

'Yes. She's been reading up ever since we went to see *Coriolanus*.'

'Take her to another Shakespeare play, then.'

'I have it in mind.'

'Sometimes I don't seem to understand you at all. Unless you're deliberately trying to rile me.'

They talked on, not exactly in agreement. She spoke to him as if he were one of her erring pupils. He wryly reminded himself that she'd talk to her chairman of governors in just this way.

Two days later Helen telephoned him. He'd just finished eating his evening meal.

'Are you busy?' she asked.

'No. Just about to wash up.' He felt dog-tired after a long day.

'I didn't know whether to ring you about this. It's not your concern, really.'

Her voice was tremulous. He waited.

'It's Eric Davenport. He's bothering me.'

'In what way?'

'He wants to see me. I've had four letters from him this week. One every day. And he keeps phoning.'

'Um?' The monosyllable was all he could manage.

'He says he loves me.'

'You've only met him once.'

'That's what I keep telling him. But he says he knows his heart. He loves me. When I tell him he's already married, he says that's of no consequence. Irene knows what sort of man she chose. They have, he says, an open marriage. They are both unfaithful if it suits them. I argued that if he couldn't be faithful to his wife, what chance was there that he'd treat me properly. He said he was not asking me to join him in a lifelong contract. It may last weeks only, days even. But we should find such enjoyment, such pleasure, such enlightenment in that short time that it would make all the difference to our lives.'

'Does that seem possible?'

'Not to me.'

'Are his letters threatening in any way?'

'No. He writes as if he means what he says. Like a boy really, not a man of his age.'

'Are you flattered?'

'Half and half. He's a somebody, and it seems impossible that a man with his reputation as a journalist should choose to say such things to me.'

'Why not?'

'I'm a run-of-the-mill solicitor. What makes me so special?'

'What you say, how you look and dress. You're the sort of woman any man would look at twice.'

'Well. That's a matter of opinion.'

'Do you write back?'

'No.'

'But you answer the phone?'

'I don't know who's ringing, do I?'

'That's true enough. Do you want to meet him? Are you tempted, however faintly, just out of curiosity?'

'No. I don't want to harm Irene.'

'If it's not you, it'll be somebody else.'

'That would be a feeble excuse. Anyhow, I don't want him. I'd be glad to talk to him from time to time, because he's interesting. For instance, talking about eating mud crabs. I'd never heard of them before.'

'Nor I.'

'He mentioned you. He said you seemed very quiet, and asked if you were shy.'

'And you said?'

'Not particularly. He told me Irene had said you'd always been under your mother's thumb. He asked me if that was right. I said you gave as good as you got in that direction.'

'Would you like to come round here?'

'I can't. I've brought some work home.'

'I can provide you with a quiet corner somewhere. I shan't interrupt except with the odd cup of coffee.'

'Thanks, but no. I shall be all right where I am.'

'Come round tomorrow evening then.'

'Thank you.' A moment's thought. 'At what time?'

'Oh, I'll send out for something to eat. So let's say six-thirty, seven. Now you're sure you're OK? If he harasses you?'

'I can deal with a phone call. If he comes round, I'll not let him in. I shall come to no harm.' She spoke confidently now.

'Did all this come as a surprise to you?' John asked.

'Right out of the blue.'

'Odd,' he said. 'I'll let you get on with your work. Give me another ring, will you? What time do you go to bed? Eleven? Ring then and report that all's well.'

'If it's not, what will you do?'

'Jump in the car, and come round.'

'Thank you.'

There had been no phone call from Davenport when she rang at eleven. She had about another half hour's work to complete, and then it would be straight to bed. She spoke her gratitude cheerily when he said he looked forward to seeing her the next day.

XIV

John came home early the next day to prepare the dinner for Helen. He bought pork chops, cabbage, potatoes. He'd risen at seven to make a trifle which he would complete after he had come home. Work that day had been particularly tedious, form filling, arranging dates for three audits for factories wishing to be ready for 5 April, sorting out a private account for a scholarly archivist who had worked in the United States for a year and got himself entangled with their tax system. The phone was constantly ringing, and he was called upon for decisions at least five times. In the ordinary way he would not have been put out, but glad, rather, that the firm was so busy. Today he wanted to concentrate on Helen's visit. Her call had appealed to him for help, and though he was uncertain what he could do, such chivalry that he possessed demanded at least an effort on his wife's behalf.

He left work an hour earlier than usual, shopped locally near his office before he made for home. He drank a cup of tea, but had no sooner set about preparing the meal than a phone call from his mother interrupted him.

'Are you busy?' she asked.

'Well, yes I am. Helen's coming to dinner, and I'm just setting about cooking it.'

'Is this occasion for any reason?' she asked.

'No,' he lied. If his mother was to hear of Davenport's unwanted advances it would be better if the information came from Helen, or Irene, assuming she knew anything about it.

'It won't take me long, but I thought you ought to know. It's about your father.' She paused, breathing histrionically.

'What's he done now then?'

'He's taken a fancy to one of the women patients in the home.'

'Does he say so?'

'Apparently. There's no secret about it. He's hanging around her all the time. They go walking through the rooms hand in hand. They kiss in full view of everybody, and I don't mean just a little peck. He's taken her into his bedroom according to some reports. God knows what they get up to in there.'

'Is she a married woman?'

'I'm not sure about that. She's one of the women he rescued. She's either a widow or a spinster.'

'I thought he spent a good part of his time on his own in his bedroom, out of the way of the other patients.'

'Not now. He's down there all the time with his lady-love.' Her scorn and resentment rang over the phone line.

'Do they try to keep them apart at the home?'

'How can they? But it's so ridiculous. A man of his age. He should be ashamed of himself. It's a great embarrassment to me, I can tell you. I can see them grinning behind my back when I go there.'

'Who?'

'The staff. Some of the patients.'

'What sort of woman is she?'

'How do you mean?'

'How old? How ill? Is she educated?'

'I don't know.'

'Haven't you asked?'

'No. I got to know from the matron a fortnight ago. She took me into her office and told me. She thought it only right that I should know. The woman's name is Monica Powell. The matron was called away in the middle of our interview, so we had no time to go into further detail. She did say that she was a quiet, respectable woman, and also it was unusual in her experience for someone of your father's temperament and background to embark on a romance. They had been worried about your father, well, not exactly worried, slightly concerned about your father in that he seemed antisocial, unwilling to talk, apathetic, and so was not getting the quality of life he and the staff might expect. She said some people suffering from dementia seem to get pleasure from their contact with other patients. It's quiet; it may not seem much to outside observers but at least it brings some sort of satisfaction to them, makes their trouble lighter, more bearable.'

'Did she put this development down to his mental failings?'

'Not really. As I say we had to break off before she could go further. I don't suppose she knows. Anyhow, the next time I went in she'd gone away for a fortnight's holiday to Scotland. I did have a few words with her assistant who said, yes, the relationship was still going on. She hardly seemed to think it was worth bothering about.'

'Have you faced Dad with it?'

'Yes. I have. He's still very morose, laconic, when I talk to him. He said, grudgingly, that Monica was a nice lady, that they were friends. And that's about all I could get out of him.'

'And what do you want me to do?' John asked.

'I wondered if you'd come up and see him. It might shock him into more rational behaviour. And now you seem to be more friendly with Helen, it struck me that both of you might visit him together. If you could come this weekend you could stay overnight with me, or longer, the pair of you. What do you say?'

'I'll have to ask Helen,' he said.

'Of course. And if she's coming round this evening, that will be a good time.'

'I will. In any case I'll try to come myself, at least on Saturday.'

'You will ask her?'

'Yes.'

'That's good, John, and very thoughtful of you.'

'I don't think my intervention will make any impression on him.'

'We'll see. He used to speak very highly of you and your opinions.'

His mother rang off, and he concentrated on the meal, to considerable success.

'That's one sort of meal we had at home,' Helen enthused after they'd eaten. 'My mother said she was no sort of cook, and my father loved his food, exotic or homely; so she acquired no art. But on Sundays if we were all at home, not very often, we'd have one of her straightforward English meals. Rather like this. He said this outmatched all the foreign fancies people stuffed into him during the week.'

'Did he mean it?'

'I don't know. He often told you what he thought you wanted to hear. But he certainly enjoyed his Sunday meals.'

104

Her father was an engineer who travelled all over Europe and the United States. He was a boisterous, clever man but not exactly the parent one would have guessed for Helen, his only daughter.

'Speaking of fathers,' he said. 'Mine is in trouble.'

He, in an ironical distant tone, explained about his father's behaviour in the nursing home. Helen listened carefully, asked no questions but allowed him to tell the tale in his own way. When he had finished, she looked at him and said, 'Do you think it makes him any happier?'

'I've no idea.'

'I realise that it must be most embarrassing for your mother, but if she can bear it I don't see that much harm is being done.'

'My mother wants us, you and me, to go up one weekend to see him.'

'Why me?' she asked.

'One, it brings you into contact with me, and secondly she hopes that you'll speak to Dad with such sense that he'll see the error of his ways.'

'That's unlikely.'

'My mother thinks very highly of you. The trained legal mind.'

'It's no joke to her, John. You realise that I thought he'd become turned in on himself, or at least antisocial, with hardly a civil word to offer to anybody. So this love affair comes as a complete surprise. But then, so did the rescue of the women from the fire.'

'She's one of them. Will you come up with me?'

'When?'

'This weekend. Either Friday or Saturday. My mother will put us up.'

'Will you go, whether I do or not?'

'Yes. I feel sorry for them. Or for my mother.'

'I'll come with you then.'

There was a pause, then awkwardly he grabbed at her right hand with both of his, kissed it as he thanked her volubly but in a low, unemphatic voice.

'What will happen if nothing happens to change the situation?' she asked.

'My mother would have no compunction about moving him to another nursing home.'

'Do you agree with her?'

'I feel sorry for her. She'll treat him as she treats her children at school. Put them out of the way of temptation.'

He picked Helen up at eight o'clock on Friday evening. This meant they could visit his father on Saturday afternoon, and return to London immediately afterwards, or if there seemed any advantage in it stay on for a second night and drive back on Sunday. He did not feel easy about this journey because he feared his mother expected him to say or do something at the end of it to resolve the awkward situation caused by his father's foolishness. He had no idea where to start. Curiosity to see Miss, Mrs Powell was high. Perhaps to watch them together, acting like old-fashioned hand-in-hand school sweethearts would trouble him. His father had always been a reserved man, showing overt affection to neither wife nor son. His mother had packed the old man off to the nursing home as soon as it became clear to her that she could no longer care properly for him. She had done her duty by him all his life. Whether, at this stage, love in any of its manifestations remained he doubted. If it had when he entered Holmleigh, his father had dispersed it by his behaviour there. First he'd sunk into the almost savage silences he maintained during her visits, and then by his foolery with this Monica woman. She'd blame his laconic utterances on his dementia, but the second was in Ella's eyes beyond explanation or excuse. John saw no way in which he could remedy the trouble.

They travelled north in his car.

Music, chosen by Helen, played gently from the speakers behind them. As they reached the M1 the last movement of Bach's Sixth Brandenburg Concerto urged them on.

'That's my favourite movement,' she said. 'I'd like that played at my funeral. To send people out jolly, thinking well of me.' She laughed, breaking up her lugubrious expression. 'What would you choose?'

'For my funeral?'

'No, silly. Your present favourite. I know you change your mind every ten minutes.'

'The piece that makes me really sit up is the opening of *Zadok the Priest*. It's like an explosion. Otherwise it would be "Cum

Sanctu Spiritu" from the B Minor Mass. That's like a great wild dance, and yet it's so brilliantly intellectual.'

They spent the rest of the journey talking like this. Shakespeare was given a good run. She had bought Schoenbaum's *Shakespeare's Lives* and was now adding further Arden editions to her collection. Moreover she was reading them, carefully studying them, one by one.

'I find some of them difficult,' she confided, 'and, this surprises me, boring.'

'Such as?'

'Well, *Cymbeline*. I think it's nowhere as good as *Hamlet*, or *Lear*, or even *Coriolanus*.'

'Is it the subject matter or the language you dislike?'

'Hard to separate.' She rubbed her pretty chin, thinking. 'The language? I don't know.'

'Yes. I agree. Sometimes I find the subject matter is antipathetical even when the verse is great. *Othello*, for instance. I don't know why I'm so set against the play.'

'Perhaps you're a racist.' Jokingly.

'I don't think it's that. Othello naively accepts Iago's fabrications against Desdemona. He should have stood up for his wife.'

'Perhaps because of his colour he couldn't. Not that he lacked the character, but the whole of society was against Moors rising high in the service of the state, and marrying beautiful, young white women.'

'I think it's because I never did it at school. My schoolmasters never banged it into me. So I'm not up to it.'

'Well done, your teachers,' she said. 'I thought they were supposed to put you off Shakespeare for life.'

They enjoyed these exchanges. She invariably admired his driving and he knew it. By the time they had reached his mother's they were friendly without reservation and almost reluctant to get out of the warm car.

Ella Riley was waiting for them with a laden table.

'A dry biscuit for me, please,' John said.

'Nothing to eat at all, thank you,' Helen added shyly. She thought it sad that Ella had taken all this trouble for so little effect.

The three talked for an hour, with the mother playing the tactful hostess. Apart from a brief reference to her husband, but not to his lapse, no mention was made of any awkward subject. Their marriage, the failure of the Stratford trip, were disregarded. Ella grew quite eloquent about the forthcoming inspection of her school.

'Are these people terrifying?' Helen asked.

'No. On the contrary I've always found them polite and helpful.'

'Do they make useful suggestions?'

'Yes. But oddly enough fashion plays its part, even in education.'

'Especially in education,' John said.

'You know nothing about it.'

That sharp sentence made Helen giggle.

They were in bed by eleven-thirty. Ella had given them no option but to sleep together. There was a room with two single beds, he knew, but his mother had not put it at their disposal. They undressed quickly; he folded his clothes neatly together on to an ottoman. Helen used a small wardrobe which had been emptied. She stood stark naked in front of her husband without embarrassment. They made love, tentatively at first, but ultimately to the satisfaction of both. Their time was short because both were tired after a long day of work, of preparation, of travelling. He lay on and in her with all trouble dispersed, both gratified, in stretched love with the other. He almost immediately fell asleep, his arm about her.

In the morning they woke at seven and made love again, but did not attempt to get up. Downstairs they could hear his mother moving quietly around.

'What time is breakfast?' she asked, kissing him.

'Nine o'clock will do.'

'Is that her usual time?'

'No. I guess half past seven is more likely with her.'

'She'll think we're idle.' Her lips ran up and across his cheeks, barely touching him.

'She'll think we're catching up on sleep. My mother's one of these energetic people who envies those who can nod off.'

'Goodness.'

He pulled her into him.

They dallied but were downstairs in the kitchen at nine-fifteen. Ella was all smiles, as she expressed concern at the moderation of their demands. 'Cereal and two slices of toast?' she reproached John. 'I thought you'd have egg, bacon, sausage, mushrooms and fried bread.'

'And indigestion all day.'

'This is a holiday. I wouldn't want you to eat like that every day of the week. You'd be fat. But once in a while. Just to please your mother.'

Helen for her part had asked for cereal and one slice of toast and marmalade.

'You'll fade away.'

'I don't think so.'

Soon after breakfast, when John was allowed to dry the dishes, his mother asked for his plans.

'We'll visit Dad this afternoon.'

'And after that?'

'That depends on Helen. She might want to go back immediately. We'll ask her.'

'You'll stop the night?'

'A possibility. If it doesn't throw your arrangements into confusion. It will mean a very early start on Monday morning.'

Ella called out to Helen to inquire if she would like to spend more time in Beechnall.

'That depends on John,' came the reply.

'You're both too polite. I'll take it that you will.'

John offered to drive his mother round the shops.

'On Saturday morning?' she asked. 'When every man, woman and child is out?'

'When do you shop then?' he asked. 'Do you slip out of school?'

'I get my main grocery order on Wednesday evening. That's the late night here. Then I visit Will.'

'And how about things like clothes or new furniture?'

'That's rarely a concern. And there are catalogues these days. My postbox is stuffed full with them. And even in these untrendy parts we have Sunday shopping.'

'How many times have you shopped on Sundays?'

'Not at all. But the facility's there, should I need it.'

She did, however, go out to the corner shop, and they accompanied her.

'Thank God, it's fine,' she said.

'Still cold, though.'

'You expect it at this time of the year.'

John had offered to take the ladies out to lunch, but his mother was having none of it. She'd improvise, her word, a light lunch for them, and then feed them properly after the visit to Holmleigh.

'I like entertaining,' Ella said. 'Gives my mind something else to focus on. Do you like it, Helen?'

'If I like the people who are coming I'll make the effort. John's a better cook than I am.'

'I insisted he learnt how to plan and prepare a meal.'

'And I provided for myself the appetite to eat it,' John said.

They waited ten minutes for their mother, who was the only customer, as she kept up an earnest conversation with the Pakistani shopkeeper.

'She's taking her time,' John commented.

'She's had second thoughts about some treat for us.'

'At a little shop like this?'

'Oh, yes. She'll make certain she buys what she wants. My guess is it will be ice cream of some sort to go with the fruit. She's really stocked the larder for us, John. I went into the pantry when we were clearing breakfast away. She could be feeding the five thousand.'

When Ella came out, John relieved her of her shopping bag and she apologised for keeping them in the cold street. She had been discussing with the shopkeeper his grandson's progress in school.

'Is he doing well?' Helen inquired.

'Yes. He's clever. And they're determined he'll make the best of the educational system here. He'll end up as a lawyer or doctor.'

Ella insisted that they walk with her to see 'the alteration to the town'. They stared down at the place where a large factory had been destroyed, and the grounds already marked out with new curbed roads and foundations for houses.

'What are these?' Helen asked.

'Little town-houses. They're building domestic premises now whenever they pull down large buildings. It seems the council don't want to encroach on the green belt. There's a great demand for new homes in big towns now. I blame young people. They marry and they split up in no time. And so they need two houses instead of one. When I was a child young married couples often lived for two or three years after marriage with one or the other's parents until they'd saved enough to set up a home somewhere. Times change.'

'Were you born in your mother's present house?' Helen asked John.

'No, I wasn't. We moved when I was nearly two.'

'You won't remember that, then,' Helen said.

'No.'

'We wanted a larger place. We were trying for further children, but were unlucky. We lost two, stillborn, after we moved in. I wasn't teaching then, and Will didn't much mind where he lived as long as it had a respectable address and was warm and dry.'

Ella marched them on to the playing fields of a school which had been taken over for four and five-bedroom housing.

'Wasn't there trouble about this?' John asked.

'There was. Some people said it was a shame to rob the school of its open spaces.'

'What do you think?' John asked.

'I don't know. The children were not allowed out there on the playing fields in their own time, at break, in the lunch hour, and certainly not in the evening. It's a matter of insurance, they say. And there are not the out-of-school fixtures at football and cricket and so on that were usual in your time. You have to pay the staff to umpire and referee and oversee games outside school hours. So it's quite certain that the fields were underused. But what we don't know is if there'll be a change in the next few years. All the education committee thinks of is the enormous amount of money that will come into their coffers on the sale of the land. But it's only once. Once the ground is sold off there'll be no chance of getting it back.'

'Where will they play cup matches between schools?'

'Oh, there are one or two schools with adequate fields, and there's the big stadium they built long ago. They bus children out.'

She led them two streets further where the ground had been levelled outside a small playground with swings, slides and a huge brand-new machine large enough to fire off a moon rocket.

'They're extending this amusement park,' Ella explained. 'They were going to build a bus station here, but reason prevailed in the end. There was a powerful faction who wanted to know what use a bus station was out here.'

'And?' John.

'They saw it as a kind of centre for cross-town journeys. One drove in here, and changed buses for other suburbs. Certainly they're doing their best to improve the bus services in order to get private traffic off the road. I didn't see that this bus station would have made three ha'porth of difference. They did their best to give an explanation, but it satisfied nobody, and they dropped the scheme. So now they're spending money on enlarging this little place.'

'Is that a good idea?' John asked.

'It would be if parents had any sense of responsibility. That is if they took their children there and looked after them. But they won't, so it will be a hotbed of accidents and vandalism. They'll put up notices to the effect that nobody over the age of fifteen is allowed to ride on the amusements, but I've seen parents, grown men, using the swings. You'd need a policeman on permanent watch to keep the place properly safe.'

'Do you lead the opposition to these "improvements"?' Helen asked.

'I sign petitions, but that's about as far as I go.'

'You're a part of the establishment?' said John.

'In my small bit of the city and its education I suppose I am. I've plenty to occupy my time, and the powers-that-be do their best. More often than not they're not sure what it is they're doing.'

'Would you say this was a thriving city?' Helen wanted to know.

'Yes. I think so. There are plenty of jobs if you want work. And we keep hearing rumours that the government is about to move some large department or its headquarters up here. That puts house prices up. There are disadvantages to everything.'

'There haven't been any governmental people move up here?' asked John.

'No. Not yet.'

They made their way back, and Ella ordered her guests to sit down with the thick pack of newspapers. She had the lunch under control. 'I love entertaining,' she said. 'You mustn't deprive me of my small pleasures, especially in view of this afternoon's visit. I don't expect your father to be either cooperative or communicative.'

They had an excellent light lunch, cold meat and salad with home-made chutney. John was allowed to wash the dishes.

'Don't you ever use your dishwasher?' he asked, when he'd finished.

'Never. Not for one person. They must be useful for large families or for those who entertain a lot.'

Again the guests were ordered to sit down while Ella prepared to go out. She came downstairs in a dark skirt and jacket, every inch a headmistress. Both young people wondered, as they confessed later, why she took such trouble to visit her husband.

'I wonder if she always does it?' Helen asked him.

'I guess so.'

'It's not because she's going with us?'

'No.'

The three set out for Holmleigh soon after two o'clock in John's car. Ella led the way indoors and straight to the matron's office. The assistant, a young rather nervous girl, said her senior was still on holiday.

'How is my husband?'

The girl fetched out a file from the bookcase on the wall. She opened and then scanned it, explaining when she had finished that they did not keep these records at the foot of a patient's bed as in hospitals. They'd hardly be safe here with one or two of their inmates. 'They might easily destroy them. Without meaning to, you understand.' She slapped a hand on the file. 'Medically, there's no change with Mr Riley.'

'But is he still besotted with this Powell woman?'

'They spend a lot of time together,' the girl said.

'And you can do nothing about it?'

'Well, it would be difficult. I know the matron was rather concerned.'

Ella thanked the girl brusquely and led her guests into one of the downstairs recreation rooms which seemed more crowded than usual. As they entered, silence fell as if the other inmates and their visitors had been waiting for this portentous entry.

William Riley was stiffly seated by a window, the same place in the room that he had occupied at Christmas. He sat straight, and seemed better dressed than when his son last saw him.

Ella greeted, but did not kiss him.

'Look who's here to see you,' she said.

William lifted his head to look at John and Helen. His face lit up as he saw Helen. John took his father's limp hand to shake it; Helen bent over to kiss his cheek.

'How are you keeping?' John asked cheerfully.

'Much the same. No change.'

'Healthwise?'

'Good.'

'Do they keep you occupied?'

'Occupied.' William repeated the word woodenly, as if he did not understand it.

'Is there anything you particularly want?' Ella joined in, fiercely this time.

'No.' The word was flat, lacking all grace.

'I've brought you a change of underclothes and pyjamas. And a new tube of denture-cleaning tablets. I noticed you were running out.'

He did not speak, offered no brief words of thanks.

'Have you done anything interesting since I last came in?'

'No.'

'I thought they were giving you a concert last Sunday evening? A choir? The Samson Singers?'

'I didn't hear them.'

'Are you interested in music?' Helen asked. He turned towards his daughter-in-law, his face more human, more animated.

'Not really,' he said. 'They tried to teach me the piano when I was a boy, but I wasn't talented at all. I'd other things I'd rather do.'

'Do they have sing-songs?' John asked.

'No. What sort of sing-songs?' His voice was nasal, quite different from his usual voice.

'"Daisy, Daisy". "Pack Up Your Troubles". "Cockles And Mussels". That sort of thing. "Loch Lomond".'

114

'No. If they have them, I don't go. I haven't even heard them.'

Ella asked about his needs and told him again what she had bought for him and where in his room she would put it. He barely acknowledged her care with anything more than a grunt or a sulky nod. Helen questioned him about the activities in the place, and again he was far from forthcoming.

'Except when they want to clean, they leave us alone.'

'What about meals?'

'They lead us to the tables like children. I suppose some of them need it. I don't. The strength in my legs has gone, but at least I can creep up to the table.' The length of his answer showed how high Helen stood in his estimation. 'They do their best.'

'Is the food good?'

'No. Café standard. Just about eatable.' His voice trailed off into incomprehensible grumbling, as if he'd forgotten his visitors.

'What about the people?' John asked. 'What are they like?'

'People.'

'Have you made any particular friends?'

William paused over this, stroking his chin and cheeks.

'No. Not here,' he replied after long enough.

'What about Miss Powell?'

'Miss who?'

'Powell.'

'Monica Powell,' Ella snapped at him.

Again a pause, as if he tried to get his excuses straight.

'Oh, Monica. Yes.'

'What about her?' John was still polite.

'Monica. A nice girl.'

'Girl?' Ella interrupted. 'How old do you think she is?'

'I don't ask women their age. It's not polite.' His voice was clear, and the remark that of a sane man setting ignorance right.

'Is she your special friend?' Helen asked, wheedling.

'That's no business of yours.' All consideration for Helen had dissipated itself as William turned his head from them, and glanced out of the window.

'And that's very rude.' Ella spoke as to some eight-year-old. 'We only ask these questions to find out if and how we can make

115

things more comfortable for you here. And that's the sort of reception we get for our pains.'

Still William, stiff-backed, gloomed glowering out of the window.

'The staff were worried about you and this lady,' John said in as friendly a tone as he could muster, 'and so we thought we ought to ask you about it.'

William kept his back obdurately towards him. The silence grew more awkward by the second.

'If this is how you're going to treat your visitors we might as well go home,' Ella said.

They waited.

William turned again to face them.

'No,' he said. 'No.'

'No what?' John inquired. 'What are you saying?'

'We aren't trying,' said Helen, 'to poke our noses in. Honestly. We want to help you if we can.'

His face softened and he looked the girl straight in the eye.

'I don't know,' the old man said, helplessly. 'I don't know.'

'Don't know what?' Ella.

'I don't know.'

'If you're not going to talk sensibly to us we might just as well go.'

William had the appearance of a child about to cry, lower lip trembling.

They tried to forage for information, about Monica Powell, the fire, the certificate for courage that was soon to be presented, the food, the visitors, the helpfulness of the staff, visits by doctors, but William let nothing out. Sometimes he answered with a short sentence, more often with a monosyllable, most often with silence. He seemed, if his body language meant anything, uncomfortable, unable to grasp the meaning of their questions. From time to time John thought his father might be in pain, as he squirmed in his chair, and a shadow of distress contorted his features.

'Is there anything wrong, Dad?' he inquired.

William looked at his son, as if begging. John would never have spoken like that to his father ten years ago, when the old man ruled the roost in his office, and strutted home to keep quiet under his wife's aegis.

'Are you in pain?' John pressed.

His father shook his head, loosely, from side to side. Whether he could not understand the question or was answering it with this doll-like gesture John could not decide.

'I'm coming in to see you Wednesday,' Ella said. 'Is there anything you would like us to bring you?'

'Chocolate,' he gulped.

'You don't like chocolate,' Ella chided.

'Chocolate.' This time William spoke more clearly.

'Is it for you, or will you be giving it away?' Ella again.

William did not answer the boorish question. His fingers were splayed on his thighs, and his head was thrust forward. John could remember this posture from the time of his childhood when his father was about to answer a question he thought he could handle, but which needed a moment's consideration to make sure that his answer was complete and comprehensible. Now his behaviour seemed thrust upon the old man by some external power. Each piece of conversation petered out, and the visitors searched in their heads for some topic that would catch William's interest. They did not succeed. Though his expression softened when he spoke to Helen, his answers to her were as impenetrable as those to his wife and son.

In the end – they had perhaps been with him for three quarters of an hour though it seemed longer – Ella gave up first and said it was time to leave. They wished him goodbye. His wife again issued orders about his clean pyjamas and underclothes. He paid no attention. John took his father's hand which felt large and warm; there was no return of pressure. Helen spoke last.

'We're coming in to see you next week. We'll bring you some chocolate. Is there any sort you particularly like?'

He nodded, but did not answer. She went over and kissed him. He did not seem to notice.

'He'll just give it away to this Monica woman,' Ella said, rather loudly.

They withdrew. At the door John looked back. His father had not moved position, but sat twisted in his chair, like a child expecting trouble. Helen waved without result.

The young woman came out from the office to speak to them on the corridor. She was in awe of Mrs Riley, but put on a brave face to speak.

117

'How did you find him today?' she inquired.

'Uncooperative as usual,' Ella answered. 'Is there anything you think he needs?'

'No. Poor man. I like him.'

They journeyed home in silence. Ella emptied her bag of soiled clothes, and settled her guests together in the drawing room. Five minutes later she came briskly in with a tray, teapot and large mugs. She poured the tea, and instructed them to sit there unless they wanted to walk out again.

'No thanks,' Helen said. 'It's too cold and dark. I'll send John out when he's had his tea to buy some chocolate for your visit next week.'

'I don't know why he wanted chocolate. I've never known him eat any.'

'We all change,' John said.

'That was a waste of an afternoon,' Ella answered.

'You don't know. He may have had some pleasure out of us.'

'He didn't put himself out to show it.'

'Is he depressed?' John asked.

'The doctor said so. He said he realised in some way that he was helpless and had little hope of either cure or improvement.'

'I'd have thought that with his dementia he wouldn't realise what was happening to him.'

'Apparently not. Not according to the doctor. If there was a way of making the worst of all worlds, you could bet your father would find it.'

Ella looked near tears. John put his arm round her shoulders. She shrugged him away.

XV

Over dinner that night they were more cheerful. The main dish was salmon, beautifully cooked.

'Did you do this in the microwave?' Helen asked.

'No. I hardly ever use it, except for defrosting things in a hurry.'

'This is delicious. It's no wonder William said his food in the home was only café standard.'

'That surprised me. He always had a good appetite, and tucked into whatever it was I served up. In my opinion food wasn't too plentiful in his home when he was a boy. What with the Depression and the war, money was short in the Riley family. So he was no connoisseur.'

'I thought that in the war the people of England were better fed than at any other time.' John said.

'Certainly rationing made the distribution fairer, but some people never make ends meet.'

'Do you remember the war at all?' John asked.

'No. I was only three when it ended.'

After the meal they sat down in front of the television. John read the morning's *Guardian* while the women chatted. Helen gave an interesting account of an average day's work to her mother-in-law.

'That sounds rather exciting,' Ella said.

'Not really. But it suits me. I'm careful, and it pays.'

John listened to this, neglecting his newspaper. Helen had not changed for dinner, but still appeared beautifully turned out, as if her clothes had been laundered in the interval. His wife spoke well, knew how to hold her listener's interest. Helen was not only good company but looked extremely attractive. Everything about her delighted him. He wondered if and how he had changed. It seemed impossible now, but a few months

119

ago they had quarrelled over everything. If they were going to
a theatre or concert they'd work themselves into anger about
the best way to get there. Or complain if one made a slight
alteration of agreed arrangements. He could remember that he
found her face charming, but his disenchantment was so great
he did not want to see it distorted as it often was with scorn,
disdain. She had seemed to have set herself above him, to dismiss
with a snarl any helpful suggestion he made. They were caged,
at least in their minds, by hateful incompatibility. Their months
apart demonstrated for him now what she was like. The fault
then must have been his. He could not believe this. She had
acted to annoy, destroy him. He remembered shaking with anger,
too stressed to be able to utter a word, and as he remembered
he could not help wondering whether a few months in close
company with her would restore the irrational rages.

In bed, they made love eagerly, expertly. He took no precau-
tions; she'd see to that. She had been certain that she did not
want children at this stage of her career. That had been one of
the points of dissension between them. It had not seemed very
important, at first. Both were extremely busy at work when things
had worsened between them, and these pressures impinged on
home life; neither could guarantee to be at meals at the arranged
hour, or even agree about their pleasures. He remembered he tried
to arrange a pleasant surprise for her, three days in Bruges and
Antwerp.

On the Saturday before they were due to go, he had announced
it to her. He thought of himself as self-sacrificing as he did not
much enjoy walking round picture galleries, though she did, and
the trip included several of these expeditions. Feeling sure he had
picked a winner he pleasantly announced what he had done. He
received his answer immediately.

'That's no good. You know quite well I'm going to Jenny's
for a birthday party. Why don't you remember these things, or
at least check up? It's in our joint diary.'

'It was meant as a surprise.'

'Why at my age should I need surprises?'

'I thought everybody liked something pleasant which they
didn't expect.'

'Well, you're wrong in my case. I'm not a child, you know.'

120

'You said you'd never been to Bruges.'

'I haven't, but that doesn't alter anything. I promised Jen that I'd be there, and I shall be.'

'If you were taken ill, they'd still hold the party, wouldn't they?'

'Yes. But I'd have no choice then. If I am ill, then I'm ill.'

'So, you're not going with me?'

'I'm sorry, no, I'm not. It was a lovely idea, but it clashes with a date I cannot change.'

'Shall I try to arrange it for a date you can keep free?'

She waited, her lips thin and tight. This was the test.

'No, thank you. Things are pretty tight in the office as you should realise. We are run off our feet what with illness and alterations of court appearances.'

'But you can have a Saturday afternoon off to go to a birthday party?'

'One afternoon is different from three days.'

He felt his face redden with anger. He clenched his fists.

'The truth is you don't bloody want to go with me.'

'You know that's wrong.'

'It bloody isn't.'

'There's no need for you to swear at me. I've told you why I can't go. I'd love to go to Bruges, but not in the next few weeks. I'm far too busy. But thank you. It was a nice idea, and I'm sorry I can't comply.'

'If you won't, you won't.'

He stormed from the room, slamming the door, but once outside he had no idea where to go. His brain tortured itself; his muscles tensed. He flung off to their joint study and, trying to sit at his desk, knocked over the chair, barking his shin. He swore violently and marched to the window. It was a beautiful late spring day. The gardener they employed moved round tidying the ground, his sailor cap on the back of his head. He appeared to be singing, a man happy at his work. John cursed. Why could he not keep his temper? He'd tried to please Helen, but she had rebuffed him. He knew quite well that, busy as she was, she could have arranged to spend that weekend in Bruges, but she had opted to put him in his place, make it clear she was not at his beck and call.

He remembered another later quarrel when he had physically attacked her.

It had been an unseasonably cold day, the skies leaden with threat. They had barely exchanged a word over three days. They ate together in silence, the food neither soothing nor cheering them. They followed accepted procedure; if he cooked, Helen cleared away and washed the dishes. This evening it was his turn to clear the table, wash up, and lay the places for breakfast. She had risen from the table with a briefest word of thanks, and slipped upstairs to the study. This annoyed him since he himself wanted to put in an hour or two's work after his chores, but did not want to sit in the same room that she occupied. She knew he had work this weekend, and had deliberately gone up there to obstruct him. More often than not these days she did any legal tasks she brought home in her own bedroom. They had slept apart for some weeks. She had announced that she would do this.

'Yes,' he said. 'Please yourself.'

'Oh, I shall.'

Now this evening, having finished his domestic duties, he made his way up to the study. Helen was seated at her desk. Neither spoke.

He sat down noisily at his desk, knowing clearly where he should start. He drew a pile of papers toward him, ready to sort out a problem, not difficult, which his subordinates had left him. Impatiently he looked round the other tasks, and then with a burst of annoyance saw that the order of each had been changed.

'Somebody has been moving my papers,' he snapped.

'Somebody?' She looked up, mildly interested, from her work.

'These papers are not in the same order that I put them in early this evening.'

'I haven't touched them.'

'Somebody has.'

'Why should I want to move them?'

'You might have knocked them about when you were passing.' He paused. 'By accident. And then tried to put them back.'

'I haven't.'

'Are you sure?'

She did not answer, but laid down her biro and said, calmly,

'You must have put them down in a different order from what you remember.'

'I am very careful about that.' He tried to copy her reasonable tone. 'I sort them out in the office before I leave, put them into my briefcase in a certain order so that I can easily lay them out on my desk without further reorganisation. I did that this evening as I usually do.'

'Then they must have moved themselves.'

'Don't be so bloody ridiculous.'

'Give me your explanation then,' she said.

'You must have interfered with them.'

'I've told you I haven't touched them. Why should I? I've quite enough to do without poking into your business. And now, if you'll excuse me I'll go to my own room and get on, since you seem bent on picking quarrels with me.'

'I'm not. All I'm saying is somebody moved my papers.'

'And I'm telling you I didn't touch them.'

She stood up and began to collect her work together. There was too much to carry on one journey. When she came back he was in exactly the same position, head down in an angry crouch. As she picked up the final six or so files he stepped across and knocked them out of her hands. Fortunately they were securely fastened so that only a few loose sheets were scattered across the floor. She looked in disbelief at the heap at her feet, then humbly knelt and began to collect them together as in a trance. He watched her from a pace away. When she had finished she stood up and turned towards the door. Before she could take a step he had pushed her violently on her left shoulder, tippling her backwards. Again the files flew out of her arms and her head nastily hit the wall behind; she slid awkwardly down to the floor where she lay, bunched, arms crookedly out.

He gasped. He had used more force than he intended. He'd meant to move her back a yard as a warning. She made a kind of groan or muted cry: she wasn't dead at least. He held his breath as she slowly got to her knees and began to crawl towards the door. Unsure, he moved across and attempted to lift her on to her feet.

'I'm sorry,' he said. 'I didn't mean . . .'

She said nothing, her face set in shock, her mouth slightly

open. A single large tear rolled down her cheek. She attempted to shrug him away, moaning softly. She regained her feet and tottered out. He followed her. In the corridor he attempted a further apology, but she closed the door in his face. He heard her turn the key.

Next morning he tried again.

'I'm sorry about last night. I didn't mean to be so rough. Are you all right?'

After a brief pause she said without emphasis, 'Forget it.'

Two weeks later she left him and returned to her own house. He had an overnight stay in Newcastle, and she had taken the opportunity to move her belongings. She had done this thoroughly, removing bed clothes, two chairs which she owned, all the photographs and pictures that were hers, and even a favourite snap of her which she had given to him. In return was a letter on the dining room table:

Dear John,

I can stand the tension no longer and have gone.

You will find me, if it's necessary, at my old address.

Helen.

She had no idea how he had taken the move, but a day or two later his mother had rung asking what had happened. Helen let her know about his violence.

'That's not like John,' his mother had said.

'That's what happened. He knocked my work out of my hands and then pushed me backwards into the wall.'

'Were you hurt?'

'I think I lost consciousness for a few seconds, and I had a huge lump on the back of my head.'

'I never imagined anything of this.'

They discussed the few months of mounting disagreement that preceded the attack.

'I'd like to hear his account of all this,' Ella said.

'That would be sensible.'

'I realised that things were not going altogether smoothly between you, but I had no idea it had reached this sort of level. Have you thought of counselling? With Relate, for instance?'

'We have not had anything to do with each other. He's sent on one or two letters, that's all.'

She guessed that Ella would have tongue-lashed John about his attack, but had doubted at the time whether he had improved the situation.

Now as John listened to his mother and his wife talking so easily together, he recalled that at the time of Helen's leaving his mother had been much on Helen's side, and had made that clear to him. She had condemned his physical abuse, and said wherever the faults lay in the first place, he owed his wife a great debt, and should take every opportunity to pay it off.

'Whatever your father's faults he never laid a hand on me.'

On Sunday he and Helen planned to have an early lunch, revisit Holmleigh and go straight back to London. The meal passed pleasantly as Ella and her daughter-in-law made much of each other in light and often trivial conversation. He had rarely seen his mother so relaxed and happy, sometimes laughing out loud. Helen, cheeks pink, revelled in the older woman's attention; it was not insincere, nothing actressy about it, but her attitude was welcoming, encouraging Ella to further attempts at wit, silly sallies. They admired each other, these two.

As they left Ella kissed her son brusquely on the cheek and said, 'When you phone me to say you've arrived back safely, let me know how you both think your father is making out. Think about it. I can't make head or tail of him. He seems to be neither here nor there. Perhaps he feels guilty. But I don't know in his case about using such words. It's possible it's his dementia, and he can't help it. The doctor says such people as he are quite often depressed. Will you ask them about the walking? He seems to me to be getting about much more easily. I don't know. Find out if there's anything he particularly wants. I shan't go until Wednesday.'

'We've got his chocolate.'

'So you have. Though why he asked for that I do not know.'

In the nursing home they found William Riley rather sleepy, unresponsive to their approaches. He had smiled at Helen when they first arrived, but looked at the chocolate they had brought with puzzlement. Had they put a bag of coke on his bed he could not have been more put out. He claimed, monosyllabically, to be perfectly well, in need of nothing, but said he felt tired.

'Why is that?' Helen asked. 'Have you been overdoing it?'

He denied this, wearily. They talked but found no way of penetrating his taciturnity.

'Is your mother coming?' he mumbled.

'No. Not today. She's sent you clean underclothes and pyjamas. Does she usually come in today?'

'Yes.' The answer short as a pistol crack.

'What day is it?' John asked.

'Friday.'

That was one day she never visited him.

'No. It's Sunday. She came in yesterday, Saturday. With us.'

William seemed to wrestle with this, but soon gave up the puzzle. They tried several topics but he showed little interest, and in the end dozed off.

'We're getting nowhere fast,' John said.

'He's tired out. We'll try him again in a few minutes.'

'Some hope.'

'You never know.' She stood. 'Do you know the number of his room? If you do, we'll go up, and put his things away.'

'Top floor. Room 15. You go. I'll stay here.'

As soon as he'd spoken he felt a pang of remorse; perhaps he had annoyed her, damaged the new rapport between them by refusing to fall in with her perfectly reasonable request. Immediately she set him at ease.

'Good idea. He might talk to you if he wakes.'

He sat looking at his sleeping father's face which seemed drained of humanity. It was more like a death mask, so little animation showed in the yellow, drawn features. An occasional snuffle escaped from his nose and spittle bubbled at the corner of his lips; once a little groan squeezed itself free.

'Are you all right, Dad?'

There was no answer. William stirred in his sleep and moaned again. John sat, bored out of his mind. He moved his chair so that he could see the other three patients. They were also dozing. Only one had a visitor, and she was more interested in the contents of the inmate's table than in the man himself. John crossed his legs, found this uncomfortable, and straightened them. He laid a hand on his father's arm. The old man opened his eyes without moving the position of his head and immediately dropped back to sleep. John looked round the bed and table; nothing, not a handkerchief, not a sweet. Perhaps it was not his father's, and yet the man at the end with a visitor had a locker. These were puzzles. John rose to his feet and stood frowning down at his father. The old man had not made much of his morning shave; patches of white stubble stood clearly visible. He wondered if William shaved himself or whether it was done by one of the assistants. He edged along three chairs and tiptoed to the window.

The street stretched as dull as the recreation room. It was not raining; a hint of sunshine trembled; the pavements were dry. One man walked down the other side of the road, swaying, obviously returning home from the pub. He wore a cloth cap and a dirty raincoat; his shirt gaped unevenly at the neck. He looked neither right nor left on his erratic way. When he had disappeared John scrutinised the houses across the road. He deduced from the banks of bells and namecards by the front doors that many of them were divided into flats. The large windows were black and with one exception he could see no signs of life within. In that one room he could make out a young woman moving indistinctly in her underclothes. She clearly did not mind being observed as she stood at the window in full view of the street. She caught sight of John and waved brazenly at him. He raised a languid hand in reply. Satisfied, she retreated.

John returned to his chair. His father still dozed. An assistant walked leisurely into the room and inquired after him.

'He's asleep,' John said.

'It'll do him good.'

'Does he eat well and sleep at night?'

'Yes. We can't complain.' She answered without assurance, but efficiently straightened the blanket across his knees. William did not stir.

At that moment Helen returned with another woman. She smiled as they drew up together.

'This is my husband, John,' she said. 'John. This is Mrs Powell, Monica Powell.'

The woman ignored his outstretched hand.

'Sit down,' Helen instructed the woman who instantly obeyed.

Mrs Powell was mid-sized, slightly overweight, dressed sombrely. Her cheeks were red and her expression vague. She sat with head lowered and hands folded in her lap.

'All right upstairs?' John asked Helen.

'Yes. I put the clean clothes away. It was all very neat. I had a word with the woman in charge. She said your father was not particularly happy. I inquired if she meant depressed, and she said yes. I asked about his walking and she thought he was doing better. He is very confused. In fact sometimes he thinks he is still at work, and that other people are his subordinates. Quite often he issues orders to them, presumably about income tax. When he does so, he speaks much more clearly and incisively than the rest of the time.'

'And when they don't obey orders?'

'He forgets within a minute or two and never inquires about the errand. This sort of hallucination, she says, is fairly common. People think they're back at work, or on holiday. In some ways it's a good thing, she claimed. They'll often say how busy they've been, reading or writing, when in fact they've been sitting around all day.'

'Is there any improvement?'

'She thought not. Except with getting about.'

He dropped his voice to a whisper, and pointed at Monica.

'Any mention of . . .'

'Nothing. Not a word. We met on the corridor and I told her I was Mrs Riley. She said she was just coming down to see Mr Will Riley. That's how we got together. Isn't it, dear?'

The woman lifted her head. Her expression was friendly, pleasant.

William woke, and looked ahead, struggling with the light. He groaned loudly. Helen stood over him, straightening him.

'Do you know who I am?' she asked, as to a child.

William concentrated.

'Carol,' he said, in the end.

'Wrong,' she answered cheerfully. 'I'm Helen. Now, who am I?'

He shook his head. He seemed lost.

'I'm Helen. Helen. Who am I?'

'Helen,' he replied.

'Good,' she said. 'Good. Helen.'

She tried again after this brief success.

'And your son. John.' She beckoned her husband forward. 'John.'

He took one of his father's hands from his lap, pressed it, without reward.

'Who's this, then?' Helen asked.

William shook his head and groaned.

'Hello, Father. How are you?'

'Fine, thank you.' William spoke clearly. The sanity of the answer shook John.

Monica took William's hand. She stared ahead in vacant pleasure, enjoying the company, their faces, the weather. Neither she nor William looked at each other, as if the pressure of hands sufficed.

'Do you come down to sit with Mr Riley most days?' Helen asked.

'Yes. I do. They won't allow us out.'

'The weather's not fit for outings. Have you been here long?'

Monica shook her head, disappointed.

'Is it comfortable here? Do they look after you?'

'Yes. They try.'

'Mother wanted to know if you'd like her to bring in anything particular next time she comes?' John asked.

William looked at Monica as if for help. She gave none.

'No,' he said. 'No.'

'Thank you,' Monica corrected.

'Do they provide you with any sort of entertainment here?' Helen asked Monica.

'No.' The woman shook her head. 'Never.'

'Are you going home today?' William jerked out his question.

'Shortly. Do you remember where we live?'

'London.'

'Whereabouts? London's a large place.'

William shook his head again. He and Monica looked at each other and smiled. For a moment they were like children, frankly sharing a secret, unbothered by anyone else. They did not speak.

Helen and John stayed for another half-hour. The father spoke more freely though never more than half a dozen words at a time. They prized snippets of information out of Monica. She came originally from South Wales. She had a serious fall two years before and she had been admitted to Holmleigh. She had no family. Her husband had died some time ago. He was old. She liked this place, except that they never allowed you out. She said, reasonably enough, that she understood that in her case. Her balance was bad; she'd fall over left to herself and her bones were brittle.

Each time she answered she looked across at William as though seeking permission to speak, and then for approbation of what she had said. He appeared to listen, but never intervened.

When the younger couple rose to go, John asked again if there was anything his mother could bring in. William thinned his lips, but vigorously shook his head. Helen said she had put his under-clothes away, and hoped he would be able to find them. He showed no interest. She then bent and kissed him, and leaned over to kiss Monica, who stood. John shook his father's hand, and then bent to kiss Monica's cheek. She stepped back abashed.

They walked out in silence, but turned to wave to the old lovers, who were concerned with their own affairs, standing, heads down, apparently searching for something.

'What are they looking for?' John asked.

'Perhaps it's the chocolate we brought in.'

They called in at the matron's empty office.

'We can ring up when we get back to London,' Helen advised.

XVI

As he expected, John's mother rang on Sunday evening. He described their visit to the nursing home, said bluntly that they had met Monica Powell and repeated what Helen had been told about his father.

'Did you see the matron?'

'No. We called in her office on our way out but she wasn't there, or her assistant.'

'Is she back from her holiday?'

'I've no idea. Helen happened to run across a nurse and questioned him about Dad.'

'What was this Monica Powell like?'

'Woman in her sixties, rather quiet. She sat next to Dad and held his hand. From South Wales, but no accent.'

'What had she to say for herself?'

'She didn't talk a great deal, but she was more forthcoming than Dad.'

'Was she, d'you think, an educated woman?'

'She spoke quite well, didn't make grammatical errors, used no more slang than you do. She didn't raise any philosophical questions or abstruse topics. She might have been a shop assistant in one of the big shops, John Lewis, Griffin and Spalding, House of Fraser. She had been married, but her husband had been dead for some years.'

'Was she attractive?'

'Nothing out of the ordinary. Nor did my father make any great fuss of her. He smiled at her in the same way that he smiled at Helen, but he hardly said a word to her. He seemed as grumpy, as unsociable, as ever. As we left the pair of them were standing up searching for something.'

'What?'

'No idea.'

131

His mother considered this. These silences during phone calls conveyed her disapproval. He could have done better. Should have.

After the break, they embarked on a new subject.

'Are you still there?' Ella snapped.

'Yes. At your service.'

'I thought you'd fallen asleep. I was pleased to notice you and Helen getting on so well. Did either of you raise the question of your living together again?'

'No.'

'Did you not think of it? You seemed so friendly, the pair of you.'

'I don't think, Mother, that you have any sort of idea what a state our marriage was in before Helen walked out on me. I've tried to explain all this, but you don't seem willing to listen. We're suspicious of quick moves towards coming together again. I can say that I enjoyed every minute of Helen's company this weekend but I couldn't forget the state we were in. And I imagine she'd feel much the same.'

'Shouldn't you,' Ella grimly pursued her argument, 'therefore be working on those present feelings of pleasure, trying to make something more permanent of them?'

'That's exactly what I am trying to do. But I'm not prepared to rush it.' Neither statement was true. 'I've never suggested that we live together again.'

'What do you think her answer would be if you did?'

'I'm not sure. Perhaps that's why I don't suggest it.'

He could hear his mother's breathing.

'I shall put it to her. You know that.'

'Wouldn't it be better to stay out of it and leave us to settle our own difficulties?'

'You've had long enough. I don't know about Helen, but you won't face the situation. You are always dodging. That's what you've always been like. If there's an obstacle, you run away from it or pretend it's not there.'

'Anything for a quiet life.'

'That's you all over. I shall talk to Helen.'

'Please yourself.'

'I shall, don't you worry.'

132

She rang off, not the best of friends.

He considered his mother's views. If he held, as she did, that marriage was for ever then she was probably right. You fought your corner as viciously as you liked but always with the knowledge that the present contention, however bitter, could in time be set aside, and the status quo ante bellum returned to. He would like Helen back, but he feared that in a few months they'd be rowing again and the discord too great, too rampant to bear. He'd try to make it work, but the escape route was never straightforward these days.

He waited for his mother or Helen to telephone him with an account of their discussion of the matter, but they disappointed him.

On the occasion of his next meeting with Helen, a visit to see *Richard II* at the Globe, he asked her what his mother had said.

'She said she was delighted that we were getting along so well, etc., etc. And she asked if I had even discussed our living together again. I said I hadn't, and I didn't want to rush things. She said that was your point of view. I said it seemed sensible. Then she began on an outline of your character. Though you were confident and certain with what she called "actuarial activities" and accountancy, you were in yourself diffident, not sure of yourself. In other words it was my place to put it to you that we should try living together again.'

'And what did you say?'

'I told her again there was no hurry. We were both extremely busy just now, and I was quite content to leave things as they were for the present. She asked me to think about what she had said.'

'And have you?'

'Yes. Quite often. But with no result.'

'And what did she say about my father?' He changed the subject, deliberately.

'That he was getting worse, physically. He'd acquired all sorts of aches and pains. His prostate gland was enlarged, his bronchitis seemed nasty, he was losing weight and his mental faculties were melting, her word, away.'

'And Mrs Powell?'

'She got short shrift. She never comes near your father when your mother is there. She didn't know whether that was the woman's own choice or whether the staff arranged to keep her away.'

'So she's never seen her?'

'It appears not.'

'My mother is very fond of you.'

'You've said so before.'

They left it there. Their afternoon at the Globe was perfect. Helen, moved by the play which she had never seen before, seemed near tears at the end, compliant to his every suggestion. This day was, he thought, perhaps the turning point. At the end of their time together they kissed lovingly and he asked her to stay the night with him. She refused, very gently, claiming she had to prepare herself for the journey to Liverpool where she was due at a conference.

He knew that she had two conferences in the next fortnight and would not therefore be able to see him.

'Will you learn anything at these gab-fests?' he had asked.

'Yes, I'm sure I shall. John Gardiner, our principal, invited me to go at the firm's expense. "You've worked very hard for us this last two years, and so you deserve a break from our sort of humdrum law. I think you're the nearest to an academic lawyer we have in this office and so you'll profit from some of the recondite topics they'll drag up. You'll also meet quite a few bright young solicitors and barristers, and they'll teach you something. Besides, you might find an opening to a larger office than ours. There will be plenty of people on the lookout for potential high fliers.'

'He doesn't want to get rid of you, does he?'

'That's what I asked him. He said he didn't, but our office was rather small, and I should on the whole just be going over and over the same dull affairs for the rest of my life. "You do them extremely well, but I wonder in ten years whether you won't be bored stiff, and wished you'd branched out when you were younger. You're a good lawyer, Helen, and I'm not telling you that what you do now is useless and trivial. But you've earned the chance to look elsewhere. I shall be retiring in about six years, and Alfred Hartopp will take over. He'll love to have somebody like you in his office so that if anything tricky comes up he'll have you at his elbow to consult. Not that Alf will go looking for difficult cases; you know him. He'd run a mile rather than take on anything he's not already done twenty times. So I'm giving you a chance to take a peep at the wide world. I'm not saying that anything will come up; I don't know. But you'll have the opportunity to look about you."' She had felt pleased, and thanked him. He'd always seemed a devious old devil to her, but one never knew. She could not immediately see who he was putting in his place by choosing her, very unusually, for a fortnight's legal training in pleasant circumstances. The office of Gardiner, Gardiner and Hartopp did not usually waste money sending out its young people on such sprees.

'I've never met your Mr Gardiner,' John said.

'He came to our wedding.'

'I don't remember him at all.'

'He gave us that lovely set of Spode plates and dishes.'

'I remember them. But not him. I ought to, oughtn't I?'

'He'd think it a compliment that he passed unnoticed in the crowd.'

'Was he a small man with his hair going at the crown?'

'No. He's a full head of grey hair. I think he looks rather handsome and distinguished.'

'No wonder he's choosing you for his favours.'

Helen rang him from Liverpool at the weekend, Saturday afternoon. Yes, she was enjoying it. A lot of it was nit-picking and not very exciting. There were too many there who were too fond of their own voices. But one of the professors had really set about the judge's decision at a recent case. He had showed, to her satisfaction at least, that the trial justice had no humanity or common sense and in one or two small instances he had not got his law right. It was a complete demolition job by this professor, who'd delivered it quietly and politely, not like an actor or orator, but like a man explaining his point of view over a table to one or two friendly but intelligent listeners.

'Why isn't he a judge?' she had asked one of the bright young men after the lecture.

'He prefers academic life. He and his wife love the house they're in, and don't want to go chasing after new jobs. She's a consultant paediatrician. Both are satisfied. Besides, he's made some enemies. Even learned judges don't like their faults pointed out in public, especially if the criticism is just.'

She moved over to the second conference which was held in Durham. As she pointed out to a barrister, another very bright young man she had breakfast with most mornings, the aims seemed very like those of the previous week.

'They're trying to civilise the barbarian North.'

'How odd.'

'I don't think so. And they also think young lawyers may learn something.'

'Is that possible?'

'Of course. You heard Scott from Liverpool. It lifts people in our profession to hear those they most admire criticised and riddled with legal bullets. We tend to think that the law is always straightforward. It isn't, as I expect you've already found out. And these conferences make us think.'

'Some of us.'

'Yes. You're probably right.'

'Is that why you're here?' she asked.

'No, I'm a spy. Some committee of the Inns of Court have sent me up here to write a full report on what's happened.'

'Why should they want to know?'

'Economics, mainly. They don't want to throw money about uselessly, especially these days.'

'You must stand high in the esteem of the authorities,' she said, solemnly, to pull his leg.

'I'm cheap. They don't have to dole out big fees for my report.'

'They must trust you to do it accurately.'

'I don't think it matters all that much to them. These are small projects; they're not sure whether they are worth spending money on. All societies have these unimportant activities on the margins of their proceedings. It demonstrates to their members and the government that they are not stuck in the mud, but have their beady eye focused in out of the way places, so that whoever claims that industry and everything else is biased towards London and the South-East can't bring that accusation against lawyers.'

She liked talking to this young man. Dominic Tyrrell was regarded with something like awe by one or two of the few London lawyers. 'He needs to have studied a case once,' they astounded her, 'and he has it docketed away in his head so that he can not only tell you where exactly to find it, but what the main points of the decision were. His memory is marvellous.' These people who knew him also said he was married, to an earl's daughter, and had three children. He would be, they added, a judge before he was forty. 'You're lucky he's cast a favourable eye on you. Usually he flies about fifty feet above everybody else, looking down on us.'

Helen, who enjoyed Tyrrell's company, his quick and accurate summaries of meetings, lectures or judgements, his pointed but scrupulously fair criticisms of the proceedings, felt flattered when she overheard a woman refer to her and to Tyrrell as 'an item'. He made no sexual advances, not so much as laying a hand on her arm to emphasise some point he was making. On a free afternoon they walked together round Durham Cathedral; when he had invited her to spend the afternoon with him on a stroll she expected him to lead her out into the country, not to a building. She could not help being slightly disappointed; she had wondered how she would react to a kiss from those aristocratic lips in some out of the way place or even a sudden hand up her skirt; but he more than compensated by his knowledge of the cathedral and its treasures. He was a wonderfully lucid speaker, with his far-back modulated voice; if he did not know the answer to one of her questions he said so at once, but would begin to guess or deduce with convincing and intelligent eloquence.

He surprised her once or twice. As they stood outside the cathedral in cool spring sunshine he said, 'My ancestors came from round here. My great-grandfather was a miner.'

She learnt that his grandfather had made money out of mining machinery, then as an arms manufacturer. Dominic's father had been a Conservative MP and was now a life peer, still active in the House of Lords. His mother, a Dame, was massively involved in good causes.

Helen asked him how he thought he would have got on with his great-grandfather.

'He'd look on me as an enemy.'

He then told her a story his father had often repeated to him. The great-grandfather, talking to Dominic's father, suddenly lost his temper, and shouted at the boy, then at a grammar school, ordering him to take the plum out of his mouth. The boy spoke up for himself and asked his grandfather if he wished him to speak as he did. The old man swore at him, asking if that's what they taught him at school: to criticise his elders. At this point the grandmother had intervened.

'He did not criticise you. You were the one who took exception to the way Thomas spoke.'

'He answered me back.'

'Politely. It might make you think.'

'It bloody well won't, you can be sure of that.'

Dominic had put on the accents of each generation with an actor's skill.

'I think the old man had come to fear his son, and his grandson. He'd let my grandfather attend grammar school, a comparative rarity in those days, and always said he regretted it. My grandfather was the apple of his mother's eye. He could do no wrong then, or not often, and when he did, she'd fall on him like a ton of bricks. She was a woman of parts. My great-grandfather was envied on her account by his workmates who then mocked him behind his back.'

Helen marvelled at the skill with which he told these stories. He spoke with what she would have guessed, wrongly, was a tradition at least twenty generations long of authority, property, money behind him. His iron skill at summing up an argument or a situation she now attributed to his great-grandfather with his blackened face, his blue-scarred hands, his Geordie accent, who found no way of escaping from his lifestyle, who never became a union man, but who thought and argued with his mates, the newspaper he read, but chiefly with himself. He had passed on his ambition to his son, to his public school grandson, and now to this smooth, clever industrious lawyer who would become a judge, a law lord or Lord Chancellor. Dominic – she wondered what his great-grandfather would have made of that as a name – occupied his place in the world with poise, without ostentation, assured of his rise to power, a prince among lawyers, a paragon amongst men.

Her relationship with him, platonic as it was, reminded her of school. She recalled that if some popular mistress or admired prefect showed her some favour, and it had happened more than once, contemporaries who would not have dreamed of seeking her out or even exchanging a word or two now took trouble, almost too much so, to be seen with her, to share some small treat from the tuck shop with her, ask for her advice, invite her to their homes.

Now people sought her company. She was never left on her own in public. Within minutes, two or three would gather round, ask what she'd thought of the latest seminar or lecture. She was chosen to be on the committee which discussed with the staff the next day's activity or commented on the complaints which students were encouraged to make. These meetings took up little time, but were held each evening before dinner, a glass of sherry provided, and were over in thirty minutes. People listened to her, with such concentration that she decided they had accepted her as the spokes-woman of Dominic Tyrrell who at the end of the week would judge them for their paymasters. When she turned these events over in her mind, she wondered if she was guilty of misjudge-ment. One expected school children, under authority and trou-bled with the beginnings of adolescence, to act like this. But these were thrusting lawyers, thirty-odd years old, all holding down responsible posts, overseeing and solving the difficulties of their clients, attending this conference in the expectation that it would look good on their CV, would help achieve their ambitions.

She sent two further cheerful postcards off to her husband and his mother, mentioning none of these matters.

Once Dominic asked her what her husband was like.

'He's an accountant,' she said. 'And good at it.'

'Do you talk about your work, the pair of you?'

'We don't live together.'

'How modern.'

'Nothing like it. We couldn't get along; we quarrelled all the time and separated. Now we are, I think, gradually coming together again.'

'That's what you want?'

'I think so. We're neither of us quite sure. We remember only too well what it was like while we were breaking up.'

'Does he ring you here?'

'No. We decided against it. Only emergencies. I send him post-cards.'

'Do you miss him?'

'In a way. I was beginning to enjoy our reconciliation.' She stooped down to pick up her bag before running upstairs to prepare for dinner. 'Do you miss your wife?'

'Yes, and the children. But it's a relief.'

'Phone calls?'

'Yes. The baby likes to speak to father. I put that down to the influence of the au pair.' He laughed, without charm, quietly.

These intimate occasions were rare.

When the conference was finished she drove back thinking over this fortnight. She had enjoyed herself, not only unravelling the legal niceties they had discussed, but the social life where there were activities, not officially organised, what Dominic called 'aleatory', taking place every night of the week. Her sensible side had decided that she would not want such frequent jollifications at home where they would obstruct both her work and her care for her house, but here she made as much of them as she could, in her quiet way. On the final night there was ballroom dancing. Some of the people danced magnificently and obviously had attended classes, but most, like her, had learned a little at school of the old-fashioned quicksteps, foxtrots and waltzes amongst the mad on-the-spot athletics that they indulged in at the weekly discos. She watched a couple from Oldham, both solicitors, very serious and quiet, not here to enjoy themselves but to widen their minds, dance the tango together with a superb rhythmic verve. Hardly anyone else was on the floor. The rest devoured the unexpected spectacle with their eyes and burst into spontaneous, loud applause.

'That's what they do in Oldham in their spare time,' she said to Dominic.

'They could do worse,' he said.

Dominic was not at home on the dance floor, but he put his poor skills at her disposal and that of the more senior ladies. He was not awkward, merely ignorant of the steps expected of him, or unpractised. He more than made up for his deficiencies by his modest disparagement of his prowess, and his interesting commentary on the world. At the end of the evening he presented prizes in a raffle for local good causes with a charming little speech. Helen was called forward to pick the winning numbers from a black bag. Very typically the first ticket for the best prize she drew out was his. He affected no embarrassment, gently took the ticket from Helen and pushed it into his pocket.

'I think we'll try again, Helen,' he said. 'Otherwise . . .' He let his voice drift away while the audience applauded. There was no sense of superiority in his decision; he made it sound firm, as if he and Helen had deliberately arranged this to lift the hearts of the rest.

Now as she drove home she remembered their parting. At breakfast they had sat together as always, but this meal seemed scrappy, as though minds were on the packed suitcases in their rooms, or the journey, or some necessary shopping, presents for their children, some unfinished tasks at home. Dominic was, as ever, relaxed; his cases were already in the boot of his BMW. He ate his usual cereal, three slices of toast and marmalade, drank his grapefruit juice and two cups of black coffee. Once he'd finished, talking calmly about a headline in *The Times*, and saw that Helen had done with her breakfast, he asked, 'Are you packed and ready?'

'Yes.'

'Shall I carry your bags downstairs for you?'

'No, thank you. I can manage.'

'I'll just go over and say goodbye to the Watsons.' They had organised the conference locally. He did so, never hurrying, pleasantly standing, talking easily. The whole table seemed intent on him, taking delight in his every word. Helen sat alone. She would miss his attention, and wished this to be marked by their parting words. What could she say or do in view of the late breakfasters? She did not know.

Dominic returned, and she stood, uncertainly.

'Come outside and say goodbye,' he ordered. It gladdened her.

At the door he turned to wave a final farewell to the rest. It was a large gesture, and entirely suitable. She moved outside. He joined her, again without haste.

'It's been good to meet you,' he said. 'You've made this conference worth attending.'

'Thank you,' she said. 'I hope we meet again.'

'I expect we shall.' The modesty of the language matched the moment. He would not exaggerate, and yet one felt in his tone a warmth beyond the meaning. He took both her hands, and bent to kiss her cheek. He straightened from the embrace. 'Goodbye,

Helen, and thanks. Have a safe journey.' He let her hands loose, slipped athletically into his car and waved as he drove off.

She stood a moment, then without looking about her made a short way to the stairs. When she arrived in her bedroom, she saw tears on her face. She sat to recover, made up her face again, searched the room to see she had packed all her belongings before she took both cases downstairs to the hall, where she went over to the Watsons to say goodbye. They said they had enjoyed her company and her contributions to the conference, and hoped it would not be too long before they met again. As she crossed the room to pick up her cases she saw that a young man had done it for her.

'I'll take them outside for you,' he said.

The Watsons' cordiality and this offer from a man she barely knew made her feel that the conference had been a success, that she had made her mark. She drove in high spirits, the last movement of Beethoven's Seventh banging from her car radio.

At home a message on the answerphone demanded that she ring John as soon as she returned. She complied, found him unavailable, tried again later when he offered to take her out for a meal. She said she would prefer something less formal and he said he'd order a Chinese at his house at six-thirty. She thanked him; he'd said that she probably hadn't stopped to eat on her way back from Durham. That was right, and thoughtful on his part. She found as they spoke that she began to compare the sound of his voice, speaking standard English, with Dominic's easy, aristocratic delivery. John seemed an ordinary man, a run of the mill decent person, no doubt, but lacking Dominic's authority. She despised herself, dismissing herself as one too easily influenced.

Over the meal John asked about the two conferences.

Helen outlined the topics discussed or lectured on, and he appeared to listen with interest.

'Did you learn anything you didn't know before?'

'Oh, a great deal. And it was good to hear some experts talk about their specialities. Some of them were dull, but one or two were really fascinating. I would liked to have worked with these people for a month or two to see if they were just as quick on topics that lay outside their expertise.'

Later he questioned her about the people on the courses, both in Liverpool and Durham.

'Who interested you most?'

'Professor Scott from Liverpool, a man called Wentworth from one of the London hospitals who gave a talk on the ethics of using cells from a dead foetus, and an old barrister from some out of the way country place arguing that a burglar lost his rights when he broke into a house. He was one of the most lucid speakers I've ever heard, with a beautiful, silvery voice.'

'Was he in favour of depriving burglars of their rights?'

'Within reason.'

'And what about the organisers?'

'The Watsons. They presumably had a big say in the main topics chosen, and the experts to lead us. They were very good, made the course interesting, took notice of our views as to what we'd like to discuss and tried to include some of them in the week. They were both excellent in the chair, kept up to the subject, could cut off the gas bags and obsessives fairly soon. They sometimes arranged small group sessions, seminars, on points they felt hadn't been dealt with thoroughly.'

'Did you add your voice to these discussions?'

'Yes.'

'With any degree of success?'

'Well, yes, I suppose. One or two commented favourably on what I'd said, even if they didn't agree. One even asked me if I was taking, or had taken, a higher degree.'

'Who was that?'

'A man called Dominic Tyrrell. He was there as a kind of inspector. He wrote, or had to write, a report for the authorities who had set the courses up.'

'And who are they?'

'In my case, the Law Society.'

'And how did this man qualify to inspect and assess such courses?'

'He's highly regarded. He works for one of the largest chambers in London and writes a good many articles in various legal journals both here and in America.'

'And was he any good, apart from flattering you?'

'Yes. He could sum up somebody's rambling remarks in a

minute or two, and set out the pith of the speech, its strengths and weaknesses.'

'A good-looking man?'

'Yes. Tall, dark and handsome.'

'And married?'

'Yes. They said he was married to a titled lady.'

'What was his name again?'

'Dominic Tyrrell. I had breakfast with him most mornings.'

'Oh, good. Did these conferences encourage any new ambitions in you? To join a larger firm, for instance, which would give you more interesting cases?'

'Not really. I'm satisfied with what I'm doing. We've a decent reputation, and get plenty of work, and quite a few of the interesting cases land on my desk.'

'Why do you lawyers have these conferences, then?'

'For the same reasons that accountants do. Partly for pleasure and partly to let people know what's happening in other parts of their profession.'

'Aren't there law reports?'

'Oh, yes, but it's interesting to know how people set about preparing, for instance, out of the way cases, or ways of speeding up everyday business. The law is regarded as greedy and boring. Well, Chancery Lane, the Law Society, won't actively try to stop us making a living, but they do like to give members a chance to look about them.'

'But only the bright people, those who either want to advance themselves or their knowledge of the law will go to such meetings? Old stick-in-the-muds like Gardiner or Hartopp at your place wouldn't go. They think they know all the law they need to know.'

'Well, that might be so, but it was John Gardiner who suggested I attend, and at the firm's expense.'

'Did he think your appearance there would get you better known so that you'd be recommended in some tricky case?'

'I doubt it, though there were a few principals there looking about them.'

'Did they speak to you?'

'One did. He asked me if I'd consider moving to Birmingham, to head the commercial side of his business.'

'What did you say? Did you like the idea?'

'I didn't show much enthusiasm. I know, of course, that there's a lot of money to be made these days from commercial law.'

'Is it interesting, though?'

'I guess so. As interesting as anything in my line of business. The few cases I have handled I found attractive enough, and I had to work hard mastering the relevant law. If I had to do it, it would occupy me well enough, but I wouldn't go chasing it.'

'Why did the man talk to you about a change?'

'I said something in one of the discussions. It was based on a case I'd actually handled. It didn't seem in any shape or form out of the way, but perhaps he knew nothing about it, or thought I presented it attractively.'

'It wasn't your Mr Tyrrell, was it?'

'No. He works in London.'

'How old is he?'

'Not much older than you. Thirty-five perhaps.'

'Young-looking?' The question surprised her. Perhaps John now suspected he had a rival in love.

'Yes. But he had an impressive way of talking. Perhaps it was because he knew so much. There was nothing pompous about him. He spoke very quietly. But his knowledge was enormous.'

'Quite the paragon.'

Helen shrugged the remark away, and Dominic occupied no more of their conversation.

XVII

In the next few weeks, as spring approached, John and Helen met at least once a week, enjoying outings to the Kirov Ballet, to two concerts by the Academy of Ancient Music, venturing out to Croydon to hear a performance of Vaughan Williams' London Symphony and, at John's suggestion, they patronised a Russian circus troupe. To him all these seemed to take place in a kind of limbo. Not that he would have enjoyed the events more if Helen had not been with him, but he felt that her company should have been the touchstone which reassured, even caused, an increase in any pleasure he took. She seemed grateful to accompany him, but any presentable male would, he guessed, have sufficed her as an escort. They were friendly, could laugh together, could discuss seriously some news item or Shakespeare, in whom Helen seemed even more interested, but the question of resuming married life in a more normal way rarely received a mention.

John thought that since the conferences Helen had perhaps become less content with her work, and was considering a move to a larger sphere. If this were so, then it would have been natural not to tie herself down to her present house, or even his, if inside a month or two she would have to up sticks and settle elsewhere. When he cautiously raised this question, she answered without enthusiasm or resentment.

'No, I haven't even thought about moving.'

'Are there attractive jobs advertised?'

'Yes, quite often.'

'And you feel you are qualified for some of them?'

'Yes.'

'Have you applied, or at least inquired about any?'

'No. Though that man in Birmingham, the one who wanted me to take over the commercial law side of his office and expand

146

it, has written to me again to ask me to reconsider my decision not to join him.'

'He must think highly of you.'

'I'm suspicious. I tend to think the attraction was sexual, if anything.'

'What age was he?'

'Early fifties. Married. His wife worked in his office. But I think he fancied having me in close proximity every day.'

'"Close proximity",' he mocked.

As to Helen, she was disappointed at hearing nothing from Dominic Tyrrell. She told herself to expect nothing, but could not for the first week or two fail to look with expectation at her post, or her home e-mail, with a thrill of soon-quenched excitement. He had said that they would meet again, and she believed him. If he wished to see her, he was the sort of man who could arrange it. She tried to think sensibly about him. Would she become his mistress? It was unlikely that he would desert his wife and family. His approach at the conferences had been friendly, not sexual. But such was his personality she could not help being convinced that his generous warmth could switch without delay to lovemaking proper. Did she want that? She wasn't sure now, but felt certain that had he made such a pass at the time, she would not have put up much resistance. Her concern about this grew fainter as the weeks passed, but she still looked at the pile of letters on her hall floor with a glimmer of hope, knowing that if there was a postcard from Bognor Regis, St Tropez or Los Angeles or wherever he took his brood for a holiday, it would have revised, revived, quickened her spirits.

She was able to laugh at herself and her girlish presumptions. He'd be unlikely to take his young family away on holiday at this time of year. And when he did, was he likely to send off postcards to casual acquaintances, to anybody for that matter? He towered beyond such plebeian custom. The sending of postcards, even tasteful ones, was on the way out, killed by the mobile phone and its instant text dispatch. She instructed herself to expect nothing from Dominic Tyrrell; the only news she received would be through the newspapers, when he was made a QC or a judge, or took a leading role in some featured case. Their time together had not, she concluded, altered her attitude to John. With her husband she would play a sensible part, act temperately, expect to join him as his live-in wife in due course, but without hurry. If Dominic suddenly proposed that she should become his wife or his partner, she would throw herself at him. She was by no means sure he would. It was too unlikely.

Sometime in April John, who was away on business in Newcastle, heard from his mother that his father had been taken ill and was now in hospital. Was it serious, he asked?

'It's serious enough. He's suffering from pneumonia, and is on oxygen several hours a day.'

'Do you want me to call in to see him?'

'He'd love to see you, John. You know that.'

'Would he know me?'

'That I don't know. He's terribly confused, and in pain and discomfort.'

On Friday on his way back from Newcastle he called in to see his father and stay overnight with his mother. He rang Helen to tell her. She sounded distant, as she often did on the telephone, and in no way disappointed that they would not be able to meet that weekend. She made minimal inquiries about his father's state of health and, to his surprise, none whatsoever about Ella. She spoke as if her mind was deeply engaged elsewhere, and resented the time wasted on such topics.

His mother had prepared, as he expected, an enormous meal of pork pie, pickles, ham and tongue, salad, baked potatoes, bread and butter, with huge cups of tea. He drank from her fine china, and thought how much better the drink tasted than from the mugs he invariably used both at home and in his office. She had bought iced Chelsea buns from the local baker's; he had made a beast of himself with these as a schoolboy, but now found great difficulty in finishing one. He persevered, for his mother hated him leaving even a few crumbs on his plate, and marked this lack of courtesy down to her failure as a hostess.

She answered his questions about his father with garrulity as if her quick chatter could make up for her husband's inconsiderate illness.

'Is he getting any better?' John demanded, interrupting.

'No. Nor do they expect any improvement. At the nursing home he was growing much vaguer. He wasn't interested in anything. He hadn't looked at a newspaper since he went into Holmleigh, though I took his *Guardian* in when he was first admitted. Admittedly it was always a day late, but I doubt if that made any difference. He didn't know one day from another. And he had a radio in his room, but to the best of my knowledge he never switched it on. There was a television in the lounge, but he showed no interest.'

'And his pneumonia?'

'He was always chesty these last few years, and he's worse now. He could barely breathe. They were very good at the nursing home. Had the doctor in in no time. She was a lady doctor, very smart, and no hanging about. She had him in hospital immediately.'

'When was that?'

'Wednesday. Two days ago.'

'And how does he seem?'

'He's on oxygen a large part of the time, and antibiotics. He just lies there with a mask on, and barely moves. He looks bloodless and barely eats anything. They try to make him drink, it's important they say, but he takes no notice. They'll have to feed him with a drip if it goes on like this.'

'Can he talk?'

'Hardly. He appears to know me, but apart from little groaning noises he doesn't answer questions either with his eyes or by gesture, never mind his voice.'

'Is he in pain or discomfort?'

'I imagine so. And if you can't breathe it's very distressing.'

He helped his mother wash up. She talked all the time, especially about the Ofsted inspectors, who had been, with one exception, intelligent and helpful. He interrupted from time to time with questions.

'Who was that?' he asked.

'A woman, as you'd expect.'

'I wouldn't expect any such thing.'

'You know what I mean. She was full of questions, but they didn't seem relevant, and suggested all sorts of improvements,' she sarcastically emphasised the word, 'that every junior school in England had tried out sometime in the last twenty years.'

'Did you tell her so?'

'Yes, but very politely. And some of the drawbacks. I think she listened, but she didn't seem very bright. She had been a grammar school teacher.'

'And wanted you to teach everybody Latin.'

'French, as it happens. I told her there weren't enough teachers available who are trained in their own language, never mind anybody else's.' Ella laughed. 'At one stage we argued about the terms "gerund" and "gerundive".'

'What's the difference?' John asked cheerfully.

'One's a verbal noun and the other is an adjective formed from the verb.'

'Thanks very much. Clear as mud.'

'Didn't you learn anything at school, our John? *Amandum* in Latin – loving, a noun, the gerund; *amandus*, *-a*, *-um*, adjective, deserving to be loved. Hence in its feminine form the name Amanda, a girl who must be loved.'

'Where did you learn all this?' he said.

'They drilled it into us at school. Old Miss Monk. A horrid old stick, but she could teach. I'm always ready to learn. This inspector taught me a new word, "gerund-grinder". Do you know what that is?'

'Unfortunately, no.'

'It means a pedantic teacher. Would you believe that?'

'I believe everything you tell me. Not much used in the Beechnall pubs, I presume.'

'John, I despair of you sometimes.'

The inspectors had obviously done Ella well, and though she had not yet seen the official report, they had held meetings and made their views known to her and her teachers. When he asked her if she and her staff were now all relaxing, she spoke indignantly in reply.

'The pressure is off,' she said, 'but as their assessment of our work was so generally appreciative, we felt like pressing on more enthusiastically. I think Ofsted understands that, the value of encouragement.'

After the chore was over, she went upstairs to change one set of thoroughly respectable clothes for another. They then made for the hospital in John's car. It took perhaps ten minutes to drive there on the moderately empty roads, and once in the car Ella's spate of talk dried. He felt sorry for her, as he realised how embarrassing these visits were to her. He asked a few questions.

'Are the wards large?'

'They divide them now into sections. In your father's case he's one of six.'

'Are any of the other patients interesting?' he asked, at a loss. His mother tossed her head as if he implied that she made these visits in order to entertain herself.

He guided his car into a huge parking space.

'I've taken a ticket for two hours,' he said.

'An hour would have been enough.'

They walked perhaps a quarter of the way along the high Victorian corridor. The wards were well signposted, and between these informational boards were a few pictures, too small for the height of the walls, modern in style, and in his eyes worthless. He stopped to examine one more carefully. He could not for the life of him have named the subject of the painting. Rivers of broad, strong brushstrokes met others of equal power; some petered out; one or two tailed away into bluntly tapering arrowheads. He presumed the pictures were abstract. No title on the frame offered a clue. One work was signed roughly 'Laura Tatham, June 1991' near the bottom right-hand corner. His mother, seemingly resenting the pause, stood watching him, her face frozen.

'Do you like that?' she asked.

'No.'

They trudged on. A quite large display gave the names of the prizewinners in the nurses' examinations. He saw that this dated from fifty years back at the end of the war. It ceased in the sixties. Another smaller framed list featured the names and photographs of consultants, with their positions in the hospital, and their medical qualifications. These were honoured because wards had been called after them.

'Here we are,' Ella snapped.

They turned left into a sub-corridor through two right angles and began to climb a staircase. On the upper floor they stood in front of the ward door, boldly titled 'Arnold Ward'.

'This is it,' his mother said.

'It doesn't smell much like a hospital,' he said.

She turned a sour face on him. It could not have been more

menacing if he had sworn at her, or spat on the floor. She wheeled left, and he meekly followed.

What had been originally a long ward had now been partitioned into smaller bays, with six or eight beds in each. All the patients, men and women, seemed elderly with unkempt hair. One room contained tables, chairs and a television set, presumably a communal recreation area, now completely deserted.

'He's in number four,' the advancing Ella instructed him. She turned swiftly.

Six beds were lined up, three to each side. Five were occupied. William Riley lay in the middle of the row on the right.

'Huh, no mask tonight,' Ella said.

William lay on his back, head raised, fast asleep or unconscious. His face was ghastly, chalk-white. The other four men shared this pallor. Two were asleep, one sitting up, the last, nearest the door, seemed liveliest. John smiled nervously at him, and the man, seemingly pleased, raised a hand in greeting, called him 'Sir'.

'Will, are you awake?' Ella asked her husband. 'Get another chair for yourself.' She pointed John to a small stack at the end of the room. By the time he returned, less than a minute, she had straightened the bedclothes and seated herself with her bag in front of her on the bed. 'Look who's come to see you.' No response. 'It's John.' She turned her head, pointed a forefinger. 'Put your chair down there, so he'll be able to see you.' She opened her bag and piled up some neatly folded clothes.

'John's come to see you,' she tried again. 'You speak to him. See if he knows your voice.'

John bent. He barely recognised his father's waxwork face.

'Hello, Dad,' he said softly. 'How are you today?'

On receiving no reply, John bent lower, supporting himself on the bed rail, and kissed his father's pale cheek. The old man had not been shaved well; the roughness seemed uncouth, out of place. They were not a demonstrative family. His father had kissed his son up to the time the boy had started school, but not afterwards. His face, John recalled, had been rough; William used to grab him and ask if he'd like a horse-kiss, then drag his bristles on the boy's face. It was the nearest the old man ever came to a joke. John used to scream, and his mother would shout

152

out in admonition, 'Stop that horseplay, you two, or there'll be tears.' The males would back shamefacedly away, John's cheek reddened by the treatment.

Now William opened his eyes.

'John,' he wheezed.

'How are you?' the son asked.

'Not very well.' Clearly enough to be made out, just.

'Is there anything you want? I'll be coming in again tomorrow.'

'Helen?'

'She's in London. She sends her love.' The old man struggled to speak, but with mouth wide open signally failed.

'John wants to know if he can bring you anything in when he comes tomorrow.' Ella spoke with the headmistressy voice she used on naughty boys.

'No.' William gurgled, gasped, then shook his head.

'He's brought you some grapes. They look nice and appetising.' She broke one off and held it in front of her husband's mouth. 'Open up,' she ordered, 'take it in.' They watched him struggling to suck the grape. 'Bite it. Go on. Sucking's no good. You have to break the skin.' William made an effort, but without result.

'He's not got his teeth in.'

'His gums are hard enough to crush a small grape.'

'Do they feed you well in here?' John asked.

His father understood, nodded awkwardly, still fighting with his grape. He then gave a kind of groan, and nodded again.

'Do they give you plenty?' John asked.

William managed a word this time, 'Yes', and followed with a short, utterly incomprehensible sentence.

'Too much for him,' Ella translated. 'I've been here when they bring the meals round. He leaves most of it. He won't wear his dentures and so he can't chew. They give him these fortified drinks.' She pointed to an unopened packet on his table. 'I don't know how much encouragement they give him.'

Conversation was difficult, but at least the father made an attempt to talk. Little though it was, they got more out of him than they had when he first went into Holmleigh. Ella busied herself tidying his locker and replacing his dirty laundry. She tried to joke with her husband over one or two objects she found amongst his clothes.

'What on earth's this?' she inquired. 'The proverbial stick of liquorice?' This was a family joke. If they had asked William what he wanted for a Christmas or a birthday present he used to say, 'A stick of liquorice,' and leave the choice to them. What this black object was, John never discovered. He guessed it to be some sort of cleaning material or disinfectant left permanently in the locker, or perhaps it had been abandoned there by some former occupant of the bed. The cleaning firm obviously did not consider lockers their business. His father had tried to heave himself up from the bed to see whatever it was. He had failed, but had registered nothing on his face, neither curiosity nor disappointment.

When Ella had finished packing his used clothes into her bag she sat down again. She spoke fiercely to her husband as if without such effort he would not understand what was said. William tried to answer her questions, but his voice was so low and thin that the answers were largely unintelligible to his son. Ella translated for John.

After a further ten minutes William closed his eyes, worn out by his efforts.

'I think it's time we went,' she advised John. 'We're going now, Will, so that you can nod off.'

He opened his eyes wide at this, and continued thus until they left the bedside. John kissed his father again; Ella did not.

'Are you sure,' she asked in this ferocious voice, 'there is nothing you want?'

He lay flat, eyes shut, unanswering.

John picked up his chair to carry to the end of the bay.

'Somebody will be in to see you tomorrow,' she said.

As they passed the end bed, the patient beckoned John over to him and said, 'Will you tell the nurse I need her?'

'Surely.' John replaced his chair, signalled his goodbye to the man. Outside on the corridor they met a nurse.

'The patient at this end of four says he needs a nurse.'

'Don't we all? Right, thanks. I'll see to it.'

She continued with whatever errand she was engaged on. John and his mother returned to the car park. Ella shuddered. He comforted her.

'It won't take the heater long.'

154

His mother drew her coat tighter to her throat as she sat in the car.

'Seat belt,' he said. He helped her with it. 'I wonder if the nurse went to see what that old man wanted.'

'He's always calling for something,' she said testily. 'What he wants is attention.' She slumped in her seat as he drove off. His one or two attempts at conversation were answered with a brevity that equalled her husband's. Clearly the visit had put her out of sorts. When they arrived back she stood in the hall, bracing herself. 'Thank God that's over,' she said. 'Would you like anything to eat or drink?'

He chose coffee, and they sat together in her best room, the parlour.

'At least he recognised us,' John said.

'About all he did. I sometimes wonder if it's worth going.'

'You seemed to understand what he was saying.'

'What I don't hear or grasp I guess. I've a good idea how and what he thinks. After all, we've been married thirty-odd years.'

'A good run for these days,' John said cheerfully.

His mother's mouth turned down. Clearly she was in no sort of mood for flippant conversation.

'Have you spoken to Helen recently?' he asked, trying again.

'No, I haven't.'

'Why don't you phone her?'

'Occasionally. I don't want to appear to be meddling where I'm not wanted. Not long ago we'd chat for what seemed like hours. But recently she appeared rather short of time.'

'Is it since she came back from these legal courses?'

'Yes. About that time. After she came back she was full of talk about them, how interesting they were, how much she'd learnt and all the rest of it.' Ella paused, eyed him up and down as if she was uncertain how he'd cope with the next question. 'She didn't meet somebody else up there, did she?'

'She did mention one or two interesting men she'd met. One chap offered her a job, to take over the commercial law side in his office.'

'Who was that?'

'I don't know his name. It meant a move to Birmingham. I

believe he wrote to her when she'd been home a few days and tried to get her to reconsider.'

'A young man?'

'That's not my impression. A family man, married, you know.'

'Oh.'

'She thought he was a bit sweet on her.'

'Sweet? I haven't heard that expression for years. Your father used to use it about some of the young women in his office.'

'He fancied them?'

'No, he didn't. He'd say some young man was a bit sweet on one or the other of them, and would be waiting for her with his car when she came out at the end of the day. It was an old-fashioned phrase even then. Perhaps he learnt it from his father or grandfather.'

'That's where I must have picked it up. It's rather nice,' John said. 'And there was some other high-flier there who made a fuss of her. He was married to a titled woman, with a young family. He was sent there by the organisers to make a judgement on the success of the course. He was a barrister, and very impressive.' He looked his mother straight in the eye. She dropped her gaze. 'Perhaps he put her off the local talent.'

'What a vulgar expression,' Ella said, recovering. 'Remember you're speaking about your wife.'

'I'm sorry.'

'Has she heard anything from this man?' Ella had lowered her voice.

'If she has, she's not mentioned it to me.'

Ella waited until she was sure he had said all he was going to say.

'What was his name?' she began.

'Dominic something or other. They all thought he'd be made a judge before long.'

Again Ella sat silently, ignoring her coffee cup.

'You know, John, you shouldn't take these matters too lightly. I thought you and Helen were becoming reconciled. But now that's not so certain. And you don't seem to take any positive effort to set things right.'

'Such as?'

'You appear to think that if you and she go out to a concert or a meal the rift between you will be gradually healed. But it is not so.' She spoke to him with the same violence of effort she had employed against her husband in hospital.

'Go on,' he said.

'You have to make her understand how you feel about the relationship. It isn't any use just idling along, hoping it will all come out right. You have to do something about it. You either want her back or you don't. Which is it?'

He did not answer, but stared straight into his mother's eyes, rudely. Her face reddened under this scrutiny, but still he did not speak. With a slow intake of breath he turned towards his coffee cup, and drained it. He returned it to its saucer with slow deliberation, before folding his hands on his middle.

'I hear what you say,' he said.

'What does that mean?' she asked. 'That you don't agree?'

'You may well be right for all I know, but I must do it as I think fit.'

His mother looked at him, and a great tear splashed from her left eye. She raised her hands to cover her face. Now she sobbed quietly.

Taken aback by her unexpected weakness, he fiddled in his pocket for a handkerchief. He pulled it out and shook it loose. He stood and, stepping forward, held it out to her. It took time for her to realise what he was about, but she reached for it gently, not snatching, with no intensification of her crying, and held it over her face, pressing it to her eyes.

He stood, saying nothing.

Now he began to understand what she felt about her husband's breakdown, his time in the home and hospital, her visits, her struggle to continue her life, to make a success of herself. He had always considered his mother a strong woman, capable of coping with any emergency, indeed welcoming the challenges. Now she had reached breaking point. Baffled, he shuffled back to his chair as she recovered her self-possession. Her first words trembled.

'I'm sorry about that, John. Things have got on top of me lately.' She shook out his handkerchief and said that she would wash it. She'd give him one of his father's if he had only the one. He reassured her. He had two more. She rose to clear away the coffee cups, herself.

157

The rest of the evening passed without untoward incident, though slowly. They went to bed early, he at ten, though his mother rattled round downstairs for another half-hour. He could not sleep, had nothing to read. He had in the past thought about his mother's marriage, but without reaching any clear conclusions. She had always seemed the dominant personality. Her decisions were adhered to. William was given pride of place in a few areas: he was the first to open the newspaper; his meals were served exactly at the time he expected or had stipulated; he was not to be disturbed if he had brought work home or was troubled in mind, as when his father had suddenly died; he ruled the design of the garden which he set out with straight rows of civic corporation bedding plants. Once or twice she had used his name as that of some tutelary deity to her boy. 'Your father will be very cross when he sees what you have done.' That had happened when he'd broken an ornament claimed by Ella to be a favourite of William's, of great sentimental value as it had belonged to his mother. Nothing, incidentally, was ultimately said about this mishap, but whether his mother had not reported it to his father, or whether he did not care one way or the other or even notice, John never discovered.

Though she began working again as a teacher soon after John began in a local prep school, she was responsible for the household. She chose her son's clothes, helped her husband to select his suits, shirts, ties and underwear. She decided, after one-sided, tactful consultation what wallpaper they would have, when the outside of the house would be decorated, and by whom. She saw to the finances of the house. That always seemed odd to the boy, who respected his father as a wizard at figures. She would appear to listen alertly, as would his son, to the occasional story William brought from work about some tricky case he had dealt with or some error made by one of his juniors, which he had to set right. When the recital was over, ending as it always did with William triumphant, she showed her approval gravely, without disproportion or adulation, mildly approving, even once going so far as to say, 'Now that really was clever of you, Will,' which brought a shocked, delighted smile to his face.

What their personal relationships were like he had never made out. No signs of passion ever revealed themselves. When he tried to imagine sex between them he failed utterly. They never kissed or fondled in public, used pet names or showed spontaneous pleasure in each other's company or appearance. They were polite to each other as to the rest of the world, but that was the limit. He had made an effort to support his wife at crises at her work. On one occasion a child, a clever girl greatly favoured by her teachers, had died unexpectedly of meningitis. Ella seemed for some time inconsolable, so much so that John, then aged thirteen, had judged that she exaggerated. William, on the other hand, had treated her with delicacy as though he perfectly understood, indeed shared, her grief at the loss of a gifted child. John, for the first time in his life, realised that teachers, or some of them, invested emotional capital in some of their pupils.

On this Saturday morning John accompanied his mother round the shops. She seemed more like herself, pointing out alterations to the architecture of the town and its superstructure. She was not always impressed by the improvements the council had introduced. Obviously she had thought carefully over her opinions, tested them out on other people. He admired her. Such matters were not her direct concern, but she had made them so. He guessed that this was reflected in her school; the pupils would not only be drilled in preparation for the national tests (she'd see to that efficiently), but would be encouraged to look about them, to learn from credible sources, to form judgements on decisions taken round about their everyday life. He believed she'd made herself unpopular with her attempts to change their diet from chips, crisps and burgers to fruit. She was on a loser, he guessed, but a dozen or so of her children would pay attention and live longer on account of her advice.

He talked to her, and she seemed more cheerful. He shunted her into a coffee shop where she drank a black coffee and ate a single chocolate biscuit; she had yielded to him and hoped for some future reward. Such naïvety touched him and they returned for lunch more cheerfully than when they set out. After he'd helped to clear away and wash the dishes, he made for the hospital. Ella did not go with him. She had plenty to do, and she guessed that he'd get more out of his father if he went on his own.

159

At the door they kissed warmly, hugged.

'You've done me good,' he said. 'I'll ring you when I get back to tell you how I found Dad.'

William was much the same, although the staff nurse declared him slightly better. 'He'll pull through,' she said. 'He's a fighter.' John put a question or two to his father and was left with mumbled answers. He wasted time showing the old man clothes before he put them into the locker. The delicacies Ella had sent he put into a cool bag following her instructions. He tried to help his father to eat a yoghurt, a messy, unsatisfactory process, which meant walking across the corridor into the toilets to wet a flannel and back to clean his father's face. He stayed for perhaps three-quarters of an hour, and even threw in a question about Monica Powell. William frowned, said no, no word from her, and turned to his semi-comatose immobility. John did not know whether his questions had upset the old man. When he said goodbye his father tried to lift himself, but failed.

'Bring Helen next time,' he croaked.

'I'll do my best.'

After all this, it was a pleasure to drive down a not too crowded motorway. He was not prepared to claim that he had done well, but he had made an attempt.

XVIII

As soon as he arrived home, he unpacked his clothes, and set out the work left to be completed from the week in Newcastle. He rang Helen; there was no reply and her answerphone was turned off. He rang his mother, reported on his father's condition, complained that his wife could not immediately be reached.

'Where will she be?' Ella demanded.

'I've no idea. She's plenty of friends she could visit. She's capable of going off somewhere on her own.'

'To where?'

'An exhibition. London's full of 'em.'

His mother seemed to have lost some of the cheerfulness she had exhibited at the end of his stay with her. She looked forward to the Easter holiday, was considering going to the coast for a few days with a friend, but gloomily prognosticated that William would put an end to the plan at the last inconvenient minute.

'That would be just like him,' she said.

'It wouldn't be his fault.'

'No. Not entirely. But it's the story of my life.'

He rang Helen again. Nothing.

His cleaning lady had been in and left the windows and furniture polished, his laundry washed, ironed and put away. Everywhere was tidy. Her habit of moving vases and photographs to different places did not now annoy him, seemed an endearing characteristic, showed that the world had remained much as it was. He watched television until midnight sipping whisky and water and browsing through the morning's newspaper.

First thing on Sunday he made another vain call to Helen, and then he set about completing his papers from the Newcastle job. This proved easier than expected, and by eleven-thirty he was finished. Reading the Sunday newspapers he decided he would go out to lunch. A colleague had recommended a little place, newly opened, not three streets away.

'As long as you don't order anything exotic, they're magnificent,' his friend had warned.

'Roast beef and Yorkshire pudding? Apple pie and thick custard?' he'd queried sarcastically.

'Something like that.'

'How long has it been open?'

'Two months, perhaps. But go and try it for yourself.'

He ate his lunch there, and enjoyed it. The food was good, the service rather slow, but the number of people so soon after midday suggested it had already acquired something of a reputation. He recognised none of the diners, mainly young couples of about his age. He wished Helen was with him.

On leaving the restaurant he turned away from the direction of his home. Few pedestrians ventured out; gutters were lined with cars. Though it did not rain, skies loured grey, and an east wind nipped. He walked quickly to keep warm, swinging his arms. From time to time he wondered why he was on the streets on such an unwelcoming afternoon. Lights shone dimly in the windows. It was almost as if the world had ceased living.

An elderly man, in trilby hat and raincoat, stopped and greeted him.

'Not very pleasant,' the man said. 'I'm still waiting for spring. We ought to get something better than this.'

'We ought.'

'It suits my life,' the old man said. 'Nothing to do, and nothing to look forward to.'

'We can't do anything about it,' John answered, 'except live in hope.'

'Fat lot of good that'll do us.'

The man touched his hat-trim as if grateful for these few hushed words, and shuffled off.

John Riley, man of the world, pushed on. The rest of his afternoon walk was uneventful. When he was within three streets of his home it began to rain, a thin, miserly drizzle. He smartened his pace so that his coat seemed barely damp. The warmth of his house comforted him after his hour and a half in the streets.

At half-past five when he was eating sandwiches and wrestling through the Sunday papers, Helen rang.

'I'm just back,' she said, breathless.

'From where?'

'The Midlands. Like you.'

He waited for her.

'How was your father?' she asked.

'Not very well. They say he's improving, and if that's so he must have been in a very poor way. It's pneumonia. He can barely talk. He wasn't saying much before.'

'Is your mother very upset?'

'It's hard to make out exactly what she does feel. All this began just after she'd finished her school inspection. It's a good job it didn't all happen together. I don't exactly understand how she views his illness, and I don't want to misdirect you. I came to the conclusion, wrongly perhaps, that she was pleased rather than otherwise that Dad was suffering from a real disease, pneumonia, not Alzheimer's.'

'But that's a real disease.'

'Not to my mother. She's very old-fashioned. To her, Dad had gone off his head, gone gaga, and it was shocking and shameful. If he had conducted his life properly he wouldn't have contracted Alzheimer's.'

'That's not true.'

'I guess she'd agree with you if you put it straight to her, like that. But it's the way she feels. Nobody in her family has ever gone mad. Or having done so has fallen for some other equally foolish woman. He couldn't behave himself even in his illness.'

'But he rescued two women.'

'That makes it worse. If he can recover his wits on that occasion then he ought to be able to act rationally at other times.

'But it was brave.'

'You don't have to go off your head to be brave. It's a coincidence, but sometime during the war her father rescued a family from a burning house in London. He was passing, saw them at the window, found a ladder, got all five of them down. Just about in time, before the fire broke into the room. None of them was hurt. Shocked, yes, but not a scratch on any of them.'

'Were they grateful?'

'I've no idea. That same year my grandfather moved up to Beechnall, and lost touch.'

'Were they young children?'

'Yes. One was a baby. The husband was away in the forces.'

They talked easily enough, and she invited him over for an hour.

Once he had arrived she provided him with coffee and a warm armchair. She announced she mustn't be too late as she wanted to be early to her office in the morning. She then began on an account of her weekend. Apparently he had no sooner rung her on Friday than an old friend, June Fletcher, who lived in Leicester, had phoned. Within minutes, to the amazement of both, it was arranged that Helen should drive up straight from work to her friend's house. June, a university lecturer, e-mailed detailed instructions and a map.

'It all happened so quickly,' Helen said.

'Not like you at all.'

'No. It surprised us both. It happened that her husband was away for the week in Oxford, and she was at a loose end. She said she'd try to get in touch with another university friend of ours and get her over for a meal.'

'And how did you get on?'

'It was as if we'd never been apart. We write letters moderately often so we had the outlines of each other's lives at our fingertips, but we talked and talked.'

'So you just sat about the house?'

'No. On Saturday morning June got me up early, and took me out in the country to look at an Iron Age fort.'

'Interesting?'

'Yes. Nice walking country. Up and down. The weather was a bit cold; we had to keep moving.'

'What was this fort like?'

'I was surprised how big it was. It was perched on a hill, and had ramparts all the way round. Now they looked just like continuous mounds of earth, grassed over, though you could see some stones embedded in the ground. From what June said they would have dug out this earth rampart and moat and then built a stone wall on top of that, and then to crown it all a wooden palisade.'

164

'There was no sign of these?'

'No. Apart from the stones. And they might have been natural for all I knew. When the fort was abandoned finally, about 600 AD, the local farmers and peasants helped themselves to the stones, and there'd be plenty round a thing of that size, for their own walls and buildings.'

'When was it built?'

'They think in the first or second century BC. Anyway, before the Romans came.'

'Were there any signs of battles between the locals and, say, the Romans?'

'I don't know. Perhaps the museums in Leicester might have that sort of evidence. The council had cleared the paths and put in a car park and loos, and an information board.'

'Interesting then?'

'Yes. It gave us an objective. And I'm always interested to see what our ancestors were up to.'

She giggled.

'What about this other friend? Did she come with you?'

'No. She came over for dinner on Saturday night. She has a family.'

'And June hasn't?'

'No. They've decided against it. She still enjoys her teaching, she said, though her university's like every other: in a muddle, short of money, reorganising itself every five minutes. She thought she might be promoted this year but she hasn't been.'

'And your other friend?'

'Leonie Steadman. She worked in a library. Now she has three children, and they seem a right handful. One is autistic. The other two are normal, but energetic. Never give her a moment's peace, dashing everywhere, wanting everything. It sounds awful.'

'Does she think so?'

'Oh, yes, but as she says: "I brought them into the world, and it's my job to help them through it."'

'How old are they?'

'Seven, six and four.'

'And her husband?'

'Does his best. He's just been promoted to senior librarian in Middlesbrough. Conscientious man, something of an expert on

165

Swinburne. I think he tries to help, but he works late hours, and is always away at conferences.'

'It's getting her down, is it?'

'When we were at uni she was always the cheerful one. All that's gone now. If I heard she'd had a breakdown it wouldn't surprise me.'

They discussed Leonie's case at length. Helen seemed distressed.

'I'd never make a good mother,' she confessed.

'We could afford a nanny.'

'But that's not so good for the children, is it? They'd be my responsibility.'

'A good number of the people who run this country were brought up by nannies, and sent off to boarding school at a very early age, and recent research, according to the newspapers, suggests that they are none the worse for it.'

He left at ten o'clock, and as he walked home he wondered if Helen weren't issuing him with a warning. 'If we join up again I don't want children.' He had no strong views, but he remembered overhearing his father telling a colleague that his son was his greatest achievement, that no success at his work would match the birth and upbringing of his boy. His father was well over forty when John was born, and he was the only child. Perhaps that made a difference. William did not usually confide such intimate thoughts to friends, however close. John felt he had never exactly requited his father's trust or pride in him. Now the old man was on the point of death, and drew no comfort from his greatest joy. His mind had gone, and soon his breath would disappear. It would have been the same, he guessed, if the old man had written *Lear* or the Ninth Symphony or painted the Sistine Chapel.

The thought slightly excited him. For an hour he took to whisky, his armchair and television. What would his greatest achievement be when it was his turn to die? He went to bed discomfited, but fell asleep almost immediately. When his alarm clock woke him at seven, he recalled to himself that it was Monday, washed and shaved gladly, went off to the office ten minutes early and found himself ahead of the postman.

XIX

On Wednesday Helen rang him. She sounded breathless, excited.

'I've had an idea,' she said.

'Well done.' John had had a good day at work and felt cheerful. 'What is it?'

'I think we should have a week off work and spend it together.'

'Yes? Doing what?'

'I don't mean immediately. You'll want to go up to Beechnall at the weekends to see your father and mother. But soon the weather will improve and we can go away and just please ourselves for once.'

'To the seaside, do you mean?'

'That's one idea. Or a week of theatre or opera. Or go somewhere abroad where neither of us has ever been. Or one of those places where we can physically exert ourselves in boats or on horseback. Does that appeal?'

'No. I'm afraid not.'

'Never mind, then. It was only a suggestion.'

'I like the idea. It's rowing boats or diving or exerting myself at activities I know I shall make a mess of that turns me off. I'm no adventurous soul.'

Helen laughed.

'Go on, then,' she answered. 'Tell me what you'd like.'

'Classical music or your favourite Shakespeare in a place I know nothing about.'

'I doubt if we can manage that at this time of the year. If it were August, we could go to Edinburgh.'

'We can't wait for that?' he asked, tentatively.

'I'd like us to try ourselves out rather sooner.'

'Try ourselves out?' he queried.

'Yes. Living together every minute of the day for a week or a fortnight. But doing exciting things. Things we really enjoy.'

'I see.'

'I know what you're thinking,' Helen said. 'You think we should have this week or fortnight on working days, when we're both up to the eyes in work, and have no time to be polite to each other, nor time to break off for a treat. I just can't help thinking of the state I was in when we parted, but I can't now understand how we worked ourselves up into such chaos. And so I'd just like us to try living together, but in some extraordinary way.'

'A second honeymoon?'

'That's it. Do you remember that?'

'Yes,' he said. 'But we were so head over heels in love we could have spent it in somebody's coal shed in the backstreets of Beechnall.'

'You speak for yourself,' she said.

'Let's go to Florence again,' he said. 'I'd like that.'

'Let's think about it a bit. Florence was the first place that came into my mind.'

'And why did you dismiss it, then?' he asked.

'It seemed too easy, going to where we went abroad for the first time together, before we were married. And I feared it might prove a disappointment.'

'It will be different,' he said. 'Make no mistake about that. But the very fact that we're trying to think these things out means we're on the right track. We're consulting one another for a start, and spending all this time on the phone discussing it; making sure it's just the thing is marvellous. You have some good ideas, Helen Riley.'

'After Easter, do you think? You'll be less busy.'

'Yes. Think again, if you will, though I must say Florence is a hot favourite with me.'

She arranged to go up to Beechnall with him on Saturday morning to see William, and to return the same day. Then they would spend Sunday together.

'I feel excited,' Helen said.

'Dad will be delighted. He asked to see you.' They hummed their pleasure over the phone. 'And Mum. She thinks you're too good for me.'

They set off on Saturday morning and were in Beechnall by eleven o'clock. Ella hugged them both, seemingly in high spirits.

She held on to Helen as if she drew cheerful strength from her proximity. She said William was better, though that was not saying much. He was as laconic as ever, to such an extent that one wondered if he'd forgotten the language. He'd be pleased to see them, as long as they didn't expect miracles.

She questioned them about their health, their marriage, their future. She approved their plan for an Italian holiday. She and William had been to Florence when John was only four. They had left him behind with his grandmother, Frances Stokes. He remembered nothing of it.

'I tell you what I remember,' Ella said, 'and that is how guilty I felt leaving you, though I knew my mother would look after you, if not spoil you to death.'

'Was it a good holiday?' Helen asked.

'We were not used to going abroad. The Costa Brava didn't appeal. Nor France. Italy was unknown territory to us. Once I knew we were going I borrowed books from the library and bought a guide so that we knew what to look for. What we didn't reckon with was the heat. That summer was boiling. And your father didn't dress as people do nowadays. He wore a suit and a collar and tie. Another thing was that he wasn't altogether interested in museums and picture galleries and sculpture. He'd visit a cathedral, though he wasn't religious in any way, and he was impressed. He particularly liked the baptistery. Besides, in these big dark churches it was cooler. When you stepped outside, I remember quite well, it was like walking into a furnace.'

Ella kept this account running over their two cups of coffee. They learnt later that part of her geniality was due to the inspectors' report on her school. This had been so good that the Director of Education had sent for her to congratulate her in person, and had told her that the headship of the 'most prestigious' comprehensive school would be vacant next year, and he hoped, sincerely, that she would apply for the post. He could promise her nothing, of course. It would have to be advertised; she'd understand that. 'That means I shan't get it, for sure,' she confided, 'but it was his way of offering me his congratulations.' She also commented adversely on his use of the adjective 'prestigious', which had adverse connotations for her. '"Prestige" meant conjuring trick

169

originally, so the idea of the illusory is always present in my mind.'

'It's like "sophisticated",' Helen said.

'What about it?' John inquired.

'It's a word of praise today, but in Shakespeare's time it meant adulterated.'

Ella was delighted. Here was a daughter-in-law exchanging knowledge as an equal. She sat John down in a chair with the *Guardian* and Radio 3. Helen she led off to the kitchen where, John guessed, she'd cross-examine her about him and the marriage. They ate a sumptuous lunch. He used the word to describe the quiche she provided. She asked for its derivation. He did not know.

'It means costly, from the Latin word for expense,' Ella explained.

All three had second helpings so by the time they reached the pudding, spotted dick with sweet white sauce, they were almost full. John, however, managed to do this boyhood favourite justice. He helped his mother with the dishes, and then sat with Helen while they waited for Ella who had gone upstairs to change into suitable outdoor clothes.

'Your mother seems to have come to terms with your father's illness,' Helen whispered.

'Yes. This inspectors' report has done her no harm. And now she has plenty of time to herself. If you ask me, she's more resigned to the fact that he's in hospital.'

'She doesn't visit him every day?' Helen asked.

'I hope not. Twice a week is the usual; three times if he's really ill or there's some sort of panic on.'

Ella reappeared to issue orders.

'We'll go in your car, and not stop for long. Then you can bring me back here. I'll make you a cup of tea, and you can set off whenever you're ready.'

Ella seemed again in good spirits and congratulated him on the warmth and comfort of his BMW.

'He's delicate,' Helen said, fitting in with the mood. 'Mustn't let him catch cold.'

The ward seemed stifling and William was in the chair by the side of his bed, well propped with pillows. He looked at them imploringly, but smiled when he saw Helen.

'Is this the first time you've been out?' Ella demanded, but received no word or expression of reply from his stricken face.

Helen bent over him.

'How are you, then?' she asked. 'Better?'

He made some grunting noise. She kissed his cheek, but he did not move.

'He's more colour than last week,' John told them.

'Do you think so? That's good. You talk to him a bit, and I'll go through his locker, and square that up for him. The nurses haven't the time to tidy personal belongings.' She busied herself.

'Do they get you out of bed every day?' John tried. They understood from the groans he made, the hand movements, the facial grimaces, that he answered in the affirmative.

'Good,' John said. 'It shows you're on the way up.'

They inquired about his oxygen mask, his meals, his drinks. Could he feed and wash himself or did they help him? Apparently they did.

'What about the lavatory?' John asked.

The old man glared and gestured to rebuke his son for asking such a question in front of Helen. His mind and body might have warped, but the manners, the propriety of his youth prevailed.

He appeared to listen to them, but did not always reply. What was noticeable was that when Helen spoke to him, he smiled. Sometimes he did not answer, but his thin face seemed changed when he looked up at his daughter-in-law.

For perhaps half an hour they kept up this attempt at communication while Ella reorganised the locker from top to bottom. Twice she bustled out of the ward, though the visitors had no idea why. They guessed she interrogated the senior nurse about William's progress, and once she took the clipboard with her husband's medical notes from the end of the bed and scrutinised them at length, clicking her mouth with exasperation. Finally she rubbed her hands together.

'I think it's time we went,' she instructed the others. 'Is there anything you particularly want?' she asked her husband. When she received no answer, she dipped her shoulders swiftly and lightly kissed the crown of his head. He did not appear to notice. When Helen bent and kissed his cheek, he moved his eyes to meet hers and smiled so that his face became human again, not an immo-

bile mask of pain or lack of understanding. When John shook
hands there was no reciprocal pressure from his father. As they
left the ward William did not even turn his head to follow them.

'What do you think?' Ella inquired once they were in the car
park.

'He seemed comfortable enough,' Helen answered.

'I think he is. And he eats a little now, with help.'

Subdued, they drank a cup of tea at Ella's house and set off for
London. For the first hour on the motorway they barely spoke a
word, and when they began to talk their sentences seemed to die
on them. They arrived at Helen's house and she offered to make
bacon sandwiches. As they ate Helen seemed to have restored herself.

'What do you think your father thinks about all day in that
hospital?'

'I've no idea. He seems interested in nothing.'

'Does he ever read a book?'

'I don't think so. He wasn't a great reader when he was younger
and fitter. He'd look at the *Guardian* every day. Some teacher at
the grammar school had recommended that and he remembered
and followed the advice once he came to the age of buying his
own paper. But I imagine now that he's in discomfort, if not acute
pain, all the time and feels so weak and physically distressed that
he's little time for consecutive thought. He'll see the nurses rushing
past and the other patients doing whatever it is they do and it'll
be momentarily distracting. But I don't think for a minute he's
wondering about dying, for instance.'

'I felt so sorry for him,' Helen said.

'I'll tell you one thing. He was pleased to see you. His face
fairly lit up when he heard you say anything. That really did him
good.'

'I'm glad. But he takes no notice at all of your mother. Never
a word of thanks; not a word of any sort. She might as well not
be there for all the attention he pays to her. She organises his
clothes, and harries the nurses if they don't look after him properly, and brings him treats, but he never offers a word of thanks
or gratitude. Not even a look. Why is that do you think?'

'Habit, I guess. That's what she's there for. All through their
marriage she's prepared his meals and done his laundry and all
the shopping. She did all the thinking in his life, outside his work.

She'd tell him when he needed new clothes and she would go
with him to see he didn't make terrible howlers.'

'Was he likely to?'

'No. He'd buy the same white shirts and grey suits every time.
She'd have the main say in buying things such as ties or pullovers
or scarves. The odd thing is that she ran the household finances.
He was very good at arithmetic and dealt with people's money
all day, but she went to the bank to draw cash and wrote cheques
and fixed up direct debits and matters of that sort.'

'What about spending money?'

'She handed some to him, and me, every Saturday morning
out of the petty cash. She was very well organised, kept all the
bills for a period, made alterations here and there to arrangements
for paying.'

'Without consulting your father?'

'No, I won't say that. If they were going to change some
option, such as a new bank or building society account, she'd
always ask him. And she showed him the bank statements when
they arrived. She'd ask him to check them, having gone through
them herself first.'

'And he didn't object?'

'No. He'd ask questions, and even made suggestions from time
to time. But she did the donkey work, the everyday chores. It
was sensible in some ways. The bank was just over the road from
her school and she could nip across in her dinner hour.'

'Was she satisfied with her married life?'

'I'm sure she was. She took to doing all these jobs when I was
small and she was at home all day. After I'd started school she
went back to teaching again, but hung on to these chores. From
choice, I believe. It made her feel that she ran the house, the holidays and trips.'

'Was your father generous with his money?'

'He was very careful. Especially as far as he was concerned
personally. He was careful with everything. He'd brush his clothes
before he hung them away in the wardrobe. But if she decided
on a new piece of furniture or new curtains or a picture for the
walls she'd give him the chance to air his views because she
knew he'd bow to her judgement.'

'It's unusual,' Helen said. 'I bet there aren't many families

173

which work like that. And now he pays no attention to her at all.'

'She's a talented woman. She'll run the finances of her school like clockwork. And no tradesman or company will put one over on her.'

'It's not much like love,' she said.

'They've been married thirty-odd years. And neither is a very demonstrative character. They'd be different when they were young, though my father was getting on for forty when they were married.'

'If we get together again,' Helen spoke very slowly, 'shall we be like this?'

He considered this carefully before he spoke.

'We shall certainly get into habits. You do this, and I do that. And on the whole that's not a bad thing, because it gets work done. But all sorts of extras, holidays or visits or weddings will come up and we'll have to discuss the ins and outs. You think the sitting room carpet's getting worn, and we go off together and make a choice.'

'But it isn't love. It's convenience.'

'It may start with love. The sexual urge, they say, will be less demanding. But we may try to suit the other in that. If on the other hand the libido in one of us dies more quickly than in the other, then that may cause trouble. But if we care for one another then we should be able to work it out. It depends just how much we think of each other.'

'Do you think we shall be all right?'

'There is one thing, Helen, that troubles me there. We both remember what we were like before we split up. You do, don't you?

'Yes.'

'We couldn't bear the sight of each other. Every little mishap or misunderstanding led to a steaming row. It was as if every time we differed about something, however trivial, we made it into a shouting match inside ten minutes.'

'Will that be the same again?'

'I don't know. That's what troubles me. I wonder now if we were envious of one another. He's doing better at work than I am. I earn more than he does.'

'How can we prevent that?'

174

'I think about that all the time. If when we were at logger-heads,' they both smiled at his euphemistic metaphor over which he paused, 'someone had asked me if I loved you, I should have answered yes, without hesitation. And yet sometimes I hated you, wanted to hurt you, deliberately thwart you. I ask myself now how that can have been love. We were good at the sex; that joined us. But . . . oh, I don't know. At least we've looked it straight in the eye. We aren't trying to claim it didn't happen.'

They held this discussion over again three or four times in the next fortnight, as if they were making sure that they left nothing relevant unexplored. She could suggest the advantages and snags better, more clearly, more completely; she could describe their distress with more poignancy than he; she was not afraid to say what she thought. In the end it was she who put the question bluntly whether he wished them to try again.

'I'll tell you what I suggest. First we go on this holiday together in three or four weeks. I'll see what I can find on the Internet. And if that goes well, and I don't see why it shouldn't, we will, if you agree, start life together in my place.'

She stopped, looked at him, her face serious.

'Here am I, deciding everything, just like Ella,' she said.

'Good,' he said.

'I don't know about that.'

John was surprised that they could dissect their past and plan their future so coolly, with so little disagreement or contention. He put this to Helen, asking if they were talking on the surface only, and neglecting the deep differences beneath.

'I don't think so,' she answered. 'The fact that you can mention this, bring it up when we're right on the brink of agreement, suggests that we are being serious about it. You want to live with me again, don't you?'

'I do. And I shall do my best to make it work.'

'Right.'

They looked about the room again, unwilling to be found wanting.

'What are we going to do before we go to Florence?' he asked.

'Meet at weekends, phone if there's something to be talked about, and get ready to live together when we come back from Italy. And think about what we've decided. You'll have to keep going back to your house, because you keep some of your work there. We'll have to think about your keeping an office there. And what are you going to do with your house? You won't want it standing closed up, will you, even in summer? No, we get ready to live together again, and think what it means, and what's still to be done.' She grinned almost ferociously. 'It means in my case I shall have to change my will again. That's not difficult for me. But what do you think now you know I cut you out of my will?'

'Sensible move.'

'Did you alter yours?'

'No. I wasn't thinking of snuffing it just yet.'

'But I was so angry with you,' she said. 'I knew it was the end of our marriage.'

'But you didn't institute divorce proceedings. You didn't even make our separation legal.'

'That's so. And that's why I think we should use these weeks before Florence to consider everything, scrutinise everything. We don't want to change our minds again in just a few weeks.'

'Good,' he said. 'Good. That seems very sensible to me. Now there's one other thing I'd like you to do for me.'

'Well?' Her expression seemed both cautious and playful.

'I'd like you to ring up my mother and tell her what we've decided.'

'Wouldn't it . . .'

'. . . be better if I told her? I don't think so. She's very fond of you and she admires you greatly. I'm her little boy still. I don't know my mind. I'm likely to make mistakes or daft decisions. But if you tell her she'll believe that it's serious, she will know we mean business. She'll be delighted, I'll tell you. And you can bet she'll put me through several inquisitions. And one of the questions will be, "Why didn't you break the news to me, John?" I know she'll put me through it, but she'll be so pleased, so over-joyed with what you've told her that . . .'

'She'll let you off the hook, treat you gently.'

'Something like that.'

They fell into each other's arms.

The next month they lived through as in a dream. Both were busy at work, but they met on Saturdays and Sundays to go to a concert or out for a meal. On two of the days he stayed the night with his wife. He had half a suspicion in his mind that she'd ban sex until they began to live together when it would celebrate a kind of honeymoon. She made, however, no demur, threw herself into carnal love with an enthusiasm that was almost lust. Both looked forward to the day when they'd take up residence together in Helen's flat. He made contact with an estate agent about letting the rest of his house except his study, but warned that the final arrangements could not be made until his return from Italy.

His mother was on the phone to him very shortly after Helen had broken the news to her.

'What's this I hear?' she asked, in mock annoyance.

'Helen and I are getting together again.'

He described for her the arrangements, though he was sure Helen had already done so, more clearly and concisely than he could.

'What made your minds up for you?'

'A slow process. I'd been thinking about it for some time, and so had she. But when we came up to Beechnall together we began to discuss it seriously. I knew I wanted her back.'

'Yes, but on what terms?'

'On any that had at least an element of reason in them.'

'I would have said that your house was more convenient than hers.'

'Don't tell me why,' he said. 'We've made up our minds, and aren't going to change them now. She seemed to want it, and I didn't argue.'

'That's not like you.'

'Are you trying to throw a spanner in the works?'

'No,' Ella replied. 'Not at all. I'm delighted. But that doesn't mean I can't think about your arrangements.'

'Did you mention this to Helen?'

'I did not. I just expressed my pleasure that you'd come to . . .'

'Our senses?'

'Had come to this arrangement.'

They talked in this fashion for half an hour. Both were pleased, but his mother seemed less keen than he to show her pleasure. He said he would come up to Beechnall on the Saturday before he and Helen left for Florence.

'What day do you set off?'

177

'A Monday.'

'That's a curious day to start a holiday,' she objected.

'Never mind. We'll come back on a Saturday.'

'You're going for less than a week?'

'No,' he corrected her. 'Nearly a fortnight.'

'Do you fly direct?'

'No. Via Pisa.'

'You'll be able to see the Leaning Tower then.'

'I've already seen it.'

'Has Helen?'

'No idea. I expect so. She's keener on travel than I am.'

His mother seemed to let him go. She complained about fly-posting in her district. Every telegraph pole, every electricity box, every unused shop window was disfigured with them. 'Beechnall Marches Against War', or 'No, no, no', or 'Myth, Reality and Racism, Beechnall Marxist Society. Do our workers benefit from Third World low pay? Oppression?'

'What's wrong with them?' he asked.

'They're an eyesore. And all sponsored by mad left-wing groups.'

'Have you been to the meetings then?'

'No, I haven't. But you can tell from the small print what sort of people are plastering them all over the streets.'

'Yes. I suppose it's illegal.'

'It gives me the impression that this city has been taken over by anarchists.'

'What about the graffiti you see everywhere? Are these posters worse?'

'Two wrongs don't make a right. Both are bad.'

'Would you ban all advertisements then? No more hoardings. Is that the idea?'

'Don't be so ridiculous.'

They put down the phone on good terms, still arguing.

XX

Helen and John travelled to Heathrow separately. This was Helen's suggestion.

'It'll be more expensive,' he objected, only half joking.

'I know. But to me it will be like a second wedding. Nobody objects to the bride and groom arriving in different cars. You don't really mind, do you?'

'No,' he said. 'Now I come to think of it, it sounds very romantic.'

'Thanks,' she said. 'It probably is a daft idea.'

He was surprised that level-headed Helen should think in this way, but was pleased that she was attempting something he'd remember.

'You're a good girl,' he said. 'You come up with great notions.'

He arrived first, as was proper, and was waiting when she left her taxi. He hurried to greet her.

'You've made it,' he said. 'I'll wheel your case across to where I've left my luggage.' As he trundled away he asked prosaically, 'Are you excited?'

'Of course I am. I'm always a bit scared of travelling by plane. You know that. It keeps one quiet.'

'Well. I'm not saying anything marvellous. I ought to come out with some grand flourish of words to greet you, but I can't think of anything. Can you?'

She laughed, a low chuckle.

'Yes,' she said. '"Oh, she doth teach the torches to burn bright." *Romeo and Juliet.*'

'Perfect,' he said. He stood up straight from her case to be kissed. She obliged. He lifted her case in triumph.

'Don't do that,' she shouted. 'You'll burst it.'

'And scatter your underwear all over Heathrow.'

They checked in their luggage and went into the departure

lounge to wait. Through the window on their plane they watched Concorde take off.

'It's not really big,' she said.

'No, but it's beautiful. And soon we shall see no more of it.'

'It's a marvel,' she said, 'that in an hour or two the people in it will be in America.'

'Isn't it? Three hours twenty minutes.'

A well-dressed woman of perhaps sixty sat on the other side of John. Her look was severe, as if she found the company aboard the plane beneath her socially. The plane took off; John's most enjoyable experience of flights was to watch great lumpish clouds moving close but obliquely across the window, filling the mind as the sky.

'It's magic,' he told Helen, who clutched his arm. When they burst into sunshine, the effect seemed to galvanise their fellow passenger.

'Have you been to Italy before?' she asked.

'Yes,' John said.

'It's my first time. I hate aeroplanes.'

'They're useful though,' John said. 'They get you from A to B smartly.'

'My daughter and her husband have bought a villa in Tuscany, and want me to stay with them. It seemed too good a chance to be missed, but I was terrified. Now I'm speaking to you it doesn't feel too bad. They'll be at the airport to meet me. I'm really pleased you will talk to me. It makes me feel safer. I know if anything went wrong you wouldn't be able to do anything about it, but I wouldn't mind dying amongst friends.'

'Oh, I don't think it will come to that.'

'I don't suppose it will. I know my fears are irrational and that air travel is really very safe. I saw you in the lounge where we were waiting to board, and I thought, "What a handsome young couple." I don't know whether I ought to say this, but I thought to myself, "They look as if they're on their honeymooon." You looked so happy, so content with each other. Are you?'

'On honeymoon? No, we're quite old stagers in the marriage game.'

Helen, listening with interest, thought his language betrayed him.

180

'Oh, I'm sorry. It's a sign of old age.'

'Well,' he said, 'we could say that it's a kind of second honey-moon.'

Helen, leaning on her husband, beamed at their fellow passenger.

'I ought to introduce myself,' the lady said, 'My name is Amy Gibbs-Smith.'

'And we're the Rileys, Helen and John,' he replied. He felt a proprietary responsibility for Mrs Gibbs-Smith.

'I'm a widow,' she told them.

'Did your husband mind flying?' Helen said.

'No, not at all. He was rather older than I am, and was a pilot during the war. He never flew another aircraft once he left the RAF.' She pronounced the letters as an acronym, 'Raff'. 'He was perfectly content to take his holidays in Scotland or Cornwall. We had a cottage there. He took over his family business, and this meant occasional trips to America and more frequent ones to the Continent, and he always went by air, but I never accompanied him. On that account.'

John explained how much he enjoyed watching the clouds as the plane left the ground. 'It seems impossible. These great bundles or mattresses of cloud crossing your window at an oblique angle seem unearthly. We ought not to be able to pass so easily through such marvellous shapes, which we never see except at a tremendous distance when we're on the ground.'

'I missed it all,' Mrs Gibbs-Smith said. 'I had my eyes shut tight.'

By the time the hostesses were bringing round a meal, she was in full spate. The food, uninteresting in itself, silenced her so that John could now concentrate on his wife, who smiled and chatted to him as she ate with neat enthusiasm. Helen was determined to enjoy this holiday, despite their neighbour's non-stop flow of information about her family, her son-in-law's business acumen, her daughter's success as a journalist and teacher and the children's beautiful fluency in Italian and English.

'I think I'd sooner listen to Italian than any other language,' he confessed, 'though I don't understand a word of it.'

'I'm hopeless at languages,' Mrs Gibbs-Smith said, 'utterly inadequate. I'm usually reduced to pointing.'

181

Later, when Mrs Gibbs-Smith seemed overtaken by drowsiness, Helen suddenly jabbed John with her elbow, and took his hand in excitement.

'Look,' she said. 'Look at that.'

Below them black, wet peaks of mountains stood clear and shining from the floor of cloud.

'I've never seen that before,' she gabbled. 'I've seen the whole mountain, or nothing at all but clouds, but this is really something. It must be the Alps. Do you think so? Isn't it wonderful?'

Helen's breath came in short gasps of stimulated delight. This was the holiday he had longed for, pleasure in the unexpected.

When they were ordered to fasten their seat belts Mrs Gibbs-Smith held tightly on to his right arm. Her nails bit sharply and her lips trembled. The pilot put them down with a slight thump.

'There we are,' he said. 'On terra firma again.'

'Are you all right?' Helen called. 'We're here.'

The lady opened her eyes, and sighed deeply. John helped her with her seat belt and lifted her hand luggage down. The three left the plane together. As soon as they were at the luggage carousel she recovered and seemed what she usually was, a calm, collected woman of the world. When they were through customs, a tall, handsome young man appeared with two small girls who came modestly forward to be kissed. Mrs Gibbs-Smith introduced them as her son-in-law and her grandchildren.

'Er . . .' she indicated the Rileys, 'looked after me on the aeroplane. I felt quite safe with them.' But, Helen thought, she had already forgotten their names.

'Very kind,' the young man said, and shook their hands. The little girls smiled up at them.

'It was a pleasure to meet you,' John said.

Helen wondered about the tense of his verb. They parted company, delighted all round.

The rest of the journey passed without incident. In a new country, under overcast skies, they enjoyed the Italian railway. They took a taxi from the station to their hotel in the Via Nationale.

'We could have walked that bit,' he complained, as they arrived.

'You wait until you've finished your holiday and built your strength up,' Helen mocked.

The hotel suited them to the ground. It was not large, but well looked after, and it took them no time to register at the desk. Replete with advice and pamphlets they staggered upstairs with their luggage.

'We're here,' he said as he unlocked the door, on the third floor.

The room was a curious shape, narrowing from the door to the windows and taking a kind of lurch to the left. The furniture was spotless, but John was disappointed to note that there were two single beds, clean sheets neatly folded back, instead of the king-size double he had wanted. He said as much to Helen.

'What did you expect, then? A four-poster? We should have booked the honeymoon suite.'

'The beds are close together,' he said. 'We'll manage.'

'Have you lost the use of your legs? You go and look round while I just get things that'll be ruined if I leave them too long in their cases all creased up.'

He looked out of the window. A plenitude of people walked the street, past the small shops. A little way along he saw a flat roof which had been transformed into a garden with plants and trees in pots. There stood a table with three white wooden chairs. He looked again with affection at the shrubs and seats. It suited his mood. This was a place to escape the crowd, to sit out of the way generally unobserved. He moved back into the room where Helen concentrated her energies in emptying their cases. He opened the door of the refrigerator and looked over an array of small bottles of spirits. He passed on to the bathroom, which was narrow but adequate. Helen had already laid out his shaver and the rest of their washing kit. Surprised that she had unpacked his cases, he wondered where she'd stored his boot-cleaning brushes. He liked to leave the place in the morning well dressed, however dusty and ruffled he appeared in the evening after a day's walking. He pushed out of the door and on to a crooked, ramshackle passage which led to a main corridor, itself not wide.

A few steps along he came to a glass-walled room. This was not exactly free from grime, but he could glimpse a piece of flat roof with a couple of tables, a bench and three chairs. This was no garden; no plants sprouted from pots or hanging baskets. He tried the door and found it unlocked. He walked over to the wall which protected him from the street, where he leaned on his elbows. It was noisy, mainly because of the building work in a tall hotel to his left, where an old-fashioned crane stood. The machine creaked and rattled but seemed efficient enough. Workmen shouted to each other, and from the street the buzz of mangled conversation of pedestrians mixed with the braking and hooting of cars and motor cycles. He listened with pleasure to the obtrusive noise.

Now he turned to his right and could see over a haphazard variation of tiled roofs all at different heights, and each oddly placed in relation to the neat two great reddish domes, commandingly high. One of these he thought must be the crown of the cathedral, Brunelleschi's dome, that masterpiece of architectural daring. He could not remember the second, and wished he had his maps with him. He would enjoy working out what was what from his papers. He'd come, he congratulated himself, well prepared. Helen would laugh at him. She liked to be surprised, to come suddenly on to something unexpected. 'You miss too much that way,' he had chided her.

He sat for a moment on one of the chairs, listening to the street noises and the broken jigsaw of voices. Though the sky was cloudy, the weather was warm; he breathed deeply. The city smelt, he thought, little different from North London. Nobody moved about on the corridor outside. He stood, stretched his arms, flapping them, an action he could not remember practising since he was at school. Why he did it now he could not imagine.

He left the roof, carefully closing the door behind him.

In their room Helen was sitting relaxed and smiling on her bed.

'Oh, there you are,' she said. 'I wondered where you'd got to.'

'Is it all unpacked?'

'Yes. Yours is in there.' She pointed to a wardrobe. 'Thank goodness there's plenty of room for everything.'

'Shoes?' he queried.

'On the bottom. All together.'

'Thanks. You're very efficient. Do you fancy a little walk out now?'

'That'd be lovely. We'd better leave our passports and money and so forth in the safe downstairs. Street robbery's still prevalent, according to that notice.' She pointed.

She had made a pile of the money, cards and travellers' cheques she meant to stash away. She handed him a small pile of Euros held together with an elastic band. She then changed her shoes, had her valuables in a small bag, looked carefully round the room, apparently checking everything, and then announced her readiness to leave.

Having locked away their money and documents downstairs they stood outside, eyeing the crowd, enjoying the musical rise and fall of Italian voices. She held his arm, as if for protection. They turned into a side road, quite broad, with numerous stalls, and handsome shops.

'This is why I don't want to bring too much money out. I shall spend it like water.'

'Why not?' he asked.

'Because I don't want to be eating nothing but dried biscuits for the last few days.' Her voice changed. 'Look at those handbags. They're gorgeous.'

To John they were about as interesting as school satchels, but he hummed agreement. They made leisurely progress, arm in arm, dodging oncoming pedestrians.

'Where are we going?' she asked.

'Just a stroll. We'll make for the Duomo. It's down this way, I think. I haven't brought my maps.'

'That's not like you.'

'We're tourists today. Going everywhere, knowing nothing and nobody.'

'In these high streets you can't see any landmarks.'

'As long as we can remember the roads we came down.'

In time they reached the cathedral and the baptistery. Young people sat on the steps of the Duomo lounging, laughing, eating, kissing. They could not get near the famous doors of the baptistery so great was the crush outside.

'We'll have to get here early in the morning.'

'Yes,' she said, 'I suppose so.'

'There seem a lot of Japanese people here.'

'They're everywhere. They're great travellers.'

'They all look young. The schools and universities won't be closed for holidays yet, will they?'

'I've no idea.'

185

'What a lot we don't know.'

At that moment a young Japanese girl approached them, smiled broadly and asked, 'Take photograph, please?' She handed the camera to John saying, 'Press button, please.' She then joined her companion on the steps of the Duomo. After the first snap, the girl asked, 'Again, please.' She and her companion changed places.

'Smile, please,' he said. 'Cheese.'

The girl took her camera, made some quick adjustment to it. 'Thank you,' she said, eyes bright. Both girls bowed swiftly and stiffly. 'Very kind.'

'A pleasure.'

After this interlude Helen said, 'I tell you what I forgot to put in.'

'Yes?'

'A knife. We'll have to buy one.'

'I don't know the Italian for butter knife. Or any kind of knife for that matter.'

They found an ironmonger's. The proprietor beamed at them. Helen was the first to spot what she wanted. She pointed. The man handed it over, fixed to a card.

'That do?' John asked Helen, who nodded.

'Quanto, per favore?' he ventured. The shopkeeper pointed to a price label and followed with a volley of Italian. John took out his small wallet and counted out the notes. The proprietor nodded approvingly, said something in Italian which they did not catch. John slipped the knife into his coat pocket.

'Grazie.'

They parted in mutual admiration as if they had bought a house or even a gunboat. They were smiling still in the swirl of the street.

'I think we should buy biscuits and cheese,' Helen said. 'Something to nibble at in the middle of the day. Do you know what the Italian for "cheese" is?'

'Formaggio, I think.'

'Oh, well done. You've come prepared.'

The grocer, just over the road from the ironmonger, spoke English, strongly accented but perfectly understandable. They bought cheese, biscuits, butter and some kind of cakes, and apples. That surprised them. 'Englishmen always eat apples. Makes them both strong and thin.'

'Slim,' John said.

'Ah, yes. Slim and handsome.'

While they were waiting for their change John said, 'I wish I'd learnt Italian at school.'

Helen suddenly looked at the shelves near where she stood, laughed and pointed. She read the label, 'Bicarbonato di soda.'

'I shall know where to come if I get indigestion.'

They left the shop carrying their parcels much pleased with themselves. The shopkeeper accompanied them with histrionic gestures to the door.

'I like the people here,' Helen said.

'Have they altered since last time, then?'

'Their behaviour then seemed exaggerated. Now it's friendly, neighbourly, or perhaps I've changed.'

They reached the hotel without difficulty, staring into the shop windows, briefly stepping into the covered market, and in Helen's case scrutinising and feeling the leather handbags once more.

'I've a suspicion one of those will be coming home with us,' he said.

'You ain't seen nuthin' yet,' she answered in her best Reagan style.

They had an hour in the hotel. He with his Fodor guide, she with E.M. Forster's *A Room With a View*. With apparel slightly altered, they followed advice from the receptionist about restaurants, and ate an excellent meal. This time they had no difficulty with the menu. Helen complained she felt bloated. He told her not to believe all she read in the newspapers about overeating. Later, in darkness, he led her out to the roof where they sat looking at the stars. In their bedroom they made love.

'I don't feel the least bit tired,' she said, stretching luxuriously then pulling him to her.

'I thought we'd fall out of bed.'

Breakfast in the hotel was simple with delicious coffee. They set out to be at the Palazzo degli Uffizi by nine-thirty, easily managed by the invigorated pair. They'd decided to visit that first to try out their taste. She had claimed that she could spend the whole holiday looking at pictures, but he was uncertain. A couple of half days would suffice him, she thought. She spoke to him like a stern but loving schoolteacher.

'I want you to decide which pictures you like best. Write their names down. Just two or three,' she instructed him.

'When I get to the top of these stairs,' he pointed upwards, 'I shan't be able to breathe, never mind see to write.'

'There's a lift.'

'This is as good as any skiing holiday. If only all culture had such exercise attached.'

Arrived at the galleries, John was impressed by the vast altar-pieces of Cimabue, Duccio and Giotto, but thought the babies did not look like modern infants.

'They're like dolls,' he said. 'Very wooden dolls.'

Once he knelt down to examine the paintwork, to see if he could make out the brushstrokes laid on in 1310. How he was going to decide he did not know, because he felt certain in his mind that the pictures must have been restored several times in the last seven hundred years. A heavy hand descended on his right shoulder. An attendant signalled him to stand, and a second man stood behind the first.

'No signor,' the man said. 'Not too close.'

'No, signor. I am sorry. I just wanted to see the paint. I would not do this any harm.'

He spoke hesitantly. There was no sign of Helen about. She must have moved on to the next room.

'Thank you,' he said. 'I am sorry.'

He bowed slightly, and then stood back a step towards the door. One guard followed him, but made no attempt to impede him. Slightly shaken, he searched for Helen, and after a few moments of panic found her at last in front of Botticelli's *Birth of Venus*. This was heavily protected by a huge blue screen, presumably of bullet-proof glass. Helen was complaining slightly.

'That must affect the colours,' she murmured. 'But there are all sorts of lunatics about who'd damage anything. If it's only one in a million it must take tremendous trouble to protect all these unique pictures. Once they're harmed, there's no real restitution. Even if they make it look right, it's not the same. It's not the real painting over again.'

'When did Botticelli live?' he asked.

She fiddled with her small guide.

'1445 to 1510, it says here.'

'Some restoration must have been done since then.'

'That seems likely, but I don't know. It's wonderfully beautiful, isn't it? Out of this world.' He stared ahead. 'They've protected the *Spring* too. She pointed him towards it on a wall at right angles to the *Venus*.

He nodded dumbly, guiltily. They parted again; Helen seemed to know where to look, and at what, as she busily consulted her small guidebook.

Some minutes later he found what he wanted, a bench, placed in front of the Portinari altarpiece. He was glad to take the weight off his feet as he let his eyes casually flutter over the huge central sector of the painting. Three shepherds adored the naked child, laid out for whatever reason in the middle of the stable floor, upheld in light. He noticed that all the adults held their hands together in prayer, angels, shepherds, Mary with her hair, shell-shocked Joseph. The expression on the face of the oldest shepherd was beautifully caught; he smiled, as if God had got it exactly right for him. Such satisfaction glowed from a man with work-worn hands who expected little from the world, but who had this day been somehow rewarded, not beyond his merits but sufficiently to transform that grizzled face. Even the ox and the ass at the manger looked on delighted, though the ass's first consideration was the hay he bent to eat.

He thought of a story he had read in the sixth form at school. They were reading William Cowper for A level. He'd enjoyed Cowper, a bit of a wimp for sure, but decent with his pet hares and his women mothering him. Cowper was a clinical depressive, and had attempted suicide. Quietly though he lived in Olney, his depression grew worse and he turned to religion, aided, John's schoolmaster had said, by the vicar of the parish, an ex-sea captain of a slave ship, converted now, and celebrated for his hymn 'Amazing Grace'; Cowper, the most harmless of men, feared that God had failed to number him amongst the elect; he was, he had convinced himself, 'damned below Judas'. A relative described how painlessly he had died, after years terrified of the outcome, so that the watchers round the bed, even his doctor, expecting his death, could not be sure of the moment when he'd

189

left them. Later the expression on his dead face, so onlookers said, was one of calmness and composure, mingled, as it were, with holy surprise. Those last two words exactly described the looks on the faces of the shepherds.

He'd not thought of the Cowper anecdote since he was eighteen to the best of his recollection, though he had used it in the A level answer he'd written fourteen years ago. John suddenly felt pleased with himself, that the picture had had such an effect on him, conjuring up literary reminiscences.

Two hands were placed on his shoulder, very gently, but strongly enough to recall the guard touching him as he knelt before the Giotto. He jerked up. Helen stood behind him.

'There you are,' she said. 'I thought I'd lost you. Isn't this a wonderful painting?'

'I like it,' he said.

'There's a northern air about it,' she said. 'It's not Italian. You can tell that.'

'What date is it?' he asked.

Helen seemed so caught up with the picture that there was a pause, quite painful to him, until she consulted the notebook.

'1475–6,' she said. 'Painted by Van Der Goes for a banker in Bruges, Tommaso Portinari, to put in the church of Santa Maria Nuova in Florence. Portinari's ancestors had been responsible in some measure for building the church. That's him, on the left panel, with his sons Antonio and Pigello. His wife Maria Baroncelli is on the right, with her daughter, Margherita Portinari. All in the book.'

'The little girl doesn't look Italian,' he said, after consideration. 'She's more like a Dutch or Belgian girl. Pudding-faced. And look at her hands. They don't seem right. They look big and not very clean.'

'My word,' she said, 'you're getting to be quite the critic. But perhaps he got it right. Even the daughters of rich bankers had to work or play in the mud. You see he can paint smooth hands if he wishes. Look at the angels; their paws are small, and smooth, and very clean.'

She asked him which part of the picture appealed most to him.

'The shepherds,' he said at once. Then, a bit hesitantly he told her his Cowper story. She listened, one delicate hand to her mouth.

'You're right. Look at the man at the back. It's as if he can hardly believe his eyes.'

John knew he had pleased her, and was encouraged to press on.

'I'll tell you another thing I liked,' he said.

'Go on, then.' She might be a teacher speaking in expectation to a favourite pupil.

'It's those flowers in pots at the bottom in the middle.'

'Yes?'

'They look real, and modern. Just like ones in our garden. They're flags, aren't they? Up at the top, white and blue?'

'Yes, they're irises.'

'And the orange ones?'

'They're lilies. Look at the leaves. Like those I had in pots outside my back door. And the blue flowers on the glass affair, they're aquilegias.'

'I beg your pardon?'

'Aquilegias. Columbines. I guess they're all symbols of something, but I don't know what. I'll look it up for you.'

'I'm amazed that they had flowers the same as ours in 1470-odd.'

'I've no idea about such things. I suppose they were all developed from wild flowers. How ignorant we are.' She giggled. 'It says here that there are fifteen angels, and they represent the fifteen joys of Mary. Don't ask me what they were.'

She tried to count the angels and twice failed before she arrived at the required fifteen.

'I don't know why I'm counting,' she said, 'when I've an accountant for a husband.'

They then worked their critical way round the picture.

'Look at that man's legs,' he said, pointing to a figure in the distance behind Signora Portinari.

'Yes,' Helen answered. 'He's a cripple pointing the way out to a servant of the three wise men, who are sitting on their horses just a little distance back from their outriders.'

'Why a cripple?'

'Again, I don't know. Perhaps it meant something. A cripple, a disadvantaged person may sometimes be able to help wise men. Why he wanted to say that I don't know. I believe he was like

Cowper, subject to depression, and had at least one breakdown.'

'We used to sing a hymn to that effect when I was at school. "Though wise men better knew the way/It seems no honest heart can stray." Why did he suffer from nervous trouble?'

'I believe that when he went into the monastery, the prior didn't subject him to all the usual harsh disciplines, but allowed him to paint, and to go into the outside world to do so. He even tried to cure his melancholy by playing music to him, like David with Saul.'

'How odd.'

'Yes. And it's said when he went out he lived on the fleshpots and felt so guilty when he returned that he was suicidal.'

'Did he recover?'

'I think so. But he died quite soon afterwards.'

'He saved his life by dying,' he joked.

She slapped the sleeve of his coat playfully. She glanced again at her notebook. 'In this it says he was bold, fiery, uncertain, passionate . . . striving for more than he could accomplish.'

'Who said that?'

'Sir Martin Conway in *The Van Eycks and their Followers.*'

'This picture isn't fiery,' John said. 'It's peaceful. Calm. And as to striving for what he couldn't accomplish, well, this seems to me to be as near perfection as any I've seen.' He spoke with a kind of solemn pedantry.

'This is the picture you'd take home if you were given the choice?' she asked. 'From all these?'

'Yes.'

'Not one of the Botticellis?'

'Not unless you wanted it.'

She slipped her arm through the crook of his, passionately.

Later as they sat outside, staring up at the tower of the Palazzo Vecchio against the fervent blue of the sky, to drink coffee and eat an exotic chocolate delicacy that would, Helen said, spoil their lunch, they were quietly at ease. John photographed his wife at table, and then they exchanged places. A passing patron asked if they'd like their picture taken together. It was an ideal moment. The air was clear. Even the maddening motorcyclists seemed to have deserted the streets.

They spent most of the day in the gallery, and on their way to the hotel they found the Casa Buonarroti, the house Michaelangelo bought for some member of his family still open, so that they could spend a half-hour there carelessly. They walked round, hardly released from the heavy dazzlement of the Uffizi, amazed at the early works of the master.

'He wouldn't need much teaching,' John said. He felt happy as never before, pleased with his own intuitions, modestly ready to offer his judgements or even his jokes.

In the Uffizi they had stood before the *Doni Tondo*. Both expressed admiration.

'I don't remember seeing this before,' Helen said. 'I suppose they had lent it out to America, or were having it cleaned or reframed.'

'What's a tondo?' he asked.

'Any circular painting or sculpture. Do you like it?'

'I do.' Then laughing, '"*Holy Family Waiting On the Wall of a Nudist Camp*".'

'John Riley.'

But he had not gone too far, and that night as they swayed back from their evening meal, heads spinning with the cheap glasses of Orvieto Classico, 'I think that's what the waiter called it,' John had ventured, replete with a plateful of tagliatelle al salmone ('twice the size of the tondo' John exaggerated), Helen, an arm round his waist declared, not keeping her voice down, that this was the happiest day in all her life.

XXI

The Italian early summer days passed with a temperate beauty. The weather was warm, but not unduly so; John and Helen walked the streets, eyeing the white clouds which sailed across the shell blue of the sky. In one of the shadowed streets they saw a scooter suddenly swerve off the road, across the pavement and into the wall of a shop, narrowly missing doorway, window and, miraculously, pedestrians. In no time a crowd gathered, garrulously giving orders or asking for information. There seemed no reason for the accident. It was almost as if the cyclist had acted deliberately. It could not have been suicidal; his speed had been nothing out of the ordinary, but now as he lay on the pavement beside an upturned yet unbroken plant pot and shrub, his eyes were closed; he seemed unconscious. An ambulance carted him away.

On the same day they were involved in another incident. A gang of dark-skinned gypsy children had snatched a tourist's handbag, and had hared off down the street with their booty. The woman herself stood shocked, unable to talk, face set but with tears already flowing. Her companions had made no attempt to chase the thieves. Presumably it had been over too quickly. A stout middle-aged man was inquiring with a strong American accent where the police station was. 'We must report it,' he kept repeating. All the woman's companions seemed incapable of action. An Italian spoke fluently but in broken English to them, pointing out where they'd find the police, blaming a culture which allowed these children to maraud. In the end the party led away the victim, her face still a mask of horror, her hands shaking violently.

'We're getting our money's worth, today,' John said.

'I guess if you strolled in London with nothing to do, we'd see incidents like this all the time.'

At this moment another child, dirty like the thieves, came skidding past them, and impeded the Americans. She held up the stolen handbag now completely empty, seeking a reward. The girl had no English, but a full gamut of gesture, and attempted to explain where or how she found the trophy.

'She must be one of the thieves,' John said, once they had passed the group.

'How do you know?'

'Because she knew where to bring the bag.'

'She might just have seen all that happened, and thought when the gang slung the bag away that she might make a few Euros returning it.'

He didn't believe this, but was glad they could argue without any residue of resentment.

One day they turned by chance, or so it seemed for they had made no precise arrangements, into the Galleria dell'Accademia to see Michelangelo's *David*. They moved down the gallery lined with its half-finished pieces of sculpture to where at the end of the hall the enormous masterpiece dominated the place. People crowded round, staring, like creatures amazed at the huge achievement.

'He did it from a piece of marble somebody had abandoned,' she had told him previously.

'Who's the somebody?'

She consulted the ever-present little notebook. 'Agostino di Duccio.'

'How long did it take him?'

'1501–04. This says he'd had his eye on the block for some time, and put himself forward as a suitable candidate to finish the sculpture. It belonged to the cathedral's Office of Works. So they chose him in the end.'

'By God, they chose right,' he said, concluding the conversation much later in front of the statue.

She knew immediately what he meant.

Most of the people who swarmed at the foot of the statue were silent, heads tilted back, as if overcome by the size and power of the masterpiece. Helen had taught him a word from her book, *contrapposto*, when one part of the body is twisted in an opposite direction from the other. She had said that one side of his body was relaxed while the other was tensed as for action. This seemed not right to him, or overindulging in some theological interpretation, good and evil, he could not accept. There was no need for such interpretation, the expression on David's face demonstrated how well he knew his own strength, and his anger. This was no young, undeveloped shepherd boy setting out to face Goliath, neither was it a figure in triumph, but rather a calm master of his own powers. John especially admired the hands which exemplified aggression itself.

Out of the low hum of talking round the building they suddenly heard a coarse voice which croaked, 'He's not very well endowed for such a big man, is he?' The question was not loud, yet somehow the English words carried to the people round him. Immediately there was silence, a dumbness of shock, as heads were turned to glare at the perpetrator of this blasphemy. The man was perhaps forty, with his hair greased down from a middle parting in an old-fashioned way. He was tall, wore a yellow T-shirt, and casual slacks. He seemed not to notice the accusatory eyes, or perhaps not to have understood that his voice had carried beyond his wife not two feet away from that impious mouth. She had realised, and her face had flushed furiously. She clung now to her husband's arm. Another voice, equally penetrating, whispered, 'Filthy bastard'. That settled it; the crowd began to break up, to go its separate ways, John and Helen with them; the two turned back and once again walked round the main hall, looking behind them to the huge figure from time to time as if they could hardly believe the evidence of their eyes. Twice they repeated the route, speaking in subdued voices, but on mundane matters. Helen asked him the time, as her watch had stopped. She wound it up; he was surprised that she continued with such an old device but then admired her for it.

They, returning to the statue for the third time, stood frozen in awe. John shook his head in disbelief before they moved on to the anticlimax of lesser works of art. Once they were outside in the street, he said, 'That was something. It would be worth coming to Italy just to see that.'

'Yes.' She seemed rapt at her husband.

'I tell you another thing that impressed me. You remember those blocks of marble that somebody had attempted to carve

196

and hadn't finished, well there was one with just some slight chiselling at the top left-hand corner. I think they claimed that it belonged to Michelangelo.'

'Yes?' Helen encouraged him.

'It showed how he started. I'd never thought of that. You have to take a first chip off the block but I'd no idea whether it would be at the top or the bottom.'

'I'd never thought of it either. You're getting to be quite a critic. Do you think Michelangelo would have taken these pieces out?'

'How d'you mean,' he asked.

'I thought some assistant might have done it. He'd know roughly how much to take off, because the master would have made drawings, and would have given instructions. I don't know how much di Duccio had done, and how much his initial carving would have limited Michelangelo's work.'

They enjoyed these discussions which they conducted without rancour. Once or twice in the evening they turned over the success or otherwise of the holiday in their minds.

'Do you think we're doing all right?' he asked.

'I'm enjoying every minute,' she answered.

'We don't seem to quarrel over anything.'

'No. It was work which was in the way before. We were both taking on more and more responsibility and I thought that you made no allowances for that. We were both downright selfish. We were both sure we had a God-given right to put our work first and hang the consequences for our partner. So we made no allowances. That's why I wanted to test ourselves on holiday.'

'But shall we be back to the old ways once we're at work again?' he asked.

'I don't think so. I've seen no signs of it here. We argue a bit, because that's our nature. We like to be one-up on the other from time to time.'

'But we're on holiday now. We've nothing to do but please ourselves.'

'And you're managing to do that?' she asked.

'Yes. I'm learning a great deal as well.'

'You wouldn't sooner be lying on a beach all day, eating big

197

meals and ice creams, and spending all the late hours drinking?'

'No, I don't think so. I'm too old for that laddish stuff.'

'We're a little bit,' she ventured, 'like one of these university adult education trips, aren't we? Studying the Renaissance?'

'Nature of the place.'

She had taken her comparison from a group of such people who had arrived at the hotel on their second week, and with whom they were going out the next day. John had talked to a couple of their leaders who had chosen to eat at their restaurant, the Buca d'Orofo, and learning that there were a couple of seats empty on the bus had gladly taken them. The trip was to Siena and San Gimignano.

'We'll have to behave,' she said.

'It means somebody else will have organised the expedition and it will be a sight cheaper than if we'd done it for ourselves.'

They enjoyed every minute of the trip, the drive through the dusty countryside, the fonts in the Baptistery of San Giovanni, the ornate cathedral, the streets running steeply downhill, shadowed between the tall houses. They were too early for the July Palio, when horses and riders representing ten of the seventeen districts race madly round the Piazza del Campo.

'I wouldn't like that,' Helen confessed. 'I'd be expecting accidents all the time.'

John said, in his jokingly English way, that the public lavatories were the finest he'd seen in Italy.

'Finest?' Helen answered him back in kind. 'The first.'

It had been a great day reminding John of school outings, and the tales with which his mother had regaled him in childhood about the Sunday-school anniversaries of her youth, when the scholars in their best clothes were packed into buses and bumped along a few miles of country roads to run races, eat picnics, shout, scream, climb trees, get lost in some park or, once even, to the seaside. This had been a failure. Too many were sick on the charabancs on the overlong journey, and had been delivered silent, pale, best suits and frocks stained, groaning, smelly and half asleep. Helen listened to his regurgitation of his mother's tales, giggling and delighted at his skill in the retelling.

They heard brief lectures about Italian hill towns, of the former seventy-two towers of San Gimignano now reduced to a still impressive fourteen. They stood listening to an aristocratic trio of buskers playing two pieces, Helen said, from Bach's *Little Notebook for Anna Magdalena*. She recognised them, she grinned, from the piano lessons of her youth.

'Ah, education,' one of the university party's leaders breathed.

They returned exhausted, but not so much so as to miss their expansive evening meal or the nightly lovemaking. They lay naked, holding hands, and were asleep in no time. Next morning they did their best to recall what one of the university lecturers had quoted, surely in the purest Italian of Siena, that the fields round San Gimignano were the place where God occasionally came down to earth to be reconciled with men.

'Do you think we're trying to do too much?' Helen inquired. They were waiting for a bus to take them up to Fiesole, so that they could look down on Florence.

'Probably.'

'You're not looking forward to going home?' she asked.

'I shan't be sorry. This has been the best holiday I've ever had.'

In his shorts, with his rucksack on his back, he looked healthy and energetic and slightly bleached.

'Will you want to come again?'

'Oh, sure. When we've seen Rome and Venice. Italy's the place.'

'The light's so beautiful.'

In Fiesole they ate ice cream after the climb upwards to see the Roman basilica and gaze down at Florence, which was lightly shrouded in mist.

'I didn't notice that when we were down there,' he said.

'No. It seemed the sky was washed clean.'

Helen had collected, John's word, some further favourite works of art: the lovely, little young *David* by Donatello in the Bargello, Mary Magdalene in the Cathedral Museum, which John said could be modern, but above all the *Pietà* of Michelangelo.

'That haunts me,' she said. 'Jesus's body is broken. And we can see the place where his other leg was to be fitted in.' And there at the back towered Michelangelo himself with his broken nose. The little book seemed unsure whether he represented Joseph of Arimathea or Nicodemus who came by night. The book had not found favour with Helen, in that it said the figure on the left was too small, out of proportion. 'You don't look at that,' she said. 'You look at the crucified figure and those lifting him down.' She sounded heated about this, and went back twice to stand and stare. The effect took away her breath. She stood herself like a piece of statuary, barely breathing.

On the morning of their last day they went out shopping. Helen had, at last, decided on the handbag she wanted, and then suggested to John that he should buy a similar one for his mother. She fell immediately into the routine of comparison, saying why this was more useful than that, or more beautiful. He was as taken with her care as the stallholder, who fetched out for her his finest. He spoke in fast Italian, with a stern, incredulous face, and when he named the price she made him write it down for her in her notebook.

John, amused when the salesman reduced his prices for both bags, paid willingly for both.

'I'm not sure,' she told him later, 'that I don't prefer your mother's to mine.'

'Well, you have hers. Make a swap.'

'That's not fair. Anyway, I'm not sure.'

They both laughed out loud.

They had decided to cross the river, climb up to the Piazzale Michelangelo and then higher to the Church of San Miniato, a favourite of John's.

'I feel tired today,' Helen said. They were seated on a low wall.

'Your holiday's wearing you out, is it?'

'Doing me good.'

They laughed, as he retold, not for the first time, the old joke about a man who went to visit a mate who had just come back from a seaside holiday, only to find that the friend had died and was laid out, as was the custom of that time, in the front room. The widow invited the visitor in to see the corpse. He looked the body over and having nothing to say, muttered to himself. The wife suggested that her late husband was very brown; he obviously had spent a fair time in the sun. 'Ah,' said the not very articulate new mourner, 'yes. His 'oliday done 'im good.'

This was one of William Riley's two or three creaking jokes.

At that moment Amy Gibbs-Smith walked stately past them.

Helen called out to her. She turned her head as they waved, but did not seem to recognise them. On hearing her name again she took a hesitant step or two in their direction.

'John and Helen Riley,' Helen called out. 'We met on the plane.'

Now she came more confidently up towards them.

'Hello,' she said. 'I wasn't expecting to see you. What are you doing today?'

'We shall have a cup of coffee here, any minute,' John said. 'Then we'll make our way up to the Piazzale Michelangelo where we'll eat our picnic, and then we'll go up higher to San Miniato.' He rolled the Italian names fluently off his tongue. 'A lovely view from both.'

'I'm waiting for my daughter,' Amy Gibbs-Smith told them. 'She's some business to do, and told me to be in this square. She'll be back in a hour.'

'Come and have a cup of coffee with us then?'

'Do you mean that? I'd be very grateful.'

They sat outside to drink their coffee, and told her, one interrupting the other, how they had spent their time.

'You sound as if you've enjoyed every minute.'

'We have. And what about you?'

'I'm afraid I've not been so lucky.' Her face fell. 'My time here has been a complete disaster.' They waited for her. 'My daughter and her husband are thinking of splitting up. It's a dreadful atmosphere up there.' A tear fell from her left eye. 'When I think of those little girls. They seem so happy. They don't seem to notice the trouble between their parents. I suppose it's a credit to the adults' behaviour that they have kept it away from the children.'

'What's going to happen?'

'They'll separate in the summer. Miriam will go back to England and stay there with the children. The younger one, Jane, will start nursery school. Chloë, the older, goes to school here in Italy and enjoys every moment. She speaks the language like a native. Both parents were delighted to bring them out here. That is, at first. They both speak Italian. Peter has been out here for some years travelling round, and his mother was Italian so he's spoken Italian from his cradle. He works in IT, and his firm wanted him out here permanently for two or three years. Miriam was pleased.

She did Italian at university. That was what attracted her, perhaps, in the first place to her husband.'

'Were they happy?' Helen asked.

'Blissfully, I'd have said. But not now. They snap and snarl. That is when they're talking to each other. They have nothing in common. Miriam says he leaves all responsibility to her, and does nothing for the children.'

'Have you spoken to your son-in-law?'

'Yes. He's very polite to me. He always sounds reasonable, but that's only my view. They are never reasonable or polite to one another. I said to him that if Miriam went back to England, he'd see next to nothing of his children. He said this was so, but he had considered it and he thought it would be better than their living in a house of bickering and quarrels. I asked him why the relationship had become so bad, and he said that work had split them up. He had to travel, and it left her with all the domestic responsibilities. I said that had always been seen at one time as a proper division. He said Miriam wouldn't have it. I told her there was no sense in throwing in a well-paid job.'

Mrs Gibbs-Smith gabbled all this out to them, and in five minutes was crying openly. It was clear that she blamed her daughter for not trying harder to resolve the situation. She'd put it times without number, she said, to her daughter but the only answer she got was that she didn't understand the effect of all this on the girl. 'I'll tell you, Mother, if I have much longer here I shall commit suicide.'

'Was she unbalanced, your daughter?' John asked.

'I'd have said not. But now she seems utterly unlike herself.'

'Was it loneliness?'

'She has the children and countless friends out here, English and Italian. No, it's as if she set up some impossible standard for herself, and when she couldn't reach it, blamed Peter. I'm not saying he's perfect. He isn't. But I don't think he understood her behaviour any more than I did.'

'Was she ambitious?'

'In a way. She did very well at university and was starting on a doctorate when she met Peter, and married him almost at once, and came out here to live, in Rome at first, then Tuscany, and Chloë was born within a year after their marriage. It might have been that. She'd perhaps have done well to finish her PhD, but, no, she knew best.'

Mrs Gibbs-Smith described her daughter's beautiful house. It was a picture, with expensive furniture and fittings. The climate was ideal, and Miriam came back to stay with her mother at least a fortnight in the summer, sometimes longer.

'Did Peter come?'

'Perhaps for a week or so. For the rest he was quite prepared to get on with his work and look after himself.'

Again Mrs Gibbs-Smith repeated her story. She could not understand it. Miriam would not be able to take a job until Jane started school full-time, and that usually began, as they knew, with a whole set of minor illnesses caught from the other children so that she'd have to take time off. She'd do her best to help them out, but it depended where Miriam could get some sort of work.

This double recital of her daughter's trouble seemed to have calmed the woman. Her tears had dried; she sat straighter, held her coffee cup without trembling.

'I'll tell you something,' Helen said. Her voice was strong. She might have been in her office speaking to a client who would not see sense. Mrs Gibbs-Smith's face did not change. She expected nothing. 'My husband and I,' she waved towards John as if to make certain there was no mistake, 'were in the same predicament. There were differences from your daughter's case. We had not been married nearly as long, and there were no children to complicate the issue. But we had worked ourselves into such a state that every small disagreement became a major quarrel. We could not agree about anything. We shouted at each other. Sometimes one or the other of us refused to talk. We never got to blows, but we did throw crockery about. It was awful. Two people living in the same house hating each other. I'm not exaggerating, am I, John?'

'No,' he said.

'And the worst thing, when I think about it now, was that there was no real, deep-seated cause for our anger and resentment. We were both taking on extra responsibility at work at the time. Doing well, other people would have said. And we put work before the other's convenience. I remember John bought us expensive tickets for the opera, *The Marriage of Figaro*, and kept it as a surprise, didn't tell me until the night before the performance what he'd done. I refused to go. I had a late, six o'clock interview with a client, and had a whole lot of work which would take up all the nights of the week. Thinking about it now I see I could have put the interview back a day, and caught up on my work later. But no, I refused to go. I bawled John out for not giving me notice. He knew how busy I was. He intended it as a birthday surprise. My birthday was the following week, but by then the opera company had closed their season. It was affairs like this that drove us to our state of fuming anger. Little differences built up into major rows over other unimportant differences, and to such an extent that we separated. I had a house of my own, and I went to it. I could no longer stand the strain of constant, maddening quarrels. I see now that we acted childishly, but it was serious enough at the time. To get out was my only option. We each had just become convinced that our partner was absolutely selfish, and made sure our partner knew it. It was dreadful. I packed my bags and fled; I could do no more. I expect John was equally pleased to see me go.'

She looked over at her husband, who nodded with a pained expression.

'We had nothing or next to nothing to do with each other. He forwarded my letters, and once let me in to pick up one or two of my belongings I had left behind. There was no prospect of reconciliation. We did not want it, nor did we think it either likely or possible. Our marriage was finished, over and done with. I did nothing about divorce, nor did John.'

Mrs Gibbs-Smith shook her head.

'Then we made occasional contact, and one of the reasons for this was that John's mother was always pressing him to make it up with me. He paid some attention to her. He always did as he was told. She and I got on extremely well, but when she encouraged me, as she did in the end, to reconciliation with John, my first thought was, "What the hell does she know about it?" We had an occasional meal, or an outing. Nothing much at first, but we didn't get across each other. Then we had a day or two in Stratford, and that was different. If you'd asked me about it a week or two afterwards I'd have said it had revived my interest in Shakespeare.'

'What about sex?' Mrs Gibbs-Smith asked bluntly, even brutally.

'After these outings?' said Helen, surprised. 'We both enjoyed it. That had never been a great difficulty between us. I am surprised now that it hadn't saved us before, but it hadn't. Let me cut a long story short. This fortnight in Florence was the final test. We move back in with one another, in my house, not his, when we return this Saturday. So far the omens are good. That's so, isn't it, John?'

'Yes,' he said. 'We start to live together again.'

'And that's something,' Helen echoed, 'I never expected. I can think back now to the time we were breaking up, and when I do I can't imagine we would ever become man and wife again. But we have. I can hardly believe it, except that I feel so content about it. I tell you this, so that you won't despair, so that you'll keep putting in a word here and there as John's mother did to him, if you think there's anything at all to be made of the marriage. There now. I've said my piece. I don't know whether any of it applies to your daughter's case. But I don't want you to give up too soon. You may think you're getting nowhere, but . . .'

'I perhaps haven't the personality or the energy of John's mother.'

'She's a headmistress, and used to laying the law down, and has never given up on her son, but she's rather quiet in her way of doing it.'

Mrs Gibbs-Smith stood up, noisily pushing her chair back.

'There's Miriam,' she said, 'my daughter, looking for me.' Her face flushed with excitement. 'I'd like you to meet her, if you would. Please.'

'You go out and greet her then, while John settles up here.'

'Oh, no, let me pay. You've been so kind.'

'First things first. I'll come with you.'

Out in the square Mrs Gibbs-Smith introduced them as the couple who had been so kind to her on the plane. The daughter was as well dressed as her mother, and seemed quite at ease. There were no signs of the troubled wife about her. She spoke in a plummy voice and gave the impression that her mother was inclined to become too excited over nothing. They went off to find their car, and then to pick up Jane who was spending the

205

day with a neighbour, then collect Chloë from school. John watched them march away, both with backs straight as ramrods.

'She seems on top of life,' Helen said. 'Capable.'

'Do you think Ma's exaggerating?'

'Possible.'

'That was a good talking to you gave her,' he said.

'I was afraid you might be cross with me.'

'I thought how well you did it. Like a Dutch uncle, whatever that is. And . . .' he laughed ruefully, 'you didn't make me out to be the villain of the piece.'

'I was as bad as you, if not worse. But what still amazes me is how we let the situation . . . we let the situation,' she stuttered on, 'deteriorate to the state it was. I just hated coming home; I didn't want to see you or speak to you. We'd lost control of ourselves. It wasn't as if I had found you in bed with another woman or chanced on compromising letters. These little things had just built up. You always put your job first. You saw the time coming when I should perhaps have children, and have to stay away from work, and therefore it was important that you were earning well.'

'Any sensible person would have thought about that, but it's no excuse for getting steamed up as we did. It made me think that there was something wrong with us, that we were temperamentally incompatible, and that's why we acted as we did.'

'Do you still think like that?' Helen asked.

'I've heard you say how suicidal you felt, and God knows I was as bad. I don't think like that now, but it frightens me that we might slip back when we're up to the eyes with worry about something or other.'

She kissed him, in the open, ignoring passers-by. As they sat eating their lunch on the Piazzale Michelangelo they were quiet, as if the attempt to comfort Mrs Gibbs-Smith had served only to trouble them. Helen walked about with her camera, while John leaned over looking out to vineyards, not the proud city or the second *David*.

'If you were allowed to take only one photograph in Florence, what would it be?' he asked.

'Michelangelo's *Pietà*, she replied without hesitation.

'Not *David*?'

'Not *David*.'

They repacked the rucksacks, crossed the wide road, and made their way uphill to the church.

'This is the thing I remember most,' ventured John, puffing.

'Why's that?'

'It takes some getting to,' he said, 'what with these roads and then all these steps.'

'But it's worth the effort?'

'Oh, yes.'

'Dante must have made his way up here as a young man,' Helen said. 'The roads would have been much rougher then. And he never forgot it. He put it in the *Divina Commedia*.'

'Did he, by gum?'

'He did.'

'Well, Gaw' bless the man.'

They became breathless as they climbed.

XXII

Outside the Church of San Miniato al Monte they stood to regain their breath and admire the view.

'This is one of my favourite places,' she said. 'And once we're inside it's like a jewel box.'

'That's right,' he agreed, laconically.

'It's old,' she said consulting her book. 'It was started in 1013 and finished in the thirteenth century.'

'I remember coming here with my mother and father. My mother thought Roman and even most Anglican churches over-fancy, but she really loved this. My father was different.

Even though my father had lost interest, he'd turn up for harvest festivals and Christmas carols, that sort of thing, but I don't think ordinary services had much appeal. He liked figures, arithmetic, things he could understand, and make use of. I remember his saying after one of his forays into church life, "I don't get along with all that praying," and my mother had to shush him because I was about.'

'He didn't try to influence you?'

'No, he'd ask me if it had been interesting at Sunday school.'

'And you'd say?'

'Mostly neutral. If there'd been anything out of the way I might mention it, and he'd say, "Good".'

'I think if I lived here I'd visit churches, attend services, I mean, more than I do at home.'

'There are plenty of churches which are both old and beautiful in England. And have marvellous music, if you like that sort of thing.'

'I don't see you rushing to go,' she said.

'No, I served my time as a boy. That's why I'm so good.'

She punched his arm, quite hard.

They walked the length of the church not saying much to each other. He recalled his visit as a boy and his father's amazement, even scorn, at the screen.

'It's a bridge. Why do they need a bridge?'

'Why do churches have such high ceilings?' John's mother had asked.

'To show off.'

'If by that you mean to be different from domestic architecture then you're right. God's house had to be fit for him to live in, as a king's palace is. Just look at that beautiful floor. You couldn't afford marble at home.'

'I wouldn't want it. It's too cold on the feet.'

There was barely a soul about as he told this to Helen.

'Is your mother a religious woman?' Helen asked.

'I wouldn't say so. She was an orthodox Methodist. But she thinks that those who are serious about what they believe should do something about it, and she doesn't do much.'

They paused by the Cardinal of Portugal's chapel and sepulchre.

'He'd suit your mother,' she said.

'What date is it?'

She consulted the small book.

'1461.'

They paused and stared around them. The air was cool, mild, holy, very still.

'It's so rich,' she said. 'It makes me feel good.'

'You like it better than the Duomo, or Siena Cathedral, or Santa Maria Novella?'

'Yes. They're magnificent, and huge and breathtaking, but they seem empty. This seems to concentrate its wealth.'

'I think I see what you mean.'

She did not attempt further explanation. They walked a yard or two away from each other. A shadow of fear crossed his mind. Could even this beautiful place, with its plain frontage, be the beginning of a break-up of their marriage? He loved his wife, and admired her. But was this only in old foreign cities where every few hundred steps you chanced on some outstanding work of art, of architecture, of human ingenuity. When the common people first saw Masaccio's *Trinity* they were staggered thinking a hole had been knocked into the church wall, so persuasive, convincing was his use of perspective. It was not so with him. When he first saw the painting he thought God was wearing a muffler, so implausible was the dove, the fluttering Holy Ghost. He decided he was not fit to view such masterpieces. When Michelangelo first saw Ghiberti's bronze east door of the baptistery he showed neither envy nor made any attempt at reduction but pronounced it at once 'The Gate of Paradise'. That was the sort of magnanimity that was lacking in John, or so he condemned himself.

He breathed deeply, but that proved unsatisfactory. The air was too warm, sluggish, soporific. He laughed silently to himself. Helen's lecture to Mrs Gibbs-Smith had kicked the confidence out of him. This mountain top, this jewel box should have set him right, but had merely served to demonstrate to him that he was nowhere near Helen's class, quite undeserving of her, had shown this holiday for what it was: a gateway to a fool's paradise. He dismissed the thought impatiently. Helen had acted as childishly as he when they had lived together. True, in a place like this, when she held the little book in her hand, her superiority was obvious. But they'd soon, tomorrow, be back to the mediocrities of life.

Helen, walking away from where he sat, turned her head and smiled broadly at him, teeth perfect. Immediately his dejection lifted and he knew that he was in the early summer in Tuscany, and that he was loved and in love. Helen stared out to the ancient city wall, lifted out of herself, on top of her world. She turned and made her way back to him.

'A penny for them,' he said cheerfully.

'I was just thinking,' she said, 'that I wouldn't mind being buried up here.'

'Good God.' The ejaculation jerked out of him.

'It wouldn't matter then whether there was an afterlife or not.'

'Why such morbid thoughts?' he asked, awkwardly rough.

'It's not morbid. I'm not thinking of dying at all. But if I had to choose the most peaceful place on earth, this would be it. You can see all the turmoil down there, or imagine it. I can hear the scooters up here, I'm sure. But faintly, and that makes this seem all the more quiet. And I'm sure that Dante would want to walk up here from time to time.'

'I don't know whether that would suit me. He looks a serious man. And he had it in for some people.'

'Oh, I shouldn't want to talk to him. Just to see him pass by.'

At that moment three small girls came running past. Their fair hair tossed about as they ran, and they breathlessly spoke English. The smallest of them, a child of two, perhaps, struggling to keep up with the others, fell over. Quick as a flash Helen darted out and picked the child up, straightening her dress. The girl was doing her best not to cry, though the corners of her mouth turned down ominously. Helen's help had come so swiftly that she was back on her feet being held and comforted almost as soon as she had registered her fall.

'There. That's a brave girl. Have you hurt yourself?'

'My knee.'

The child pointed. The other two had now walked back and lined up to watch. The mother arrived at a sharp pace, a pretty blonde.

'Thank you,' she said to Helen, who immediately released the little girl to her. 'You were running too fast,' she said to the others. 'I keep warning you. She can't keep up with you.' She then turned, inquired from the youngest daughter the extent of her injuries, examined the knee, dabbing at it with a fold of tissue. 'Your daddy has a tin of plasters in his pocket, and when he arrives we'll put one on. How's that?' The child thanked her mother with a kind of gravity beyond her years. 'I don't know where Daddy's got to,' the mother said.

'He's come across something really interesting,' the eldest volunteered. She, at perhaps six years old, spoke with an adult tone of criticism in her voice at his shortcomings. 'He won't be long.'

At that minute the father arrived, a tall, handsome man who looked down quizzically at his family, and on instruction took out, and used, his first-aid kit; he said cheerfully, 'There you are, my poppet. As good as new.' He then looked at the strangers, and his expression changed.

'Helen,' he said. 'Helen Riley.'

'Yes.' She bowed her head.

'We met at those solicitors' courses in Liverpool and Durham,' he told his wife.

211

Introductions were made. All were standing. John now learnt that this was the Dominic Tyrrell who had so impressed his wife.

'Are you still working in the same office?' Dominic asked Helen.

'Yes.'

'There was one man there who was particularly impressed by something you said and wanted you to take over his commercial department. You weren't tempted?'

'No. He tried to get in touch with me twice, but I didn't want to join him. Did I throw away a great chance to improve myself?'

'Walker's office has a good reputation. I don't know anything about the commercial side of it. Perhaps he was just wanting to open up, and thought you were the sort of bright young person who'd handle it for him. He'd want his pound of flesh from you.'

'A pity.' John had no idea what she meant by this. She looked excited, like a schoolgirl to whom the head or a prefect had spoken kindly.

'There was another post that I thought might well suit you,' Dominic said, 'but I imagined that if you wanted a move you would have seen the advertisements. Roland, Drew and Parkyn. A good firm. Interesting cases all the time.'

'I did see it, but I was preoccupied just then.' Tyrrell turned to John.

'Would you say your wife was ambitious, Mr Riley?'

'You think that this is the time to move if she is?' John threw back the question.

'Ideal. That is if she wanted a change. Whenever I sit on appoint-ment boards, candidates invariably claim that they like a chal-lenge. I always construe this as meaning that they're growing tired of the humdrum tasks that occupy them in most solicitors' offices.'

Lady Daphne, Tyrrell's wife, who had been keeping an eye on her children, joined the conversation.

'I should think it depended on their temperament. I find bringing up a family a thoroughly engaging, full-time occupation. My brood see to it that the domestic chores, meals, shopping, the school run, keeping them busy and out of mischief, are well varied with illnesses and accidents and demands.'

Her voice was deep, and superior, and she spoke as if those

who worked for money had little idea of the dangerous variety of a mother's life.

'I'm sure you're right,' John said.

'You mustn't agree with my wife quite so easily,' Tyrrell answered. 'She sets these arguments up for us to examine and tear apart.'

'Rubbish,' said his wife.

There was no malice in her reply. She smiled at Helen, then John, not as if seeking allies, but as if she was slightly annoyed at him for letting her secrets out, instead of allowing the newcomers to light upon them for themselves.

They all laughed, even the children, who bounced boisterously. Helen held her hands out to the smallest girl, who took them without shyness and commanded, 'Swing me round.' Helen complied, and was rewarded by delighted shrieks. 'Again,' the child shouted.

'If you please,' her mother corrected.

'Please,' and they whirled once more.

This time as they stopped Helen said, 'I shall be as dizzy as a cricket.'

'What's a cricket?' Miranda, the eldest daughter asked.

'An insect,' her father said.

'Why is it dizzy?'

'I don't know, but I guess because it hops about. It jumps.'

'Jump, jump, jump,' said the smallest, again taking Helen's hands.

'Don't be a nuisance now, Rosie,' her mother warned. The child wrapped her arms round Helen's legs, and closed her eyes. Helen stroked the little one's hair and back.

Dominic Tyrrell now began to explain what they were doing in Florence. They had arrived yesterday and on Monday he'd attend a three-day conference on arbitration.

'It seemed too good a chance to miss.' It meant Miranda had to take a week off school, but he concluded, 'I know it will soon be an offence to take your children on holiday with you when they should be in school. She's in a private school and I don't think they'll embark on a law suit.'

'Mightn't she miss something important?'

'Nothing as important as this.' He waved his arm at the distant city.

'She won't be examined on this,' John said. He felt he ought to contradict.

'True.' Tyrrell smiled dismissively at such a trivial objection, and told them a little about the local private day school she attended. 'They know their way about, these people. They also know that if they don't do their work properly, the likes of me and Miranda's mother will soon have their child out of the school and into another where they are giving value for money.'

'I heard somebody say that these schools teach people to speak properly, in standard English, and that's the advantage,' John said.

'And when they've learnt to do that they then acquire in their teens the glottal stops and other vulgarities so that they sound like cockneys. We can't win everything. They also start to learn Latin quite young, which is an advantage. Or perhaps you don't think so?'

'I'm an accountant. The bit of Latin I learnt at school doesn't do much for my clients, I'm afraid.'

'I'm glad I learnt some Latin,' Helen said.

'You did more than I. And if you've spent a long time on it you don't like to confess that it was time wasted,' John answered.

She did not contest her husband's argument, but turned to the oldest girl and asked if she enjoyed school. The child did not answer at once, gave the question some thought. The grown-ups waited politely, making no attempt to interfere.

'Yes,' said Miranda, 'yes. I like it very much. And it will all be useful when I'm an adult. Besides I meet my friends and that's good. The teachers tell us some interesting things.'

'Such as?' her father asked.

'Greek legends about people being changed into trees or animals.'

'Expound.' Tyrrell again.

'A princess called Io, I-o, it's a funny name, was changed into a cow.'

The middle child laughed.

'"And lovely Io metamorphosised",' Helen quoted, mellifluously.

That stopped them momentarily. Miranda recovered first and began to regale them with an account of the end-of-term play which she would not miss. Her enthusiasm lifted their spirits.

She was to be a fairy who could cure all troubles and illnesses with a touch of her magic wand. As Helen watched, she almost believed that the child had these powers.

'Is it a real play?' Helen asked.

'Yes. It's put together by our teacher from *A Midsummer Night's Dream*. We sing as well as speak.' Without embarrassment she began to sing in a pure, unwavering voice, '"You spotted snakes with double tongue Thorny hedgehogs be not seen." I don't do the solo part there. That's one of the bigger girls who has a superb voice. But we all know all of it. "There'll be no shortages of stand-ins for any part," Mrs McElroy says.'

'Good,' Helen said. 'That's lovely.'

'I know what you think. That I made that up about being able to cure illness with my wand. That's true. But the teacher told us each to imagine for ourselves what we could do with our magic, and that's what I chose. But we weren't allowed to tell each other what it was we could do.'

'And you didn't?'

'No. Except now to you. But one girl told me the same day what she imagined she could do.'

'And can you tell us?'

'Oh, yes. She could make the stars come out, millions of them, on a dark night.'

'I wish I could do that,' Helen said.

'Yes. But it's not so good as my choice. Think if you could stop pain. Sometimes I have earache. It's excruciating.' The last word was pronounced without difficulty or ostentation.

'And you haven't tried your wand on that.'

'No. It's only make-believe.'

Tyrrell listened to his daughter in the manner he would employ before some respected, learned judge in court.

'You'd sooner be a doctor than an opera singer?' John asked, guilelessly.

'Yes, but I might change my mind. I'm only seven.'

Lady Daphne began to question them about their stay in Florence. It appeared that at Miranda's age she had lived for almost a year in the city.

'Did you go to school here?' Helen asked.

'No. I was taught at home. My father was out here, pursuing

one of his academic whims, to do with mediaeval or Renaissance religion, this time, I think. He was something of a scholar, or that's how he liked to think of himself, but all his other duties prevented full-time study. While we were here he had to keep scuttling back to England. But he thought if he brought Mother and me out, he'd be that little bit less likely to be distracted by the thousand and one things happening in England. My brothers were at school, and they came out in their holidays.'

'Was that good?' John asked, surprising himself.

'My brothers coming out? I was pleased to see them. Oh, you mean living out here. When I think of Miranda's school, I'm sure I missed something. She enjoys it so much. But I guess things were different nearly thirty years ago. I don't know. It makes no difference now.'

'You learnt to speak Italian, I guess?' Helen asked.

'Not really. I didn't see much of the local children. I didn't go to school here. I spoke to the servants in their sort of Italian, but I've forgotten most of that. My father or my governess taught me in a very old-fashioned way. But I could read, I could recite the multiplication tables and do mental arithmetic, French verbs, and learnt history and geography and botany from out-of-date books. And I could browse through encyclopaedias and a great lot of fiction left over by my brothers. Father kept quite a library out here, and I was allowed to take what I liked from that. When I went back and was sent to school they knew things I'd not heard of, but I knew a great deal that was new to them. I was well prepared to learn. Especially the new things. We did Latin and algebra before too long.'

Daphne Tyrrell smiled to herself remembering those experiences.

Her deep voice was as impressive as her accent, but she spoke lightly as if she did not expect what she said to be taken seriously. She had lived here as a child; perhaps these strangers would be interested. If not, she had not wasted much energy on the telling.

Helen listened, intently it appeared, but did not say a great deal. Her initial excitement at meeting Dominic Tyrrell had evaporated, and now she gave her full attention to what the Tyrrell family had to say. Dominic himself now seemed to John to be set apart, listening with interest to the conversation of his inferiors, or perhaps seeing himself as a puppet master who had set the show in motion. Rosie clung on to Helen's hand, quite content to stand undemandingly with her heroine.

After exchanges on Italian weather, family matters – especially the responsibility of parents for the educational upbringing of small children – the plays they had seen recently, and concluding with a curious rhapsody from Dominic about musicals, his favourite form of theatre, they parted. This latter made John suspicious of the man. If he was as Helen had described him, likely to be a QC, then a judge and the rest, then he should have pitched his leisure pursuits elsewhere and higher. John had no particular dislike of musicals, rather the opposite, but Sondheim was not Shakespeare or Mozart. He began to argue with himself why this should be the case. Why was *Sweeney Todd* inferior to *The Magic Flute*?

He put this to Helen on their way back to the hotel.

She made no attempt to answer the question, but confessed her surprise at Tyrrell's preference.

'Perhaps he's not very musical,' she said, 'though I should have guessed he would have been a Wagner fan. Little Miranda could certainly sing in tune.'

'And talk like an adult. I've never heard a child speak so clearly. "Excruciating." As bad as Macaulay.'

'She must have heard her parents use the word,' Helen said, 'remembers it and is not afraid to use it.'

'It impressed me. Just as you obviously impressed Tyrrell on those courses. Did you say a lot?'

Helen felt a pang of fear. Had her husband noticed her excitement at the appearance of Dominic Tyrrell? Was he jealous? Perhaps here was already a threat to their second attempt to live together. She must be careful.

'No, not really.' She tried to speak as naturally as possible. 'If anything, the opposite. Most people on these courses try to impress by the breadth of their legal reading. That takes time. I just stood up and said my piece, that is if I had any knowledge or ideas on the topic we were discussing, and sat down without a lot of ceremony. And once or twice I was supported by the experts. Once by Dominic and once by one of the lecturers, a very learned professor at the LSE.'

217

'Good. You never told me.'

'I didn't think I'd said anything out of the ordinary.'

'But you had.'

'I didn't think so,' she murmured.

'It's a good thing to have some notable like Tyrrell backing you.'

'Yes.'

'Do you ever think of applying for another job? You're well set living in North London, aren't you?'

'I read the advertisements, and think about it. But I'm quite satisfied where I am. They're talking about a partnership, and the work's interesting. Anyway, we can live pretty well on what we earn.'

'That's true enough. But I'd keep in with Tyrrell if I were you. Knowing people who have some influence never did anybody any harm in any profession.'

She felt a surge of pleasure and confidence. John was thinking of her foremost. And with an added dimension from Tyrrell's praise.

'Did you know they'd be here in Florence?'

'No. I've heard nothing from Dominic since those two courses. What did you think of them as a family?'

'Very upper crust. Impressive. He speaks very quietly, absolutely confident that people will listen to what he's got to say. And I imagine if he's as good as you say he is they'll not want to miss a word when he's talking about the law.'

'Would you say he was trustworthy?' she asked.

'That's a rum question to ask after a quarter of an hour's talk. I just couldn't tell. As I say, he looks and speaks impressively, even strikingly, in his quiet way. I'd say he's going to be a notable.'

'And his wife?'

'She was quiet, too. But arresting. With that voice. Obviously she is used to catching and holding people's attention, but isn't making any great effort. We can take her or leave her, because she knows she is a somebody, a personage in her own right.'

'You can see the children going the same way.'

'Except the middle one,' he said.

'Yes, the firstborn and the youngest often receive special treatment at the expense of the middle child or children.'

218

'You were neglected, were you?'

'No,' Helen answered. 'They did their best for me. But I was the only girl. Perhaps that made a difference.'

Helen was still shell-shocked at the appearance of the Tyrrell family. She had often tried to imagine what Dominic's children were like. They were beyond her imagination, and yet in spite of this, somehow more specifically human. She could imagine them arguing with their parents, or sulking over a disappointment. Their mother too seemed less vivacious than in her imagination, but more serious, inconsequently substantial, not to be crossed on important matters, having gravitas. Helen smiled to herself as she piled these attributes on a woman who had barely spoken to her.

They walked downhill to the Arno, crossed it into the city. Back in the hotel they showered together before Helen began to pack their cases.

'I know we've plenty of time tomorrow morning,' she said, 'but I don't want to rush. Tell me what clothes you'll need.'

'These will do.'

'Are you sure?'

He liked her in her bossy moments. She was on the lookout for snags, suspicious of last minute changes of mind. Perhaps it was her legal training. She did not rush, or lose her cool, but carefully sorted difficulties out. He threw his arms round her, and they made love before they set out for their last dinner of the holiday. Once that was over, they walked back hand in hand to the hotel.

'Home tomorrow,' she said.

'Yes.'

'Are you sorry about that?'

'No. I don't think so. This is the best holiday I've ever had.'

'We haven't done much out of the ordinary.'

'Oh, I don't know.' John knew he was right. 'We've seen all sorts of marvels, and we've seen them together in a way that seemed different.'

'In three days we shall have done a day's work.'

'In a way I'm looking forward to that. I shall be thinking that I shall be going back to you in the evening.'

'It will be all right?' she asked.

219

'I'm sure it will. We've been preparing ourselves here. We've not agreed about everything, but we've never quarrelled.'

'That's true. I can't help remembering what a state I was in before we separated.'

'I know. And I can't help thinking how lucky I am to be with you,' he said.

'Have we changed? In ourselves, I mean. We're not just deceiving ourselves because we're in a foreign place with all kinds of interesting sideshows to keep us from clashing?'

'In my view, Helen Riley, you are the most fascinating of the wonders to be seen in Florence at this moment.'

They kissed in the street under the darkening skies.

XXIII

They arrived home on Saturday, and spent Sunday lumbering about in Helen's flat. She encouraged him to walk over to his house to examine the e-mail and phone messages and letters. He found fewer than he expected. The firm, it seemed, could do quite well without his guiding presence. Having sorted this out to his satisfaction, he telephoned his mother. He had called her three times from Florence, and found her cheerfully tired with end-of-term activities. Now she was even more cheerful.

'I'm relieved you're back,' she said.

'Air travel's utterly safe these days, you know. Safer than walking the streets.'

'I'm sure you're right.'

'How's Dad?' he asked.

'No better. Worse in some ways. He doesn't make any effort to help himself. You're living with Helen now, aren't you?' She knew quite well, but fished for information.

'I am. I'm ringing from my house because I'm up here to look at the correspondence.'

'What are you going to do with your place?'

'Give us a chance. First of all we'll see how things work out at Helen's. That's only a flat.'

'And?'

'We'll perhaps take over the whole house, give her tenants notice. That'll occupy some months. Or if we want a whole house quickly we'll move into my place. We might even choose to live elsewhere altogether. Start again.'

'Why didn't you do that in the first instance?'

'Helen seemed to want the present arrangement. So did you as far as I remember. And I put as few stumbling blocks in anybody's way as I could.'

'And it's going well?'

'Steady on. We've had less than a full day together back home.'

'You will try to make it work, won't you? I was so pleased at your decision. I really was.' Headmistressy tone.

'We're doing the right thing, then?' He hardly kept the sarcastic edge from his voice.

'You don't know how glad I am. I'm convinced that Helen is the right woman for you.'

He guessed from his mother's tone that the end of term was wearing her down. He invited her to London once the summer holiday began.

'Will you be able to put me up?'

'Yes. Helly's flat's pretty big. We'll put you in what was the butler's pantry.'

'What's there now?'

'Books. Her desk and two computers. And there's still room for a single bed.'

'Thank you. I'll think about it. I've already fixed a holiday in Egypt.'

'With whom?'

'Mary Oldham.' Mary was her deputy, a cheerful woman near retirement who'd never married and never, it appeared, missed it. The two were close friends as well as colleagues.

Helen and John found plenty of work back at their offices when they reported well before nine on Monday morning. Both complained to the other when they arrived home that evening, Helen half an hour after her husband, who had already peeled potatoes, sliced beans, put in the pork chops and made the apple sauce. On his way from the office he had called in at the local delicatessen for small trifles and cream.

'It smells delicious,' she said as she entered. She noticed that the table was already laid. He'd even set out candles, though where they came from she'd no idea. His house, perhaps.

'I'm glad you're here,' he said. 'I don't know what I should have done with the grub if you'd phoned to say you'd be late.' He'd asked her what time she'd be home, and when she said just before six had organised his day to have the meal cooked and ready to serve at about that time. Both were pleased with themselves. A good start.

They ate heartily and complained how lacking in initiative their subordinates at work were.

222

'You'd think these young men would be only too glad to be left on their own. But, no, they leave the decisions until I'm back.'

'They're probably terrified of you,' she said. 'But our lot are just as bad.'

The meals, the talks at home were admirable. One evening Helen ventured to bring some work back with her. Her husband seemed to think this reasonable and cleared the table and washed the dishes and then occupied himself, successfully he said, with the easy crossword in her *Times*. They did not even arrange to go out to the cinema or theatre at the weekend, but took a long walk on Sunday.

'I've never seen so much of the district,' she said. 'Or the neighbours.'

'Not so interesting as Florence,' he answered.

'I don't know. Some of the things are just as strange. All those joggers. And that man with a moustache.' An elderly gent stood blatantly in the broad Victorian bay window of his house, dressed only in vest and underpants, gently going through the gymnastic routines with arms and legs that he'd learnt at school sixty or seventy years earlier. They waved to him, and he bowed deeply and ironically in reply. They hurried past, grinning.

Next a young man had stopped them to beg for a drink. His manner was quiet, unaggressive, his eyes dark and watery. John, in his euphoria, fiddled in his pocket for a pound coin which the man held down in his palm as if he expected it to leap away. The beggar thanked them in a whisper. Helen suddenly said, 'Give him another, if you have one.' John sought amongst his change and handed over the second coin, so that the two lay together, naked, uncovered. Again, the mutter of thanks as the Rileys marched on.

'I know we shouldn't,' Helen whispered. 'But . . .'

'You think he'll spend it on drugs? Two quid won't go far.'

'We're so happy, it seemed right to share it.'

'I should have given him a ten-pound note, or a twenty, or a hundred.'

She kissed him, reaching up for his cheek.

A quarter-mile on, a schoolboy dribbled a football along

the pavement dangerously near them. With a neat flick John had the ball from him, slipped past him, and then with equal, unobtrusive skill backheeled it smartly to its owner, who stood open-mouthed.

'I thought rugby was your game,' she said.

'We played soccer in the schoolyard with a tennis ball.'

Next he carried an old woman's big battered suitcase, bursting with articles from the laundry, along the street for her. At first she viewed them with suspicion, but then gratefully speeded her pace to keep up. The case was damnably heavy, and the handle malformed and sharp so that John was not surprised that the woman made such heavy weather of lugging her burden along. He was pleased when the old dear stopped them at her front door in a row of terraced houses, to tell him they had arrived at her destination.

'Thank you,' she croaked. 'I don't know how I'd 'a managed it without you. Them sheets was like lead.'

As they parted he looked at his right hand which was marked into lumpy red and bloodless white stripes. He stretched it, showing it to Helen.

'Was there something wrong with the handle?' she asked.

'I'll say.' He blew into it like a boy just strapped at school.

They made good time with the walk before they entered a small park. They took the path up to a shallow pond. The water, brownish and still, seemed wonderfully clear.

'I can't see any fish or frogs,' she said.

'Nor I.'

He felt a small finger poke his leg. A boy directed them.

'There look, mate. There.' The grubby finger pointed. 'Dozens of 'em.'

'What are they?' They could see the small cloud of dancing fish.

'Sticklebacks.' A note of scorn sounded. 'They come up the river.' He pointed.

'Great,' Helen said. 'Lovely. Thank you very much.'

The boy suddenly darted away.

They sat for a few minutes on a seat by the gate licking ice-cream cornets. In spite of the fine weather there was hardly a soul in the park.

'I didn't know there was a park here,' he said. 'It's a wonder they didn't fill it with other houses like these round about.'

'Sometimes they think about amenities for taxpayers.'

'And sometimes not,' he said grumpily.

They left the park and caught sight of a golden cockerel flashing, a vane, from the roof of the pub.

'That's unusual,' she said. 'More suitable to a church tower.'

'It'll be a brewer's trademark, I guess. Let's go in and try a pint.'

He ordered his beer and for her a still orange.

The pub was better patronised than the park. It was clean: no muzak disturbed the clients, nearly all men, who seemed to take their drinking seriously. They talked quietly to each other, earnestly, not like people who enjoyed themselves. There was one exception when a huge burst of coarse laughter rocketed from a group in the corner.

All eyes searched round for the cause. A small man with a pinched face and ginger hair had obviously been telling the tale. The laughter died down for a few minutes until another blaze of sound startled the pub. The storyteller sat, hands on knees, a smirk of satisfaction on his lips. A wilder laugh screamed loose as if one of the listeners had suddenly seen the point.

A dark, sober man on the table next to John said, 'By God, somebody's been at the wine gums.'

His companion nodded, acknowledging the understatement. Helen giggled. They finished their drinks at leisure, thanking the barman on the way out. The sun now shone brightly. They made a happy way along a wide straight road.

'I've never been along here,' he said.

'We're provincials,' she said.

'Not you. You've lived in London most of your days.'

'We thought of it as Kent, my man.'

Far ahead they could see two motorbikes abreast, approaching. The drivers were not speeding, riding with the stately balance of a police escort. When they were perhaps 150 yards away, the one on the inside deliberately, or so it seemed, turned into the second bike and pushed it, with almost quietly ruthless force up the kerb and into a garden wall. A metallic clash and both machines lay across the pavement, their owners stretched out.

'Good God,' John said.

They quickened their pace.

Though there had seemed very few pedestrians about, at least a dozen formed a ragged circle round the accident. Both drivers wore black leather suits and strong helmets. One had now forced his way to his feet, and then crouched by the wall. The other lay where he had fallen, unconscious.

'What happened?' someone inquired from the conscious man.

'He ran straight into me.'

'Why did he do that?'

'Don't know. Unless he had a fit or something.'

People came out of their houses. The noise, minimal in John's estimation, must have disturbed them indoors. Someone had run back into his home to phone the police and an ambulance. The motorcyclist on the ground now begun to groan softly and his eyes flickered. His comrade, face white with shock, moved across to stand by the stretched-out body.

'We wasn't goin' anything like fast,' he said.

The crowd stood by sheepishly.

'The ambulance will take about seven minutes,' one offered.

'If you're lucky.'

'You sit down again,' a tall man advised the standing cyclist. 'Somebody's gone along to the doctor's just down the road. We don't know if he's in, but it's worth trying.'

'He swerved, right smack into me.'

The doctor arrived in a cardigan, his hair unkempt; he gave the appearance of just coming from bed. He wore shiny brogues quite out of place with the rest of his attire. He carried a small bag, and knelt down beside the body, and made some sort of examination. He said nothing to anybody, but continued his work.

Finally he stood and asked, 'You've phoned for an ambulance? How long ago?' He listened to the answers. 'He'll be all right,' he said finally, 'until the paramedics come. I've moved him slightly.'

'Is he unconscious?' someone asked.

'He's coming round. He doesn't answer questions yet.'

Helen had not heard him speak to the victim. Within a few minutes the ambulance arrived, and the crew took over after a brief consultation with the doctor. They gave the impression of

226

complete efficiency, hurrying nothing. The police appeared, began to take names. The victim was stowed away in the ambulance, and one of the paramedics questioned the other motorcyclist, who now claimed to be unharmed.

'We can run you up to the hospital. They'll check you over.' He refused in a wordless mumble. 'Right,' the answer came, 'but get down at once to your doctor if you feel any bad effects in the next day or two. You don't usually run into walls with motorbikes and get away with it.'

The ambulance left; the police took over. Now the crowd was quite large, blocking the pavement as if a message had gone round the neighbourhood to call out witnesses to the unusual incident. Old hands began explanations to newcomers. One man offered to take the motorcycles into his backyard.

'I've got room for one in my garage and one in the garden shed. It'll keep them out of the weather.' The sun now shone quite brilliantly.

The policeman told him not to touch anything yet. They laboriously recorded names. 'We'll have to measure up.'

Helen took John's arm.

'Let's be off,' she said. He nodded agreement. 'I'm not quite certain where we are,' she muttered as they moved.

'No. We'll go back the way we came. We should have brought a map.'

They walked now at a brisk pace, only half sure of their way.

'It's been quite a walk,' she told him. 'As full of incidents as Florence.'

'More so. In not quite the same way.'

'What do you expect?'

'Well, nothing like Florence. There you came across something historical or artistic or architectural every few hundred yards. You don't get that in London suburbia.'

'We saw an accident in Florence.'

'So we did. And it didn't surprise me either, the way they drove.' John now began to think of the motorcyclists. 'I can't understand how this happened.'

'One of them swerved into the other, and they both crashed into the wall.'

'Yes, I know, but why?'

'Didn't one mention a fit?'

'Yes, but they were going along so slowly. They weren't roaring round the streets like lunatics. They were dawdling. That's not like motorcyclists. It's altogether odd.'

They walked on and within ten minutes knew where they were. Within half an hour, it had taken nearly an hour on the way out, they were back at home.

'Twenty to two,' he said. 'We're late.'

They drank a cup of coffee and ate a slice of date and walnut cake Helen had made first thing after breakfast. She had also taken a piece of roast beef out of the freezer.

'Would you like Yorkshire pudding?' she asked.

'Let's not complicate things.'

'There's no difficulty there.'

'May we have Yorkshire pudding, please?'

He sliced the beans and scrubbed the potatoes. She then dismissed him to read the Sunday newspapers.

'By the time you've read your way through all the sections and magazines we'll be ready to eat. I'll join you in a few minutes. It's too early yet for the vegetables.'

She did not in fact join him; he could hear her busying herself in the large bedroom. He nodded off for a short time, unusually, and felt bad about it as if he was wasting part of this precious day together in sleep. She looked in to say the meal would be on the table in ten minutes, so he'd better get himself ready for it. He washed hands and face thoroughly, recombed his hair and straightened his tie, before going to the wardrobe to change his shoes.

It was nearer twenty minutes than ten when he helped her bring in the food, but there was no doubt it was worth waiting for. He watched her skilfully carving the beef while he turned on the television. As they ate they listened to *Songs of Praise*.

'Food for the soul and for the body,' he said.

'Is the beef cooked to your liking?'

'It is. And your gravy is a marked improvement on their music.' He paused as the camera drifted over the multifarious faces and mouths of the singing congregation.

On his suggestion pudding consisted of tinned peaches and cream. When he was a boy, tinned fruit was always provided at

Sunday teatime, and served in special dishes carefully lifted off a shelf in the larger of two china cabinets.

'It's like a birthday party,' Helen said.

'I never had one. My parents gave me presents and my mother made me a cake and iced it.'

'With candles for your age?'

'No,' he replied, 'they didn't overdo it. My father loved cake with icing sugar and marzipan on it, and he didn't want to spoil it with candle wax.'

'But no other children?'

'No. My aunt Irene as far as I remember. And that was about it.'

'Were you pleased?'

'Yes. My mother took care to give me presents I wanted. I always got a box of handkerchiefs from Grandma Stokes. Irene was good and surprised me. She once gave me a farm, with stables and byres and beautifully made lead animals.'

'You didn't play any special games?'

'Apart from the presents and the cake. My father often had two slices. I was only allowed one. When I complained once, my mother said it would ruin my digestion, and my father claimed that I wasn't properly grown yet and slices of sugared cake might well interfere with my manhood. I didn't know what he was talking about, but I could see from my mother's expression that he was venturing near forbidden topics. She ate her cake with no obvious signs of enjoyment. She cut it into small cubes and ate it like that, picking up every crumb between thumb and middle finger. I suppose there weren't many obvious signs of affection between them. But as long as she was allowed to choose the furniture, and the decoration and the holidays . . .'

'And the meals?' Helen asked.

'That was her prerogative. Not that she put herself out. She made a list which rarely varied from week to week. The puddings, stewed fruit, changed a bit with the seasons. And on Sunday, when our main meal was at midday or thereabouts, we had a real steamed pudding, made in a basin. Fruit, sultanas, raisins, apple, pear. Sometimes we had jam roly-poly made in a cloth tied with string. They were the highlights of my father's week.'

'He'd a sweet tooth?'

'Must have. He always seemed so dry to me, and old. But

229

these times with boiled puddings and Christmas and birthday cakes seemed to demonstrate a different man.'

'Did he never show pleasure elsewhere?'

'He congratulated me if I did well at school. He'd fiddle with the change in his pocket, which always seemed full, and give me a fifty-pence piece. But it didn't seem real. He knew from my mother what he had to do. She'd be quite different. When I brought a good report home, she'd fling her arms around me, and smother me in kisses.'

'No money?'

'No. But there'd always be some little treat due. A visit to a theme park, or a zoo, or a museum or Tussaud's in London. Of course by that time she had gone back into teaching, and was doing well.'

'And your father?'

'His work satisfied him. He was on his best behaviour at home. And every advance he made at work was a kind of obeisance in my mother's direction. I'm doing well for you.'

'But he didn't mind?'

'Didn't seem to. I suppose he buried some parts of his character. There's one incident I specially remember. I was about eight or nine at the time. A friend of my mother's had come in and was telling her about a funeral she had attended. I was sitting there reading, but was all ears. The clergyman had spoken eloquently about the dead man, and this had affected some of the congregation, especially a Mr Greensmith, an elderly man, let's say sixty-odd. This friend of my mother's, a Mrs Pickervance said that Greensmith was touched by what was said. My father was passing through the room, and he suddenly stopped and said, "I always found him eminently sane." This intervention in a conversation in which he was taking no part shook my mother and her friend. Mrs Pickervance, a nervous, jerky woman tried to set things straight, but my father, right out of character, affected not to understand her. "But you said he was touched," my father objected. "I didn't mean it in that sense." Mrs P. said. "But you said it," my father continued. Even I, child as I was, thought this was going too far. My father knew quite well what the woman meant. "He had tears in his eyes," she said, almost hysterically, "and he had to wipe his cheeks with his handkerchief." "Oh, yes,

I see," my father mumbled, and rushed out of the room. Mrs P. was red in the face now, almost crying herself. "You didn't misunderstand me, did you?" she asked. My mother comforted her with a second cup of tea. "He knew, as well as I do, what you meant. He was making a joke of it." "About a funeral?" Mrs Pickervance said mournfully. "That's no joking matter." It was right out of character, this making a joke of sorts, and worse carrying on with it. But it must have been a throwback to his younger days. It was pretty childish.'

'Did your mother tick him off?' Helen asked.

'Not in my hearing. I think she thought her friend was slow on the uptake for not realising that he was pulling her leg. I'd guess she'd get on to him, in private. But I never heard him say or do anything like it again. My mother would consider it rude, mocking a friend like this.'

'And your father?'

'I never noticed anything similar again. He'd play on words with me. Quite difficult puns. "Dough" and "doh". Or "straight" and "strait", a, i, t, a word I'd never met. I think he quite liked little games of that sort. But his pulling of Mrs Pickervance's leg seemed out of place, cruel. It upset her. My mother sent me upstairs to fetch one of Father's handkerchiefs for the poor woman to cry in. And sometimes, I remember, if we went to a stately home and we were being shown round by some ancient servant, he'd ask some questions, just to get a laugh from the rest of the party.'

'She didn't like that?'

'I'd cringe with embarrassment, or stand there fearful that any minute he'd ask one of his daft questions. What my mother thought I dread to think.'

'But they stuck it out together?' she asked.

'Yes. I guess my mother would have thought divorce an even bigger source of embarrassment.'

'Did they ever quarrel in front of you?'

'No. Not really. If they had words, and I guess they did at times, it was in private.'

He could see Helen was interested. Here were a couple, not unlike himself and his wife, both successful in their work, but not ideally suited in marriage, but who kept up the pretence, at least before their son, that all was well. He guessed that whatever William saw, he might have felt rejected when his son was born. Any affection for the boy was now shown by Ella. He was important. Outings were arranged for his benefit; she chose the books and games that would help educate him. The television set was more often switched off than on, and if this meant a sacrifice of the father's pleasure then it was one he should willingly make. William spent much of his time in the garden and was graciously thanked when he brought in flowers to decorate the house, and at dinner Ella went out of her way to praise the cabbage or beans William had provided. Then his father would smile, as one justified.

His mother had, he recalled, once or twice tried to get her husband interested in the bowls club attached to his office. Why she did so was a mystery. William did as he was told, turned up, but showed no interest. Games meant nothing to him. He had not played them at home, neither chess, dominoes, draughts nor cards, the gambler's pastime. At grammar school everyone had to turn out for rugby, cricket and athletics, but he had shown no aptitude. His scorn was specially harsh against football, perhaps because Ella supported him in this, with the huge salaries paid to Premiership players and the thousands turning out every Saturday to sit in the cold watching people tapping a ball to each other. Colleagues at work had tried earlier to get the promoted William to join them at golf, but he regarded that as throwing money away. He never once turned up when John was playing for one of the school teams, though he occasionally asked about a result. There were more important ways of spending your life, William would have said, than running and kicking. He enjoyed a walk, especially on holiday, and even bought a folding stick for these expeditions.

'Would you say it was a successful marriage?' Helen asked, not for the first time.

'They kept together, and came to some sort of agreement about how to live. Money wasn't short, because the style they adopted was prudent, careful. Each had done sufficiently well at their everyday jobs to have some admiration for the partner.'

'Were they happy?'

'Within limits. He was proud of her with her shelves of books. He did as she told him to do.'

232

'Ella seems to be the dominant one.'

'Yes. But remember he could throw his weight about at work, and could spend his weekends with his garden, on his own, doing as he liked.'

'That's the way we should act, is it?' she asked. He knew that every time they discussed his parents' marriage, their own was her real subject.

'Every marriage is different. We were in love; I couldn't keep my hands off you. My mother married a suitable man who'd provide comfort, help, and an acceptable background. I may be quite wrong. It's possible there had been strong sexual attraction between them, but I never noticed it. They were elderly parents, or at least he was, and very self-contained in public.'

'My parents separated and then divorced before I was eight years old.'

'Yes, I know. That must have been a tremendous shock.'

'Oh, I don't know. I hated it when they quarrelled at the top of their voices in front of me. I used to cry, and try to stop them, and my mother made the most of it. She'd accuse him of terrifying me. "You might consider the child," she'd say, "if you don't think of me and my feelings."'

'Was he nasty?'

'To my mother he was. He made a fuss of me, as far as I remember. But once they'd divorced he'd make little attempt to see me. And then he went off to Canada, on some sort of big engineering project, and as far as I know he stopped there. I think I've seen him twice since I was an adult. He was back in England and on the way elsewhere, to build his bridges and roads and power stations in the Middle East, and he called me on the phone. He took me out to dinner, but it didn't seem real. We were polite, and he was an interesting talker, but it didn't seem all that important. He gave us a very expensive wedding present, if you remember, and turned up with his wife, an American.'

John knew all this; they had discussed her father before. Her mother had died before Helen had met John, soon after she'd qualified as a solicitor. He had the impression that her father had contributed towards her upbringing and regularly sent birthday and Christmas gifts. He had turned up on time for their wedding, had given her away, had concluded with a witty speech at the reception, and made a favourable impression on everyone present, including her mother's relations. Now they exchanged Christmas cards with his wife, his third, but saw nothing of him. According to the snippets of information crammed into the Christmas cards, he was as busy as ever. He'd still be in his fifties, and constantly travelling the world. There were three children, two girls and a boy, from his second and third marriages, but neither they nor their mothers had ever made contact.

To John, Helen's parents' marriage had not been serious. The story Helen told was of cruelty from her father towards his wife. His temper was short and his tongue barbed. He'd showed no signs of these faults before their wedding; he'd been smooth and pleasant, a success with all the wedding guests. How much the failure of his marriage could be laid at his wife's door John could not judge. He had never met his mother-in-law, who had been gentle, something of an invalid, and had died of lung cancer in her forties. She had met and married her husband at university against the wishes of her family. Her husband had felt cheated when the young, pretty, sharp girl he married turned within a year or two into a sick, complaining, unattractive, useless woman. The arrival of Helen had proved no help. It was a marvel that Helen had turned out as normal as she was. John often wondered about these matters in the first summery weeks after their return from Italy. Things went perfectly.

One Friday in July Helen came back from work with a heavy cold. On Saturday morning he insisted that she stayed in bed. He was surprised that she agreed, and he did the shopping and cooked the meals.

'I hate these summer colds,' Helen said.

'They seem so awful because everything looks so bright outside.'

He fitted her up with a radio which she barely used. She seemed to spend most of the day sleeping, as if she were worn out. He kept her in bed on Sunday morning, promising to let her up for their evening meal if she felt like it. When she did come into the dining room in her fleece dressing gown she looked pale, but talked cheerfully. Next day she went to work, and by the end of the week was fit again.

'You saved my life,' she said, 'keeping me in bed.'

The following weekend his mother appeared for the Friday and Saturday nights. Helen was full of praise for her husband.

'He's a first-rate cook,' she said. 'Did you teach him?'

'Yes. I gave him some elementary lessons.'

'Was he pleased to learn?'

'All children love doing jobs if they know they'll be praised for them. I didn't make a martyr of him. But I was surprised at how little William knew. When we were first married I went down with flu, and he seemed hopeless. He was willing, but if he attempted to cook anything he needed instruction. "If I put the potatoes in the oven, how long will they take?" He was up and down stairs all day. And I felt so awful lying there.'

'Did you give him a few lessons?'

'I did, but they weren't needed again. He knew how to look after himself when I went into the maternity ward with John, although he burnt the bottom of my best saucepan. I never mentioned it, and he thought I'd not noticed.'

'How had he gone on before he was married?' John asked.

'He'd lived in digs. Dinner on the table at six every night.'

'Poor old Father.'

'Oh, he never complained. He was the sort of man who'd eat the same meal day after day. I had to teach him how to eat properly and enjoy his food, rather than just filling himself up.'

'Did he learn?'

'Oh, yes. He was intelligent. He knew how to please me.'

Ella insisted on helping Helen in the preparation of meals and John thought the pair enjoyed talking to each other. His mother had looked tired when she first arrived but now seemed cheerful and energetic.

'I think she's pleased with us,' Helen said.

'Good. She's convinced I've married the right wife.'

235

XXIV

On Sunday morning as they were dressing Helen suggested to her husband that they should invite his mother to stay with them for as long as she wished during the next week.

'Won't she want to get ready for her holiday?'

'No. She's made all her lists. She says that in an emergency she could pack inside an hour.'

'Fine. She knows her mind.'

When over breakfast Helen invited Ella to spend a few more days with them it was as if a cloud lifted from his mother's face. She threw her hands about as excitedly as a child, though as they expected she made a proviso or two of her own.

'If you'll allow me to cook the evening meal for you.'

'We're never quite sure when we'll be home,' John murmured.

'Don't let that worry you. We've phones, and I know how to hold a meal up. If you think that Will was never delayed at work, you'd be quite wrong.'

'What will you do all day?' Helen asked. 'We're never home before six.'

'I shall look about me. I shall find out all about the district. I'm not good with my imagination, and I'd sooner know than try to make it up.'

'Is it important?' John asked.

'You don't know how often I think about you. Now some of it will be nearer reality.'

'What about my father?'

'I'll go back soon enough to fit him up with clean clothes. Not that he has any idea of time. I don't think he knows whether I visit him or not. And you've promised to go to see him while I'm abroad. I'll leave another lot of clothes out for him. He'll be pleased to see you. He always asks about Helen.'

'A man of taste,' John said.

As they were preparing for bed, John remarked on his mother's obvious pleasure at being invited to stay some extra days with them.

'Has she not said anything to you?' Helen asked.

'About what?'

'Has she not mentioned that she's been feeling down this last few weeks?'

'She said she was very tired at the end of term.'

'It was more than that.'

'No. She's said nothing. Perhaps she left it to you to tell me.'

'I don't think so. She'll let you know in her own good time. She said as much. Whether she feels embarrassed by it now, I don't know, but it was serious.'

'Was it anything to do with our marriage? Was she worrying about that?'

'That came into it, certainly, but only as a very small ingredient.'

On Monday evening John helped to dry the dishes after the evening meal. Helen had disappeared into her office. He thought he'd better ask a few questions.

'Had a good day?' he began.

'Very. I went out for two strolls before and after lunch. Just round the houses, but the weather was beautiful.'

'Did pedestrians pass the time of day with you?'

'No. No more than in Beechnall.'

'The swine. Helly tells me you've not been very well lately.'

There was a pause while she stood upright her red hands held dripping into the washing-up bowl. She seemed to be bracing herself.

'That's right,' she said. 'I don't know whether or not it was physical. I was getting very tired towards the end of term, but then I always do. There are always setbacks, a thousand things to clear up and no time to do it. One of my best teachers was off with stress, and that meant I had to take over in her classroom. But I don't think that was the main cause.'

She paused again, rubbed a cheek with the back of a wet hand.

'When your father first retired I thought he'd be well away. As indeed he was for two years. He found enough to occupy himself in the garden, and he started going to the library again,

237

and he'd be pleased to walk down for me to the open market and do a bit of my shopping. His memory was beginning to go, but that's not unusual. Sometimes I thought he looked a bit lost, and I'd send him off on some little errand to make him think he was busy. On the whole he was exactly as I expected he'd be.'

John nodded, and she turned to acknowledge him.

'In the six months before his seventieth birthday he had a fall or two. In the street. He said his sense of balance was a bit precarious. And the streets are very unevenly paved. But he did himself no serious harm. He was bruised and shocked but there were no breakages. He used to joke about it. "I shall have to take more water with it," he'd say, though he rarely touched alcohol. But then came this serious fall, down the stairs, he broke both his legs, and his wrist and injured his pelvis and shoulder in some way. That all meant, you'll remember, some time in hospital. He was unhappy there. He was in an orthopaedic ward full of young men with loud radios and vulgar jokes who had smashed themselves up on their motorcycles. He was glad to get home to a bit of quietness, that I can tell you. But after a little time I began to notice a difference in him. It was as if he had lost his confidence. He'd talk about something that made no sense to me, and expect me to understand. Once I got him up and out of bed, the district nurse and the doctor came in and saw to him, and he went back to the hospital a time or two for physiotherapy, I thought he'd be better, improve with it, if you know what I mean. But he didn't. Not only was his mind clearly on the way out he found it difficult to walk, even clinging on to the furniture.'

'Yes,' John encouraged.

'The worst thing was that he knew his mind was going. There were great gaps in his memory, and he couldn't read. He once said if he started to read, or even say a long sentence, by the time he'd reached the end of it he couldn't remember the beginning. "I don't know what's wrong with me, Ella," he'd say. "It's as if I'm lost." I used to try to cheer him up. "You're at home," I'd say, "and you're waiting for your dinner. And the garden's outside looking a picture." In the end I had to have a woman in all day to look after him, and a man to keep the garden tidy, a thing I would never have dared to do when he was well. He'd look at me so pitifully, and say, "There's no strength left in my legs. Only pain. But my mind's worse. There's nothing there. Sometimes I don't know what I am." And he'd ask the same daft questions over and over again. And his hands would begin to shake. Once or twice he began to cry like a child. It was awful. As I say, he knew from time to time what was happening to him. I used to think it wouldn't be so bad with people suffering from Alzheimer's or other sorts of dementia because they wouldn't realise what was happening to them, couldn't compare themselves to what they once were. It must be awful for those married to them or looking after them, but not for the persons themselves. They wouldn't know. But your dad did, John. He knew he couldn't read properly or remember or even add and subtract, all those things he used to be so good at. And he couldn't understand what was happening to him. In the end he had to go into a home. It was the best thing for him, as you know. And I wonder how much he could understand at this time.'

'Yes.' John wondered what this account of his father's illness meant. Was his mother suggesting that she had failed her husband? No one had ever thought or suggested that. The transformation of her husband into this helpless body was not to be blamed on her.

His mother was now drying her hands with a kind of fury as if she'd tear the handtowel into ribbons. Suddenly she stopped, carefully replaced the towel on its rack, and then leaned back against the worktop. She spoke in a quietly controlled voice.

'Things were hectic at school. That inspection took it out of us. We got a very decent report, but at a price. We all felt drained. And in the last term nothing seemed straightforward. People were ill, a child was run over by a lorry in the street. She'll never be able to walk properly again. I had all the preparation for the next year to deal with, as well as all the paperwork for this year's leavers, and the summer drama performance didn't seem to run as smoothly as usually. Everything I touched complicated itself, and took twice as long. End of term has always been a rush and a strain. I told myself I was getting too old for the job.'

'How long have you got left?'

'Seven or eight years before I can retire.' She smiled grimly. 'But I oughtn't to be thinking of retirement at my age. I ought to be at the peak of my powers. And I've been a head long enough to know what's expected of me.' She paused and looked about her as if she'd lost the train of her thought. He led her gently by the arm to the table, pulled out a chair and seated her. She leaned forward on to her elbows. He sat beside her, not too close and making sure she was not staring him straight in the face.

'Would you like a drink?' he asked.

'No thanks. We had a cup of coffee.' Her voice was normal again. 'Let me get on with it. When you and Helen separated, it had such an effect on me. I was sure when you were married you made the ideal pair. You had so much in common. I thought perhaps that after the split Helen would cut off all communication with me. But it wasn't so. We wrote and phoned each other. There was nothing I could do about getting you together again, but at least I could hear both sides. The thing that worried me most was that you both seemed so certain that the marriage had broken down irretrievably. You couldn't bear each other to be near. It seemed so wrong, but when Helen told me it was so, and so often, I had to accept it. You both spoke so sensibly about it to me. It had happened, and that was that. It wasn't like your father and me; he had become a different man.'

'I see. But you're right. We could barely bring ourselves to speak. The atmosphere was awful.'

'And there was one other thing at that time. I don't know whether I dare mention it. It played dreadfully on my mind.'

'Oh?' He waited for her.

'It was Irene. I thought she was setting her cap at you.'

'How do you mean?' He spoke clearly.

'Sexually. It didn't seem possible. Apart from the family relationship, she was nearly twenty years older than you. I know such things happen these days. There are plays about older women and young lovers.'

'Did she say anything to you?'

'She did not. But I suppose her husband was away for long periods. And from the way she sometimes talked their marriage was open. If one or the other took on a lover that was acceptable by the other partner.'

'Has she done so?'

'I've no proof. She thinks I'm a fuddy-duddy and likes to shock me with her tales. How much of it is just talk I don't know.'

'It's not so in this case.'

'But she invited you up to her house. She's a good-looking woman.'

'True, but her husband was at home.'

'And he raised no objection?'

'No.'

'But if she had made a pass at you, what would you have done?'

'She didn't.'

'I thought that when she knew you and Helen had separated she might have thought it a good opportunity.'

'She didn't.'

'I'm glad. But it added to my trouble at the time. And with all this mental disturbance I seemed to be losing physical control. I was like your father just shuffling about, having terrific difficulty getting out of chairs. I wondered if I hadn't had a stroke.'

'Did you see your doctor?'

'Yes. She said I was working too hard, that I should try to relax.'

'And you couldn't?'

'No. And worse I seemed to know exactly what my symptoms were. There was no self-deception there. I knew where I felt pain. I knew all the things I could do a month or two before and couldn't begin to do them now.'

'Did the doctor say anything about a nervous breakdown?'

'She didn't use those exact words, as far as I can remember. She gave me some tablets.'

'Did you take them?'

'Yes. I'm not a fool, John. Anything to get me out of my trouble. They seemed to have some success from time to time, but then the black mood would come down again.'

'Why do you call it that?'

'I had to give it some name. I think perhaps the doctor used the expression. It wasn't black in any way; it was a sense that I was incapable of carrying out tasks I'd done easily enough for years. I think that was how your father felt before he went into the nursing home. There was reason enough in his case. He'd had a really bad fall and was lucky to be able to creep round

241

the house. Mine was all nervous, mental. I was useless. I felt guilty at putting your father in a home, but he needed twenty-four-hour care, and I wasn't capable of lifting and shifting him. I ought to have been able to look after him, but I couldn't. I knew I couldn't. But I couldn't rid my mind of the idea that it was dereliction of duty on my part. It was as if I'd chosen not to be able to look after him, or neglect all these other things I ought to have been able to do. I couldn't. I was a shadow of myself. When you and Helen started to get together again, I couldn't believe it was anything but a temporary phase. You'd so convinced me that there was no cure, that the rift would never be set right, that I couldn't believe my own eyes and ears. It was awful. And then I suspected you and Irene. I must have had a filthy mind. It was so unnatural, incest even, though I suppose it was not.'

'Are things improving now Helen and I are together again?'

'To some extent, but I keep falling back to this state of mind where I am useless, am losing myself, have no control over the simplest situations. I remember how your father looked like a lost soul when he couldn't remember words, and I don't mean rare words or medical words, "rodomontade" or "endogenous" or "ischaemia" but short, easy, everyday words like "cup", "jug", "fork". I could see him straining for them. He could see the object, could remember what it was used for, but he couldn't put a name to it. If you lose that power you become inhuman.'

'Are you getting better now?'

'Yes, yes. I must be.'

'Are you still under the doctor? Can she help you out?'

'Yes. I am. She's very good. And not in any hurry. She changes the tablets from time to time, or at least the dosage. But I don't think she realises quite how far I'd sunk.'

'Um.' He watched her. 'Is the holiday doing you any good?'

'It is. But I suddenly get dreadful days. I go to bed at peace with myself, and next morning things begin to crumble again. I know what my father would have said.' She smiled pleasantly at him so that he felt encouraged. 'He'd say, "Pray about it!".'

'And do you?'

'When I'm down I haven't the energy to pray.'

'Was your father a cheerful man?'

242

'Yes, quite humorous in his way. I know most people think that clergymen are serious all the time.'

'And he wasn't?'

'No, he'd pull our legs. And, to give him credit he didn't mind our criticising him, or joking at his old-fashioned ways. That's when we were teenagers. And I think Irene, who was his favourite, was even worse than I was. He knew he was right. But would argue his case.'

'He was never depressed?'

'I think he was. But he kept it from us. His mother died with agonies of cancer soon after Irene was born. She lived with us for a time. Even when I was quite young I used to see a kind of contradiction in his beliefs. He often preached about "God's free grace", favours granted to us that we in no way deserved, and yet in his life he worked on the assumption that we'd never get anything unless we slaved hard for it. He'd had to slog in his early days to get to university. He took a BD, and it left its mark on him. There was no such thing as a free lunch for him.'

'Did you never argue this with him?'

'Not really. His answer would have been that God's grace had been given to him in allowing him to study at a university. That was God's part, and now he had to work hard, to make the most of the opportunities granted to him. In a way, I'm not so far from that outlook myself.'

'You're like him?'

'In some respects. It's the Puritan ethic.'

'Did he preach about that?'

'Yes. But I used to tell him that it was once upon a time the Catholics who believed you worked for your place in heaven and the Protestants who said you got there because God elected you, chose you.'

'The Catholics were more sensible, then, than the Protestants.'

'Some of his ideas have rubbed off on you. From me, I expect.'

They laughed. She pushed herself upwards.

'We can't sit here all night,' she said.

'No. We could choose somewhere more comfortable. Before you move I must apologise for my part in your troubles. I knew you worried about Helly and me, but I had no idea it upset you quite so much.'

'How could you? You were up to your eyes in trouble at home.'

'I didn't see that very clearly, either.'

'How do you mean?'

'We worked ourselves into a real tangle of anger and resentment. We were both busy, very busy at the time. That should have been an advantage. We were doing well money-wise. But we'd no time for each other. We couldn't put off some piece of business for a day or two to make time to go to the theatre or a concert. And to me it seemed that if I arranged some outing I thought she would like she deliberately said no, claimed she was too busy, though she was in fact often free.'

'Who was the first to be awkward about this?'

'I don't know. Perhaps I was, though I wouldn't have admitted it at the time. I was, I think now, a bit jealous because she was getting on so well at work. Why I had such feelings I don't know. We got across each other, in small ways, and these multiplied, raced one after the other, piled up to the catastrophe. It seems impossible to me now that we could act so foolishly. When I explain it to you it doesn't seem likely. But when I sit down and think of the state we were in when Helly upped and left me there's no doubt that it was serious enough. We loathed each other. That's why we took so long to get together again. I was convinced that we could not have got ourselves into such straits, unless there had been some real flaw, something radically wrong with the relationship. Mere, small quarrels, awkwardness, scoring off one another could not in themselves lead to such a break, such division between us. We were incompatible.'

'You don't think that now?' Ella asked.

'It happened. It wasn't imagination. If you had asked me at the time I'd have said we were unfit for each other. And it wasn't the sex. For me that was the only good part. But that became savage, malevolent even. There was no doubt in either of our minds that separation was the only reasonable way out of our dilemma.'

'But neither of you started legal proceedings.'

'That's right. And that makes me wonder if subconsciously we weren't so estranged, antagonistic. I don't know.' His voice took on a cynicism. 'Perhaps it was the old excuse. We were too busy at work to bother ourselves even with divorce.'

244

They moved into the sitting room, established themselves in comfortable chairs.

'I'm glad we can talk like this,' the mother said. 'It clears the air. I wouldn't say I'm altogether better now. Such an experience must leave scars. But there are improvements.'

'Like Dad saving those women from the fire?'

'I often wonder about that,' Ella said. 'I'm sure he woke them up. But getting them down the fire escape . . . It's more likely they helped him. He seemed, even then, to be too far gone to be rescuing anybody. He could barely walk.'

'Somebody did something. At least they got out.'

'Yes.'

The door quietly opened and Helen appeared.

'Hello,' she said. 'Have your lordships delivered judgement?'

'On what?' he asked.

'You both looked so serious.'

'I think I was to blame,' Ella said. 'I've been telling John how I've been this last few months.'

Helen walked across, stood behind her mother-in-law's chair and then very gently began to stroke the top of her head.

'And we,' Helen said, 'were at least partly to blame.' The other two made no answer. The small, white hand continued its slight, delicate, courteous movement. 'I will tell you something. When John and I got together again, I was extremely careful not to say a word out of place. I remembered how bad we were. I tiptoed about the place, not literally, and whispered, and lowered my eyes like a servant in Buckingham Palace. But do you know in these last few days I've never even thought about it. Since you've been here,' and the hand now moved more animatedly, 'I've just been myself. I'm sure we could disagree about something and not let it get to us.'

'I shouldn't try it,' Ella said. 'Not yet.'

'No fear. I'm not as barmy as that.'

Helen left her slow stroking, sat down, and suddenly asked, 'Would anyone like a drink?'

'We've only just had coffee.'

'I was thinking of something stronger.'

There was a pause.

'No, thank you,' Ella said. 'I feel so contented that it would be tempting providence to try to add to it. But don't let me stop you.'

John rose to provide whisky for himself and a kir for his wife. When he returned Helen was gently smiling, and his mother, with hands clasped, seemed almost uplifted. She nevertheless refused even a soft drink. The two young people toasted each other. The mother made it certain that she somehow joined this exchange of good wishes.

'I'm sorry your father's not with us,' she said. 'Not that he'd want it. He wouldn't know what was going on.'

They made sounds of sympathy.

'It's not as though he's really old. He'll be seventy-three next. And that's no age these days. I sometimes wonder if he'd have turned out differently if he'd have married someone else. What do you think, John?'

'He'd have been different, that's for sure. But he might have been worse. His present condition can be put down to physical faults. You looked after him well enough.'

'I don't know. He seemed to look up to me too much.'

'That's what he liked. He bossed them about at work, and corrected their mistakes, and sorted out difficult decisions, and then when he came home there it was all laid on for him. His meals, his holidays, his outings were all done for him. You asked him, consulted him, of course.'

'Bullied him, you mean.'

'Not at all. You flattered him when he told you about his work or his garden. He fairly purred when you praised him.'

'I'm not so sure about that.'

'You set your mind at rest,' John said.

'I'm even wondering now whether I do any good visiting him. I take in his clean laundry and chocolate . . .'

'And trifles. He loves them.'

'Yes, bought trifles, but I could have them delivered.'

'You do well,' Helen said in her lawyer's voice. 'I've had to deal with several cases of old people in care homes, and there is no doubt in my mind that those who have regular visitors are better looked after than those who have nobody. Relatives who come in, look about them, ask questions, keep the staff up to scratch.'

246

'Yes,' John said. 'That is so.'

'I shall go along, even if he shows no sign of wanting me there or even knowing me.' She breathed in deeply. 'I've no sort of hope, but one doesn't know. He seems to indicate, signify in some way that he knows Helen, and so we can't be sure.'

'You aren't jealous?' John asked impudently.

'No. If he were quite normal he'd show more interest in Helen than in me. I'm always there, giving him orders, laying the law down. And I'm not anything like as pretty as Helen. It does old men good to have some attractive young women offering them their undivided attention even for a few minutes. But fear not, I shall be there with his clean hankies and pyjamas.'

She was as good as her word. For the next eighteen months she made her twice-weekly visits to Holmleigh. William showed no improvement, but his death came as a surprise. He was found dead in bed one morning when the carer went in to wake him. He looked different in that he had grown a beard, a decision they had put to Ella. She agreed; he was incapable of shaving himself and a beard would be more easily kept neat. But it altered his appearance. He looked sharper; it hid the downturned mouth, the thin double chin, but he was no smart retired naval officer. His eyes were as vague, his hands as wasted as before. Ella sometimes wondered if he would have looked better if he had grown the beard in his prime. He wouldn't have had it; it was no part of a civil servant's duty to go about looking like a tramp. Towards the end he no longer recognised Helen; if one fed him he ate his trifle with something like enthusiasm, though one had to wipe his beard clean.

Today their mother said she'd spend the next morning, if the weather was suitable, up in the West End.

'Shopping?' John asked.

'I might. Or it could be window shopping only.' She smiled. 'I would like to buy you two something to commemorate this day when you were really together again. Now what would that be?'

They looked baffled, pleased.

'There's no need, mother,' John said. 'You've done more than your fair share in bringing us together again.'

'Never mind that. Just pander to my wishes. What would you choose, Helen?'

'A rose bush for the garden.' She looked up, suddenly smiling. 'Or perhaps John's favourite, a magnolia.'

'I'd like nothing better,' he answered. 'But perhaps we could leave it a bit until we decide whether we'll change houses. Do you fancy moving in with us?'

'That's sensible,' Helen concurred.

'I'll do it,' Ella said, 'when and if you're ready. We'll see. But you'll have a family by then.' She stared out into the brightness of evening. 'But I shall never forget this room. Never. You think about it.'